A TERRIBLE DISCOVERY

Birdie simply stood and looked, for minutes, letting her torch play over the dark mass of trees, bushes, and vines till her eyes grew accustomed to the shapes before her, and she was able to see the narrow gaps that separated them and sense what was beyond. And then she was moving forward, bending and weaving, following the little tracks that wound, hidden, through the dense undergrowth. Cat tracks. Mai tracks, perhaps. Her feet sank to the ankles in soaking .eaves. Her nose was filled with the smell of rotting fruit. She pushed on, her skin creeping as vines caught at her legs and arms. She could hear the sound of her own heart beating and the panting of her own breath.

She reached a small clearing and paused. Whispering darkness rose around her on all sides. The torch beam caught the eye of a cat. It gleamed, unblinking, fixed. Puzzled, she moved closer. Still no movement. She bent to investigate. No cat. A jeweled comb, flashing in the light, lying where it had fallen, half-hidden in the wet leaves. She skirted it and walked forward, holding her breath.

Mai was lying on her face, half under a dark thicket of jasmine. Black hair spread out and gleaming like a silk shawl, black trousers, black shoes. Almost invisible. She was cool, wet, and quite dead.

Jennifer Rowe

STRANGLEHOLD

BANTAM BOOKS

New York   Toronto   London   Sydney   Auckland

S T R A N G L E H O L D

A Bantam Crime Line Book

PUBLISHING HISTORY
Allen & Unwin (Australia) edition 1993
Bantam paperback edition / February 1995
CRIME LINE and the portrayal of a boxed "cl" are trademarks of Bantam
Books, a division of Bantam Doubleday Dell Publishing Group, Inc.

ISBN 0-553-56819-1

Published simultaneously in the United States and Canada

Bantam Books are published by Bantam Books, a division of Bantam
Doubleday Dell Publishing Group, Inc. Its trademark, consisting of the
words "Bantam Books" and the portrayal of a rooster, is Registered in
U.S. Patent and Trademark Office and in other countries. Marca Reg-
istrada. Bantam Books, 1540 Broadway, New York, New York 10036.

PRINTED IN THE UNITED STATES OF AMERICA

RAD   0 9 8 7 6 5 4 3 2 1

For Bob, with love and thanks.

STRANGLEHOLD

PROLOGUE

Max Tully called his house 'Third Wish'. The name was greeted with surprise and interest, both in the circles in which he moved and in the wider, the very much wider, circles that made up his enormous national radio audience. No one, including his old partner Isa Truby and his longtime boss Angus Birdwood, who probably knew him better than anyone, would normally have thought of brash, tough-as-nails, wisecracking Max Tully in terms of wishes. Desires, maybe—acted on fast and decisively, with little regard for consequences or propriety; needs, certainly—met lavishly and with the necessary ruthlessness, should they clash with the needs of others. But wishes? The province of fairy godmothers and enchanted fishes? Not likely.

And yet 'Third Wish' it was. And of course, even more intriguing, once people thought about it: for there to be a third wish, there had to have been a first and a second. Friends and enemies alike (and Max had plenty of both) considered this, discussed it, joked about it, and in the end asked him about it. As did the journalists sent to interview him—about the house, ostensibly, but really in search of a juicy quote or two about the glamorous nobody Ingrid something-or-other he'd been seeing lately. And when Max was asked, he would laugh—the familiar rich, infectious belly laugh so strangely at odds with his small, wiry body and thin, tanned monkey face and say, 'Sweetheart (or mate, if his questioner was a man), I was ten years old before I saw the sea. I'd lived in Sydney my whole life, but I'd only ever seen a beach in pictures. Can you believe that? But on my tenth birthday I jigged school and hitched to Bondi. Don't know why, really. I just did it. And when I got there I went down on to the sand and I stood there, and looked, and I didn't know what hit me.' He'd shake his head, remembering.

'A skinny little kid with the arse out of his strides, with nothing and nobody, and not a hope in hell of getting them either, standing there with the whole Pacific stretched out in front of me. And I made three wishes, then and there, and I swore they'd come true. I was dead serious, too. By God I was.' His small, black eyes would soften, then, behind his horn-rimmed glasses, and he would pause.

'A house by the sea,' the questioner would say, as the silence lengthened. 'That was the third wish?' And Max would nod, and look around his gleaming clifftop palace, with its hundred and eighty degree view of the ocean glittering blue as far as the eye could see, and his glasses would flash in the sunlight.

'Took me thirty years, but I got there.'

'And what about the other two?'

The belly laugh again, the big, wolfish grin, with its glint of gold. 'Ha! The second wish was to be filthy rich and famous. What else would a kid like that wish for?'

'That came true too, then.'

A shrug. 'Yup. Guess it did.'

'What about the first?'

A little grimace, a wave of the hand. 'Ah well—two out of three's not bad, is it? Now, how about a drink? You know, a bloke I met . . .'

And so the subject would drop, as they began to talk of other things. And only when Max's interrogator was driving away from the place, charmed, flattered, dazzled and feted, would the image of that ragged little boy standing by the ocean flash back into mind, vivid in its pathos, throwing into high relief the image of the man the child had become. And the driver, whoever it was, would lean over the steering wheel, strangely moved, as the car crawled back to town around the winding narrow roads with their occasional startling glimpses of open sea and sheer drops too close for comfort. An extraordinary man, Max Tully. What a life. What an enigma. What went on in the mind of a man like that? What could the first wish have been? What . . . ? And so on. Which, of course, was the whole idea.

'Third Wish' was indeed a milestone in Max Tully's life. The fact that he knew how to make good PR out of it didn't alter that. There really had been a moment, on Bondi Beach, when the clouds of a miserable and anxious childhood had parted and a vision of hope and power had been revealed to him. And the house was everything he had hoped.

It had taken time, energy and money to achieve. The purchase of the clifftop around the headland from Paradise Beach, with its million-dollar view and only one near neighbour, had been the easiest part. The elderly couple selling, Clive and Mary Skinner, had been thrilled and flattered by Max Tully's delight in their home.

Of course, as it happened, Mary and Clive hadn't really been mad keen to sell at first. Their daughter was always asking them to come to live near her in Tuggerah, now they were getting on, and the steep steps up from the street were hard going these days,

for both of them, that was true. But after all, Clive had
built this place with his own hands. They'd brought
up Sandra and Bill here. This had been their home
for fifty years, nearly. They just mentioned it to the
real estate agent to see what he'd say about the value,
so they could think about it.

But of course he'd rung up the very next day, and
asked if he could bring someone around. Someone
who'd been looking in the area. Someone who already
knew their house, and loved it. And when they found
out who the someone was, well, they could hardly refuse, could they? They'd listened to Max Tully on the
radio almost every day for close on ten years. He'd
been part of their lives—almost like a member of the
family.

And that's how it seemed, when he came. It really
did. They could hardly believe it. He sat there, Max
Tully in the flesh, in the big old blue chair, chatting
away as funny and natural as he always sounded on
the show, they said afterwards, but more sort of gentle-
manly than you'd think, and very much smaller,
though you soon got used to that, talking about their
house, telling them he'd fallen in love with the place.
No haggling about the money, either. He offered
them a sum that nearly knocked their socks off.

They would have liked to think about it—talk it over
for a few months before deciding. Because, after all, it
would be a wrench to leave. But unfortunately Max (he
insisted they call him Max) couldn't wait. He had to buy
now. They didn't ever quite get the reason for the hurry
quite straight. Clive had thought it was something about
his work, or tax, or some such. Mary was sure it was because of the little daughter he missed so much, living at
present with his ex-wife. She certainly remembered him
saying that divorce was a terrible thing, and how lucky
she and Clive were, to have found each other and stuck
together the way they had, through good times and bad.
Fifty years, she'd told him. Fifty years in this house we've
had. This house is full of love, he'd said, his eyes wistful.
It's a real home. You can feel it. She'd felt sorry for him,
then. For all his money and fame.

In the kitchen, clearing away the tea things, Mary and Clive talked in whispers with the agent while Max gazed through the sitting-room windows at the sea. The offer's unbeatable, the agent said. You won't get another chance like this. So they decided to sell. Just like that. It was quite exciting, to think how ecstatic Max was going to be when they told him. And he was ecstatic. He shook hands warmly with Clive but he threw his arms around Mary and gave her a big cuddle, and kissed her on both cheeks. Thank you, Mary, he whispered. Thank you. And six weeks later to the day Mary and Clive were heading off up the coast, their heads still spinning, set for life with Max Tully's cheque in the bank.

Max visited the house that was now his property that same afternoon. He stood in the sitting room and looked out at the view, his hands in his pockets. He thought about Mary and Clive. A lovely old couple. Hard workers, warm hearts. He'd liked them a lot. He hoped they'd be happy in Tuggerah. He paced around the house, appreciating the simple proportions of the three bedrooms, one pink, one blue, one lemon; the spotless, old-fashioned kitchen with its glass-fronted cupboards; the little linen press tucked cunningly into a recess in the hallway. The furniture had gone, of course, but the atmosphere of the place affected him as powerfully as it had on his first visit.

He picked a gardenia from the big bush beside the front steps as he left, and the flower's heady fragrance filled the car all the way back to town. The bush wouldn't survive the demolition tomorrow. A pity, he thought. He'd have to make sure to plant another.

Max had seen the house he wanted to build on his clifftop in a magazine advertisement for some barbaric liqueur. The house was pale pink stucco and glass, curved on its seaward face like the bridge of a luxury liner. Golden light streamed from its dozens of windows, mingling with the rays of the setting sun on the tips of pale green waves in the middle distance. He showed the ad and photographs of the site to four prominent architects. Samuel Nye shook his woolly head and refused the job outright. Linley Smith straightened his tie, listened politely and then sent a note a few days later saying he had unfortunately just accepted another pressing commission. Thin and eager Jonathon Chambers expressed enthusiasm, looked at the site for himself, went away and came back with drawings of a place that resembled Max's magazine advertisement home only in the sense that it had a roof, walls and a lot of plate glass facing the sea. He said it captured the essence of Max's concept. Max said in a pig's ear it did, and sent him packing.

Hector Paine was bald on top and wore the rest of his hair in a long ponytail. He grinned and said why not, if money was no object, and started to ask about numbers of bedrooms and bathrooms. Five bedrooms upstairs, said Max. All with en suite bathrooms. Two other bathrooms downstairs. A housekeeper's apartment. A study with a soundproof radio studio attached. A decent kitchen, with room to move. I like to cook. A billiard room. A pool. Big, open living room facing the sea, good for entertaining. How does that sound? Music to my ears, said Hector Paine, tossing a pencil from hand to hand. He bought a bottle of Moët on the way home that night. And some roses for his wife. If this is selling out, he said to her over dinner, I love it. She smiled at him. She was a journalist and inclined to be acerbic these days, but she loved roses. And French champagne. And she was still quite fond of Hector, too.

'What's Max Tully really like?' she asked. 'As crass as he sounds?'

'Crasser,' said Hector. 'And much smaller. But he's got something . . .'

His wife nodded sagely, pouring more champagne. The top button of her shirt had come undone. 'He's supposed to be really hot stuff in the cot, you know,' she said. '*Really* hot stuff. Barbara Bayers says . . .'

'Bugger Barbara Bayers,' leered Hector, emboldened by champagne and the prospect of lots of money. 'I'll show you who's hot stuff, woman!' He reached for her across the table, and she laughed, but not unkindly, and didn't push his hand away.

Over the months that followed Max was forced to devote much of his considerable energy to the task he had set himself, Hector Paine and the builder they had employed to transform Hector's prettily coloured diagrams to stucco and glass reality. Fortunately he enjoyed a good fight. And he was tireless. His little black eyes sparkled behind his glasses as he squared up to each new opponent of his dream like a minute gladiator taking on one lumbering, loinclothed assailant after another. Cheering his victories, jeering at his wry accounts of frustration and delay, his audience listened riveted each day from the safety of their living rooms to his account of his battles with the local council, the next-door neighbour, the water board, the builders' suppliers, the electricity authority, the phone company. They called in to wish him well. They told anecdotes of their own attempts to build decks, pergolas, home offices, granny flats and driveways, to remove trees, dig a cellar and keep chickens in the face of enormous odds and neighbourhood ill will. They deplored the apparent desire of councils to prevent anyone doing anything remarkable, useful, practical or interesting while allowing all manner of noxious developments right next door to them. They gave him advice, commended him to God, and sent him cakes in the post.

Sitting in the kitchen of the clean, tidy house that for nearly two years now had been hers alone, Sonia Tully drank tea and listened to her ex-husband's tales of battle interspersing the patter, the jokes, the guests, the music and the news bulletins. Her mouth made a thin line as she took note of the admiring callers on talk-back, heard him laugh. This business with the house—it was so typical of him. He just asked for trouble. Why couldn't he have bought a place? He had the money. Or if he had to build, why couldn't he build something like other people had? Why go in for all this fuss and bother, and cause all this trouble? Why did everything have to be so special, with Max? As if ordinary things weren't good enough for him? It made her stomach knot up.

Always, always, Max had been like this. Her father had warned her before they were married . . . yes, Dad had known, all those years ago. 'You'll want to keep him on the straight and narrow, Sonia,' he'd said. 'You're going to have to be the strong one. I'm not saying he's not a good lad at heart. But never forget, he hasn't had your advantages. You can't rely on him to know where his duty lies.' Poor Dad. He was right, of course. And for all his faint praise of Max's good heart, he'd have tried to stop the wedding, if it hadn't been for the baby. But there it was. She was pregnant, at nineteen. Even if she hadn't been infatuated with Max the way she was, there'd have been no choice. Abortions were something she'd only heard whispered about in those days. Keeping the baby and bringing it up alone was out of the question. The disgrace would have killed her mother, and Dad had work to consider. And she could never have adopted Wendy out.

Anyway, she was still a baby herself. She didn't know what she was getting into. She was crazy about Max. The fact that he was so different from boys she'd been out with before made him seem exotic and glamorous to her. They seemed so—sort of—young, in comparison. She remembered how it was in those months after he took over from the old pastry-cook at The Lilac. It was such fun. She'd never dreamed going to work could be so much fun. She'd arrive at eight-thirty, the way she had every morning six days a week since she left school. But instead of fat old Fritz, grunting and banging away in the kitchen and never saying a word to her, there would be Max, kneading pastry and turning out pies and cakes and buns by the dozen, red and sweating from the oven, the muscles standing out under his white t-shirt, whistling and singing and ready to say hello, and tease her, and tell her jokes.

It wasn't as if he was handsome. And he was rough, and wild. She knew that. But no one had ever made her laugh like that before. No one had flirted with her, or made her feel so pretty and—sort of—like a woman, before. And she knew he'd never let anything happen to her, while he was there. He knew about hoods, and crims, and cops, as he called them. It made her feel safe in a world that she'd realised, once she started work, was far more unpredictable and dangerous than her family seemed to realise. And nothing fazed Max. If someone swore at him, he'd swear straight back. If a drunk approached them on one of their secret excursions out on the train on Saturday afternoons Max would just tell him off and make him go away.

So, even though she felt a bit embarrassed by him, when finally she had to let him meet her parents and her friends, she told herself that they just didn't understand him like she did. It was wonderful, when they were alone. And anyway she fully intended to do what her father said. Be the strong one. She always had intended that. She was going to help Max. She was going to make his past up to him. She was going to give him a home. Give him something to work for, like in the movies.

And for a while, that's just how it was. For a couple of years, everything was fine. They got a little flat—just two rooms, really, plus a kitchenette and a bathroom, but it was enough. He adored Wendy: a darling little thing with fair curls she was then, toddling around after him everywhere when he got home from work. And he was good with her, too, even if he would always swing her round and throw her up in the air and all that till she was overexcited and half sick with it. Wendy loved it of course. And Max too. But it was Sonia who'd have to calm her down and get her fed and into bed on time. Routine was important for kids. But you couldn't tell Max that. You couldn't tell Max anything.

Like, Max never did understand that he couldn't
expect things to go on just like they had before Wendy
was born. Parties, and going out to the pub of a night,
eating at all hours and all that. And he didn't understand how it was for women. She was dead tired at
night, after the day with Wendy. The last thing she felt
like was sex, when she finally got to bed. And with
Wendy asleep in her cot on the other side of the bedroom, it didn't really seem right, anyway. But it
seemed to be all he thought about. Sex, sex, sex all
the time. He went on about it like a broken record, as
if it was the most important thing in the world. It
made her feel like a piece of meat. And she couldn't
see why he wanted it so often anyway. She was sure
most men didn't. Most normal men.

Then one night she woke up and found him playing with himself in the living room, on the pretty floral couch she'd covered herself, with some disgusting
magazine open in front of him. She'd never forget the
horror of it. And all the other feelings rushing in, all
mixed up. The feeling that she didn't know this man
at all. That he was a dirty, ugly stranger. That he didn't
love her or care about their life together. That she
couldn't control him. That he wouldn't respect her
wishes and needs. That if he wanted something he'd
just go ahead and do it, secretly, somehow, whatever
she thought about it.

He'd actually tried to laugh it off. Then when she
wouldn't stop crying he'd got angry and shouted at
her. 'What do you expect, Sonia? I can't live like a
bloody monk. Would you rather I picked up tarts in
the pub?' She'd shouted back. Called him filthy and
disgusting. Shrank away when he tried to touch her.
And then he'd lost his temper properly. Raised his
hand to her, his face all tight with rage. And then he
went so white she was terrified, spun around and just
went out the door.

The next day he came back. They didn't talk
about what had happened. And after a while their
lives went back to normal. Well, there was no alternative, was there? With Wendy and her parents to con-

sider. But, of course, she could never feel the same about him. Not ever again. And after a few years he'd stopped even trying to make up to her. He just went his own way. Fighting and quarrelling with nice people, getting in with all sorts of weird types, starting that stupid comedy act at the pub on Friday nights, then, when Wendy was only five, giving up his good job and risking everything they'd worked for to do that late night radio show. And then they moved him to daytime, with that common, foul-mouthed actress Isa Truby first of all, and then on his own. And then he began to get well-known. And then the women started. Isa, of course. Always Isa. But others, too. Dozens of them. Hundreds, she sometimes thought. Hundreds of women. They crawled all over him, once he got famous. It was disgusting, and ridiculous. They wouldn't have given him a look, when he was a pastry-cook, would they?

If only they knew, those women, what it was like, living with a man like Max. Let them try it. They'd wake up to themselves pretty fast. And that cold snobby piece Ingrid Fife, the latest girlfriend—she thought she was on to such a good thing. Thought she was so great, being photographed hanging onto his arm and smiling like the cat who'd swallowed the cream. Thought she was going to marry him, according to *Hers*. Well, she'd learn if she did. She'd learn, when he started to stay out late, bring his loud friends home to drink, get that cunning, stubborn look and refuse to listen to reason or sense. And so would Max. Max would learn too. Sonia couldn't imagine Ingrid washing his socks and ironing his shirts. Or putting up with his crazy ideas. Not like she had. For twelve years. Twelve years trying to make a home for him. A home he'd just walked away from, as if it were nothing. Less than nothing.

Sonia hunched over her cup, warming her hands on it, pressing her knees together. The pain in her stomach niggled and nagged. It never seemed to go any more, no matter how carefully she ate. Wendy wouldn't be back from school for hours. The house

was clean. She'd already been to the shops. A fly
buzzed between the venetian blinds and the flyscreen
at the window. She stared into space, and went on listening to Max.

A year after Mary and Clive left their clifftop, 'Third
Wish' was complete, from the swimming pool jutting
out above the sea to the brass fire-irons on the hand-
cut stone hearth in the vast living room and the
folded piles of fluffy white towels in the bathroom
cupboards. Of all that Clive had built, only the steep
stone steps from the roadway to the house remained,
zig-zagging now through massed tropical shrubs and
tidy groves of fully-grown palms that had arrived in
trucks from sites all over the city, their roots bundled
in hessian, and now stood in Max's new topsoil obediently recovering from the shock.

   Max took possession at sunset, the day before his
fortieth birthday. He took it slowly, easing his Mercedes up the discreetly-screened driveway, enjoying the
sound of thick tyres bearing down on fine red gravel,
the tiny squeaks and whispers as bamboo and banana
palms brushed gleaming metal. He drew up in front
of the house, turned off the ignition, and sat for a moment, listening to the waves crashing on the rocks at
the foot of his cliff. It was high tide. He reached for
his overnight bag and got out of the car. He wouldn't
garage it tonight. The house stood complete, intact,
untried, and waiting, bathed in pink light.

   Ingrid had no idea he was here. If she had known,
she'd have wanted to come too—to share this first
night. So Max had taken care not to tell her of his
plans. Watching her between half-closed eyelids as she
undressed in her elegant little apartment bedroom on
their nights together, he had often pictured her with
pleasure between the sheets of the king-size bed at
'Third Wish': in the evening, cool, smooth, seductive
in black silk; in the morning, gloriously nude and
abandoned, blinking lazily in a room flooded with

light the colour of her tumbled hair. But that was for later. Tonight the house was his. Alone.

Max climbed the stairs to the front door. The key was already in his hand. The air was warm, and heavy with the smell of the sea, fresh paint, and gardenias.

The seasons went by at 'Third Wish', the days measured by the rising and falling of the tides, the months by the waxing and waning of the moon, the years by the blooming of the gardenias by the door. The pink stucco mellowed in the sun. The palms grew. The bamboo threw up spike after spike beside the drive. Bushes, shrubs and vines flourished and tangled in warm, sticky dampness. In the early evenings, men and women sprawling pink-faced and salty in late-homing yachts and cruisers saw the lights flaring on the headland and pointed them out to one another. Max Tully's house. 'Third Wish'. Vulgar. An eyesore. Worth a fortune. They edged their craft closer, stood and looked upwards, narrowing their eyes to pick out a familiar figure—leaning over the terrace railing, perhaps, in a trademark lairy shirt.

Sometimes they'd see a girl with him, her fair head adoringly tilted up as she listened to him talk—a girl of sixteen, seventeen, eighteen—Wendy Tully, only fruit of Max's long union with the embarrassingly faded, relentlessly respectable woman who had been his first wife. Sonia Tully was dead now, of cancer. And Wendy was living with Dad in the palace.

Often there'd be a woman, too—a tall, expensive-looking piece with a mane of hair swinging around golden shoulders. For five-odd years, the hair was blonde. That was Ingrid Tully. The second wife. Mother of little Douglas Tully. Married to Max at 'Third Wish' the year he moved in. 'The Wedding of the Year', *Hers* had called it. Tongue dripping honey, Barbara Bayers, the magazine's editor, had personally organised the exclusive pictorial coverage. It featured (within heart-shaped lacy borders) a pensive, pre-nuptial Ingrid, eyes downcast in misty veil, fairy-tale white flounces and flower wreath; radiantly smiling, post-nuptial Ingrid, her hand on Max's arm; Ingrid and Max kissing ('Like a monkey kissing Grace Kelly. Still—she's a lucky girl. He could put his slippers under my bed any day,' said Barbara, then adding, because he'd never shown the slightest interest in doing so, 'And think of the money!').

But after Ingrid picked up two-year-old Douglas and left—or was chucked out—whichever piece of scuttlebutt you believed (Barbara said chucked, and Barbara usually knew)—the hair colour glimpsed from the sea changed every few months as other beautiful bodies took her place by Max's side on his terrace and in his bed.

There were parties, too. Lots of parties. Noisy, crowded, laughing affairs when music floated on the light across the water from the 'Third Wish' windows. 'Stars' attended the parties. 'Stars' who were Max's friends, or acquaintances, or were the current partners of friends and acquaintances. Soap opera queens and barrel girls fell squealing into Max's pool, actresses of a certain age sang with TV and radio executives at his piano, comedians who hadn't had a club gig in a year told jokes to top models around the kitchen table while Max cooked cheese puffs and sausage rolls for the mob. Rolls Royces, Jaguars and Mercedes lined the narrow road below the house. As did humbler vehicles, for even stars, when they have fallen on hard times, must drive whatever will get them from one point to the next.

The crusty next-door neighbour growled and complained to the police, who did nothing. He planned endlessly to sell up and move. The place hadn't been the same since Mary and Clive left. He hadn't liked them much either. Hadn't exchanged ten words with them in twenty years. But at least they were quiet. And his foiling of Max's plan to build a wall between the properties had been a Pyrrhic victory. The trees on the border still stood by the sagging wire fence. And he hadn't had to pay for the stone wall that now encircled his own land as well as Max's. But it made a compound of the place. And joined him to that monstrosity next door in a way he didn't like. You couldn't pull the wool over his eyes, he thought, hunched in front of the TV while music from next door thumped through his thin walls. He knew that clown next door wanted to buy his place too, and pull it down. But he'd never let him do it. He'd sell for a handful of nails and a tin of dog food before he'd let Max Tully have his place.

So life on the clifftop went on, and the public gaped from afar, and read the gossip, and listened to Max's Morning Radio in ever-growing numbers, pushing the ratings higher and higher so that advertising spots were so in demand that they were practically impossible to come by. The proprietors of his station, including Angus Birdwood, who was by now more friend than employer, tried to remain calm at contract-renewal time, when rumours of retirement or a move to television always flew, and Max grew particularly humorous and difficult. Competitors moved in and out of rival stations like square-dancers, retreating after months or even years, indignant and rattled, to safer timeslots or 'to spend more time with their families'.

And the seasons passed, and Max Tully remained in 'Third Wish'—utterly happy, utterly self-contained, so it seemed. Then, at fifty-five, he married, quietly and without warning or fuss, the young painter Berwyn Kyte, whose portrait of him had won the Archibald Prize three months before.

Berwyn Kyte was not tall. Her hair did not tumble over golden shoulders. She was small and boyish in figure, with short, spiky black hair and an eager, mobile face that could close down instantly when she felt herself intruded upon. Wendy Tully, thirty and still living with Father, took one look at her and realised the time had come to end her spinsterhood. Six months after her father's wedding to Berwyn she was walking down the aisle herself on Max's relieved arm, to marry a kind, stolid engineer called Roger Laidlaw. He was twenty years older than she was, but lonely after the death of his wife two years before, and grateful for

Wendy's attentions and womanly sympathy. They settled down in the Laidlaw family home, and Wendy began adult life by devoting herself to the twin tasks of expunging all traces of Roger's first wife and turning herself into her mother.

Max had not expected or desired remarriage. After two disastrous liaisons, both begun in hope and ended in boredom and disillusionment, he had formed the opinion that women made far better lovers than they did wives. For him, at least. Max rarely flinched from facing unpleasant ideas about himself, and it occurred to him that perhaps because of his background, and because he knew himself to be subtly different from most of the people of his acquaintance, he was unsuitable husband and father material.

But Berwyn Kyte was different too—quite different from any woman he had known intimately before. During the weeks of sitting for the portrait in her grubby, sunny studio flat, a potted geranium dying spottily on the windowsill, a carton of milk open on the cluttered table, he found himself attracted, piqued, curious, and finally fascinated.

He began to need to see her. He would look forward eagerly to their meetings and then, climbing the narrow stairs to her room at the appointed time, feel strangely tense and shy. His natural caution evaporated in the face of her small, dark beauty, her energy, the intensity of her concentration on her work, her independence, her focused passion. He wanted her. But for the first time in his adult life, he felt diffident. For what would this fierce, talented young woman want with him? The lissom, accommodating beauties he had entertained so lavishly and so blithely for years had not prepared him for this. Nor had domesticity with Sonia. Nor elegant life in the coolhouse with Ingrid. Nor had Isa Truby, that familiar, seasoned trooper he had thought was the closest thing he would ever get to a perfect mate.

He felt that he had been sleepwalking for years, and had just woken up. Emerging from the apartment building after a sitting he would blink in the sunlight, dazzled, and sit in his car for minutes before driving home.

When the sittings were finished, and he had no further reason to visit Berwyn, he stayed away. He had no alternative. But her face, intent, absorbed, as she stood working on her canvas or sketching on sheet after sheet of paper, sitting crosslegged on a cane armchair, stayed in his mind.

He made a few half-hearted efforts to resume his old way of life, but found it had no flavour. For the first time (this period in Max's life was full of firsts) the future seemed a flat, featureless plain, without challenges, aim or interest. And 'Third Wish' ceased to be a refuge. He would prowl from study to sitting room, look out to sea through the windows, hands in pockets, and answer Wendy distractedly when she asked about the housekeeper's wages, or relayed the messages from the station that had come in during his absence. Angus Birdwood and Isa Truby found him out to their calls.

At work, his researchers found him uncharacteristically vague and easy to please, and wondered if he was ill or finally showing signs of burn-out. But on air, Max didn't falter. The microphone before him was his key to oblivion, his theme song the gate through which he plunged daily, with relief, into an intensely busy, personal place where no thoughts of the outside world could intrude.

Then Berwyn rang to ask him if he'd like to come and view the finished painting. He drove to her building in the late afternoon and parked, locking the keys in the car in his nervousness and haste, cursing and leaving it to rot. She met him at the open studio door, her face white and serious, her hands, clean for once, clasped in front of her. They exchanged pleasantries. He asked, more anxiously than he'd meant, if she'd been ill. She looked so pale. She laughed and ran thin fingers through her hair and said she was nervous, she supposed. Perhaps he wouldn't like what she had done. He hadn't given a thought to the fact she might care one way or another. She gestured stiffly to the finished work

on the easel across the room. He murmured something
and went to look.

Max knew nothing whatever of art. He'd agreed
to sit for the portrait because Berwyn, introduced to
him as up-and-coming ('a genius' several people told
him), had asked him to do so. He'd been flattered,
and interested. But watching the girl work over all
those weeks, at first punctiliously respecting her re-
quest that he didn't look at the work in progress, and
later increasingly concentrating on her rather than on
what she was doing, he hadn't really considered the
finished product. He had no idea what to expect.

His first reaction was a curious sort of shock. It
was strange to see himself translated to another form
like this. Max had been photographed countless
times, of course. He was used to his image—had got
used to the face he turned to the world reproduced in
two dimensions. But this was something else again. It
affected him powerfully, in a way no photograph had
ever done. He couldn't look away from it. There was
Max Tully leaning forward on a stool, his hands planted on his knees, trousers hitched up to show ruckled
socks, brightly patterned shirt flaring. Berwyn had
painted him looking straight ahead. His mouth had a
wry twist, instead of being stretched into the usual
broad grin. She'd caught that perfectly. He'd seen
that face in the mirror, plenty of times. The portrait
was like him. He could see that. It was strong, and
powerful. He could see that too. But what made it so
. . . disturbing?

Then Max, staring at the picture stretched on its
frame, slowly became aware that this wasn't just a like-
ness. There was a knowledge there. This girl had seen
something in him he had never articulated to himself,
let alone communicated to anyone else. He stared at
Max Tully, exposed. The sharply defined figure sat in
the centre of a large canvas filled with muted, moving
colour, hunched forward on his stool in his bright,
bright shirt, eyes sparkling behind the glasses, cockily
facing whatever lay in front of him. The figure was
filled with energy. It was eccentric. Comical. Inde-

pendent. Courageous. Ruthless. Intensely private. Utterly alone.

A paralysing ache seized Max in the chest and throat. Hot tears blurred his eyes. He stood, blinking rapidly, holding his breath, astounded and appalled by what was happening, fighting for control but unable to do more than turn his head to one side, away from Berwyn Kyte. Wave after wave of pity for the man in the picture, and more especially for the boy the man had been, beat over him. He jumped when he felt Berwyn's hand on his arm, heard her voice saying his name anxiously. 'Max, Max! Don't, Max,' Berwyn was saying. 'It's all right. It's all right.' He stiffened, burning with humiliation. 'It's all right,' she repeated, and caught her breath as though she was choking. 'Max, please . . .' And then at last he turned back to her, and saw that she was in tears herself, biting at her lips and wiping her eyes with the back of her free hand. Not embarrassed, not coolly appraising, not horrified, as he'd imagined. In tears, her nose pink and shining, her firm mouth trembling, trying to smile, gripping his arm with one hand, raising the other to her face.

'Don't cry,' he said helplessly, rubbing at her cheek himself, feeling her tears under his fingers, while his own eyes still watered and burned. 'My God, Berwyn. Isn't one of us bad enough? What are you doing to me?'

She laughed, then, and went and got a box of tissues. And they both dried their eyes. Then they had a cup of tea with brandy in it. Then they went to bed.

Max woke the next day before dawn filled with misgivings. He'd made a fool of himself. Berwyn lay beside him in the dimness, her spiky hair stark against the white pillow, her cheek in shadow. She was soft and warm. She looked very beautiful, and incredibly young. A bitter taste filled Max's mouth. He'd wanted her so badly. But not like this. She'd felt sorry for him. She'd felt responsible. She'd given her body to him to comfort him. He began squirming carefully to the edge of the bed. His only thought was to get away—before she woke. Before the moment when he'd have to meet her eyes and see the awkwardness and pity that would confirm his worst fears.

Berwyn stirred. He froze as she blinked sleepily and focused on him. She stretched out an arm and slid it around his chest, pulling him gently back towards her. 'Max, don't go,' she murmured, her eyes half closed. 'It's so early. You don't have to go yet. Don't go yet. Stay with me.' She felt him relax beside her, sighed with satisfaction and drifted back to sleep, her mouth against his shoulder.

So Max stayed. He stayed till she woke again at sunrise, and asked him quite wantonly for more of what he'd given her the afternoon and night before. He stayed to shower in her tiny bathroom, and breakfast at her cluttered table. He stayed until it was clear that if he didn't tear himself away Max Tully's Morning would have to go on without him for the first time in twenty years. Then he remembered his locked-up keys, laughed, borrowed a wire coathanger from her, opened his car with it ('Simple. At my school you learned to be a crook before you learned to read,' he told her) and set off for work. By the time he reached the corner of her street he was missing her. By the time he walked into the station building with three minutes to spare, unprepared and whistling, he was planning the studio he would create for her out of the second and third bedrooms at 'Third Wish'.

It took a long time to convince Berwyn. Abandoned and malleable she might be in bed, but out of it she grew defensive and prickly if he spoke of living together, of marriage. Why change things? she said. She wasn't cut out for domestic life. She'd make him miserable. He'd make her miserable, probably. It wouldn't do.

But Max didn't want to visit Berwyn in her flat, or have her for lost weekends at 'Third Wish'. He wanted to have her, in his home, under his eye. He wanted that intensity, that creative force that fascinated him, working in a beautiful, peaceful environment he made for it. And he wanted marriage. He wanted her to be his, in her eyes, and the eyes of the world. He wanted to be able to look at her at any moment of the day or night and think, with delight, 'She's my wife'.

Berwyn gave in quite suddenly, in the end, the night she learned that her portrait had won the Archibald Prize. Perhaps she thought that the confidence that suddenly rushed through her then would stiffen and strengthen her permanently; shield her against the threat to her independence she sensed in Max, the man she loved. Perhaps she thought, remembering that first afternoon in her flat, that the deep sense of isolation she had seen in him, the desperate, helpless and unhappy little boy hidden deep inside the strong, funny, intensely masculine carapace that was Max Tully, would be finally released and healed by a woman who understood him.

She was wrong, of course. And quite quickly, as the walls of the light-filled rooms of 'Third Wish' slowly filled with her paintings, bought stealthily by Max from galleries and shows and borne home in triumph, she saw that she had been. She was being absorbed; she was sinking in Max's life, Max's attention. He was too strong for her. His shell never cracked again. But her defences softened, weakened, with every day that passed, leaving her vulnerable to any pain or loneliness he might care to inflict. Not that he ever did. Not knowingly. She had no doubt of his love—his adoration, even. He showered her with gifts. He protected her from every disturbance, irritation and danger. He gave her everything except what she most wanted—himself—while drawing out of her everything she had. Or so she felt. The beautiful studio upstairs—air-conditioned, fitted with every artist's luxury, began to oppress her. The people she painted there (and of course commissions were flooding in now, since the prize) were impressed and silenced by the opulence. When they did talk they talked not of themselves, but of Max. Berwyn understood why. The house was filled with him.

One afternoon, about two years after they were married, she found herself sitting in the living room of 'Third Wish', waiting. Waiting for Max to come

home from work. He was late. Her portrait of him
hung over the fireplace. She was staring at it. It was a
beautiful day. The waves crashed and hissed below the
house: the palms rustled in the garden. She was listening for the sound of his car. Waiting to become real
again. The thought leapt into her mind and with it a
picture: a clear picture, of what she must look like, sitting there. A small figure, with cropped dark hair and
a checked shirt, sitting deep in a huge leather couch,
looking up at a portrait. Tense, motionless, sus-
pended, listening, waiting ...

Berwyn stood and ran upstairs. She packed a few
clothes and her sketch pad, scribbled a note. And
then she left. Got into her car and left. She was crying
so bitterly she could hardly see, so when Max met her
on the narrow road home he had to swerve the
Mercedes slightly to miss her. He swore, tooted and
grinned, but she was beyond responding, and drove
on. 'Nutty as a bloody fruit cake, my wife,' Max said
aloud and fondly, turning into the gates of 'Third
Wish'. 'I'll get a rise out of her when she comes back.'

But Berwyn never did come back. She bought a
little house in the Blue Mountains, and came to Sydney once or twice a month. She started painting land-
scapes as well as portraits. Her work went on selling.
After the first six months she started meeting Max for
lunch or dinner almost every time she was in town.
But she wouldn't return to 'Third Wish'—or to him.
Five years later she won her second Archibald Prize
with a startling portrait of the enigmatic Harriet Deal,
the deaf-blind poet. It was bought by the National Gallery. The first of many Kytes they would collect.

Berwyn was courted now by the social set. But she
preferred her little house, and solitude, to gallery
openings and premieres. The money flowing in meant
nothing to her except that now she was free to paint
only what she preferred. And after a while Max Tully
was able to shrug and smile wryly at his portrait in the
evenings, after the guests had gone, the housekeeper
had retired, and the lady of the moment was putting
on her nightie in the big master bedroom, and think

to himself that he'd been right all along. He was different. And Berwyn was different. They were better apart. Neither of them was cut out for marriage.

He grew older, but showed no sign of it. His sixtieth birthday came and went. And his sixty-fifth. He entertained at 'Third Wish'. He cooked pastries and brioche on Sunday mornings. He swam every day. He let the garden go wild. He warmly welcomed housekeeper after housekeeper employed for him by his widowed and increasingly concerned daughter Wendy, then sacked them or drove them mad and away. He alternately laughed and sparred with Isa Truby, now flush with cash and living in the house next door thanks to a new career as Auntie Dora in the Springdale margarine advertisements. He lunched affectionately with Berwyn, gently beat off Wendy's ministrations, conducted occasional, strained, unsatisfactory phone conversations with Douglas, his son, with whom he had nothing whatever in common, and continued his love affair with the microphone. His ratings hadn't faltered. There was no talk of retirement. Except by him. At contract-renewal time.

It was a good life. A colourful, but settled life. Max had reached safe harbour. Everyone said so. At nearly seventy, Max Tully had finally become predictable.

So they thought. But they should have known better.

ONE

—

The garden was a jungle now. Light streamed from the windows of the house on the clifftop, but the garden was all darkness. It rose thick, black and secret on either side of them as they climbed, their eyes on the steep stone steps, their feet crushing snails and twigs, their arms and faces brushed by fleshy leaves and tickling vines that clung where they touched. Things stirred, shrieked and scuttled in the undergrowth. Verity Birdwood stopped, and hunched her shoulders uneasily.

'Cats,' said her companion briefly.

'Sounds like there's hundreds of them,' muttered Birdie. 'Don't tell me Max has taken to cats in his old age? Doesn't sound like him.'

'Taken to them? He bloody hates them. They're Isa Truby's. Come in from next door. She's got twenty-five or thirty and counting. Max shoots them.'

'What?' Despite herself, Birdie gave a snort of

laughter. 'He *shoots* them? Isa's cats? Dad, you're not serious?'

'Ssh. Of course I'm serious. Well, shoots *at* them, anyhow. Keep moving, will you, kid? If I stop I'll keel over. These steps are going to kill me one day. Yeah— well, last I heard his favourite hobby was taking pot shots at them with an air-rifle. He says half of them are feral. Says they catch the birds. And fight. And shit everywhere. 'Course, Isa's not impressed.'

'No, I guess not.' Birdie sniggered and glanced back at the small, plump figure toiling just behind her, his gift for Max, a bottle of seventy-year-old brandy, clutched in his hand. His head was bent, and you could see that his grey hair was thinning on top. He was breathing heavily. Birdie suddenly realised with a little stab that her father really was having trouble with the stairs. She kept forgetting that he was getting older. Well, not forgetting, exactly. Just forgetting what that meant.

She sighed, and slapped at a mosquito whining in her ear. She wasn't looking forward to this party. She'd be seeing Max's kids, Wendy and Douglas, for the first time in years, for a start. Although they'd spent so much time together as children, while their parents socialised, they had nothing whatever in common. Birdie hadn't really considered that then. When you're a child you just go along with things. But the relationship had quietly lapsed as soon as she got old enough to be busy with other activities on Max's party days. She hadn't much enjoyed Wendy and Douglas's company at five, still less at ten. At fifteen she was unsentimental enough to acknowledge the fact and take appropriate avoiding action.

Birdie grimaced in the darkness. She saw no reason why she would feel differently about the Tully progeny now. But Wendy and Douglas were part of her childhood, just like Max, and this house, and in that sense they had a claim on her. A claim that Wendy, at least, would be eager to exert.

Then there were Max's old friends. A lot of them had worked for her father at one stage or another, in radio and later television. Some of them still did. Many of them had known her since she was born. To them she wasn't an enigmatic, aloof and therefore somewhat daunting, adult. She was Angus Birdwood's skinny little daughter, Verity. And they knew all about her. She could hear the voices now. Kind, interested, bitchy, gossiping. '. . . Funny little thing. Always was. Used to say the oddest things. When she was six she . . . Not a bit like her mother, is she? Angus all over to look at. Well, at least he can be sure . . . What a stunner Jane Birdwood was. Tragic she died so young . . . Car accident . . . Verity just a teenager . . . Angus alone all these years . . . Mind you, dear old Angus, it might have been for the best. A brilliant man, but so besotted he never saw it, wouldn't hear a word against Jane, but everyone knew . . . the men, darling! . . . anything in pants . . . *yes* . . . well, I heard she even . . .'

Birdie hunched her shoulders and plodded on. In the world in which she usually moved, very few people knew she was related to the almost legendary Angus Birdwood. No one knew about her mother. Very few people knew anything about her life at all, past or present. And that was the way she liked it.

'It's fifteen years since I was here, you know,' she said aloud, looking up at the house on the headland. 'Fifteen years ago, tonight. The wedding.'

'Ah, yes. Berwyn'll be here tonight, I guess.' Her father didn't look up.

'The wedding and the fifty-fifth birthday party,' Birdie went on. 'Typical of Max, I always thought. To give himself Berwyn for a present.'

'Didn't get to keep her, though, did he?' Angus Birdwood smiled.

They reached the final group of steps, and paused. Behind them another cat shrieked. From the shining pink house floated the sounds of music, the dull roar of voices, high-pitched laughter. Beyond it, and far below, unseen, black water pounded on rocks.

'Fifteen years.' Angus grimaced. 'Doesn't seem that long ago. Doesn't seem all that long ago that old

Max built this place, for that matter, and it's bloody thirty years.' He looked vacantly towards the house. 'He was forty then, and I was—what—thirty-two? Lot of water under the bridge since then, kid. We're all getting on.'

'Dad, come off it!' Birdie shifted uncomfortably.

'Angus, is that you?' The voice floated up to them from below. Steps sounded on the stone stairs, coming closer. 'Wait for me!'

Birdie's father turned and cupped his hand over his eyes, peering into the darkness. 'Berwyn?'

'Yes.' A woman climbed panting toward them, her thin, eager face turned up to the light. 'Oh, I'm so glad I met you, Angus,' she called. 'I hate going into these things alone.'

'Glad to be of service, madam.' Angus Birdwood made a small bow. The woman bounded up the last two stairs, grabbed his face and kissed him on both cheeks. Birdie looked at her with interest. She'd seen Berwyn Kyte's picture in the paper often enough over the past fifteen years. And her father often mentioned that he'd seen her lunching with Max, or at some exhibition or other. But Birdie hadn't seen her up close since her wedding day all those years ago. And it was startling just how little she had changed. The short-cropped black hair was thickly peppered with grey, and there were signs of strain in her pale face tonight, as though she needed sleep, but she was still the same intense, attractive boyish figure she had always been.

'Do you remember Verity, my daughter?' Angus was saying placidly. 'She was just saying she was last at "Third Wish" for your wedding.'

Berwyn shifted her attention to Birdie. 'Of course I remember,' she said. 'Nice to see you again, Verity.' And her mouth smiled politely, while Birdie felt as much as saw the dark grey artist's eyes automatically appraising, remembering, recording. It was an interesting, if not quite comfortable, sensation. Then the eyes dropped and looked away, towards the house. 'You're at the ABC, aren't you?' Berwyn went on, making conversation. 'A researcher for TV?'

'Not any more,' Birdie said. 'I still research, but I'm freelancing now.' She closed her lips firmly, as a sign to her father not to add that most of the investigations she did these days had more to do with crime than television. 'Private detective' was a phrase she never used to describe herself. It sounded laughable, even to her. Small, bespectacled, thin and scruffy, Birdie wasn't most people's idea of a gumshoe. Anyway, Berwyn obviously had other things on her mind just now, and wasn't interested in the details of Birdie's occupation.

In the house, someone started playing the piano.

'The gang's all here,' muttered Angus. 'We'd better get in. Get it over with, eh, Berwyn? Got your earplugs? Your oxygen mask? Your crap detector on full?'

She glanced at him quizzically. 'You must be the one person who hates these things as much as I do,' she said.

'I think it's fair to say that Birdie hates them more.' Angus flicked gently at his daughter's sleeve. 'She's being dutiful, coming with me, bless her little cotton socks. Max was very keen she should come. Getting sentimental in his old age, he said. I twisted her arm.'

Birdie shrugged, feeling ungracious.

'Ah, well, what Max wants, Max gets, right?' said Berwyn dryly. 'And tonight, you'll find, will be a perfect example.'

'Yes,' muttered Angus. 'Should cause quite a sensation.' He eyed her curiously.

'You know?' Berwyn demanded.

'Of course I do.'

'Hey, what's up?' asked Birdie with interest. 'What haven't you told me, Dad? Something wrong? Trouble between Max and Douglas?'

Berwyn nibbled at her lip. 'Only the usual. Suppressed mutual loathing. They should keep away from each other. Douglas's come over for the party, though. I must say I wasn't expecting him to, but he has. Oh, no. No trouble, exactly. A—surprise, I suppose you'd say. One of Max's little surprises. I thought I was the only one to know about it.' Her face was tense, now; her eyes unfathomable. 'Come on. He'll be fretting. He won't want to make the announcement without us.'

She turned and strode towards the house. Birdie and her father followed. 'I don't know why *she's* peeved. I thought *I* was the only one who knew,' said Angus.

'Knew what? For God's sake, tell!' urged Birdie, though it was clear from her father's expression that he would say nothing more. She felt a pleasant tingle of anticipation. For all Berwyn's bland, if belated, assurances she sensed trouble. Perhaps this evening wouldn't be as boring as she'd expected it to be. She had great faith in Max's gifts as a showman. If he was planning a surprise announcement to be the highlight of his seventieth birthday party, the announcement wouldn't be a tame one, and it was bound to be of real interest to a lot of the people present. And if Berwyn's reaction was anything to go by, not everyone was going to be pleased by it, either.

The scent of gardenias mingled with the sticky tang of salt hung about them as they climbed the stairs. The mellow pink of Max's stucco palace gleamed. Everything's the same, thought Birdie, watching the light shining through the panes of the white front door as Berwyn rang the bell. So much time has passed, but everything's the same. Perfect, ordered, familiar. I might have been here yesterday. Then she remembered and turned to glance behind her, and down, to where the garden seethed and whispered with life. From here you could see just how much it had grown. It hid the street below completely. Black, feathery shapes and reaching vines threw themselves up into the night sky, drinking the humid air, grappling and tangling together in the struggle for food and light, thickening almost as you watched. Hunched shrubs, monstrous and sprawling, massed together at their feet, covering the ground, making the house an island. That wasn't the same. In the garden there was no order now, no perfection, no familiarity. And there time hadn't stood still.

The door swung open. A wave of light and noise rolled out to surround them and pull them in out of the darkness. They stood, blinking at the edge of the huge, split-level room, overwhelmed for a moment by the moving, laughing mass of people, the peacock colours reflected everywhere on glass, the sound, the music.

'Angus! Berwyn! About bloody time!' It was Max, grinning broadly, pushing through the crowd to greet them, resplendent in a red, yellow and green floral shirt. He flung a technicolour arm around each of them and kissed them soundly on both cheeks. 'What've you been doing? As if I didn't know. Should be ashamed of yourselves. In front of the child, too.' He winked at Birdie. 'You're past that sort of thing, Angus. Give it a rest.'

'Give your own a rest,' said Angus Birdwood, grinning. 'Long service leave.' He passed over the bottle. 'Happy birthday.'

'What's this?' Max squinted at the label. He blinked rapidly, and punched Angus's shoulder. 'What's this you're trying to palm off on me, you bastard?' he shouted. 'Hell, Berwyn, this is only as old as me. I'll have to keep it till it matures.'

Berwyn shrugged and smiled. She didn't feel like playing.

'I'll love it, old mate,' said Max softly. 'I'll guzzle it with enormous pleasure, to the last drop.' His eyes suddenly gleamed wet behind his glasses in a sudden overflow of emotion that Birdie remembered from her earliest days as characteristic of him.

Angus nodded, touched in spite of himself.

'Right!' Max unselfconsciously stuck his fingers under his glasses and wiped away the tears. 'I'll get it out of the way, then. Leave it round out here and some floosie's likely to shake it up to see if it pops. Get yourselves a drink. Isa's here somewhere. Mad as a snake.'

'Mad like a fox,' Angus corrected.

'Maybe.' Max grinned. Carrying the bottle carefully he edged away into the crowd and quickly disappeared from view.

'He will too, you know,' said Berwyn, looking after him.

'What?'

'Love it. Guzzle it with enormous pleasure, to the last drop. That's how he is. With things. With people. With life. With everything.' She turned back to them, noted their bemused expressions, and abruptly laughed. 'Oh, what does it matter? All's well.' She took a glass of champagne from a hovering waiter's tray, and waved at them to do the same. 'Cheers!' she said. 'To Max!'

Angus began moving more deeply into the room, greeting people right and left. Birdie followed, with deep misgivings. In the distance she saw the gesticulating, bone-thin figure of Claudia Budd, the current editor of *Hers* magazine and an acquaintance of Birdie's own. Was Claudia here as a friend of Max's, or professionally, she wondered. Well, both, of course. That was always the answer with Claudia, who was never off duty and was far too interested in scandal to be considered a friend by anyone with any brains. Could she handle Claudia tonight? Maybe. Of course, if Claudia had other fish to fry she'd cut her dead.

The room roared and hummed with sound. Voices, laughter, piano . . . 'Do you remember when . . . And so she said to me, all right, Penelope, you're history. And I said to her . . . Remember when Max . . . drunk as a skunk, I promise you, and . . . *I'd walk a million miles for* . . . Midnight to dawn left an LP on and went to the pub across the road and it was *scratched* and . . . Like a *gorilla,* I promise you . . . Do you remember . . . ? . . . and she said . . . *Tiptoe, through the tulips* . . . afterwards. Come on, why not and I'll . . . sshh . . . ten minutes it ran like that . . . switchboard jammed you wouldn't believe at that time of night . . . God, Isa Truby looks a hundred. Younger than Max, you know . . . hard to believe . . . Oh, yes, for years and years . . . I know, I know . . . do you remember . . . ? Do you remember when . . . ?'

Birdie became aware that her father was nudging her. 'You're wanted,' he murmured.

'Oh, Verity, Verity Jane, hello! How lovely you could come! Hello, Mr Birdwood!' A bulky, beaming, middle-aged woman was bearing down on them. My God, it's Wendy. She looks older than Max, thought Birdie, and buried her nose in her glass while she adjusted her expression. We're all getting on, a voice droned in her head. Shit!

She was enveloped in Wendy's plump arms and crushed against an ample floral bosom. She willed herself not to struggle, and concentrated on not spilling her champagne.

'. . . so long,' Wendy was saying. 'And you look exactly the same, Verity Jane.' Birdie smiled feebly, aware of her father's amused eyes on her. When she was a child, coming to 'Third Wish' daytime parties with her mother and father to play in the immaculate, terraced garden and splash in Max's pool with other progeny while the adults made merry in their own fashion, Wendy was the 'big girl' of the group. She was the one who organised the games of hidings and murder in the dark. She was the one who was in charge of making sure they had enough to eat, and knew where the toilet was, and didn't drown or fall off the terrace. Toting the baby, then toddler, Douglas with her on her hip she'd bustle them about in a kindly, know-all fashion, bossing and breaking up fights, revelling in her competence and her knowledge.

For a long time the young Birdie had assumed that Ingrid, the tall, beautiful, scornful-looking lady Max was always cuddling, was Wendy's mother. It was curious, though, that they never spoke to each other directly, and Wendy never referred to her, though she spoke about her father quite a lot. So one day Birdie, swinging on the old tyre Max had had put up for them in the garden, had asked her about it. 'Don't you like your mother?' she'd said.

Wendy had stood there in front of her, clutching Douglas, her pleasant, dull face frozen. 'My mother's dead,' she'd said abruptly, and turned away. And Birdie, mightily confused, had even at eight known better than to say any more.

The next time she came to visit, Ingrid was gone, and Douglas too. Max was cuddling a quite different tall, beautiful lady wearing red and white striped trousers and a red bikini top. Her name was Bonita. She smiled much more than Ingrid had done, showing all her teeth and some of her gums too, and gave all the children chocolate eclairs from the kitchen. Birdie saw Max pat her bottom and giggled about it with the others. Wendy went scarlet. 'Don't be disgusting, Verity Birdwood,' she'd said. 'Don't make up stories about my father or you won't be able to come here any more.'

Birdie still remembered Wendy's face then. Young, plump, and vaguely pretty, with worry, embarrassment and loneliness struggling to remain hidden behind a mask of righteous disapproval. She was to see that look again, many times, at 'Third Wish', while slowly Wendy became a plump, less pretty woman, Douglas, visiting occasionally on holidays, grew husky, handsome and patronising, she herself drifted into tormented adolescence and Max, Peter Pan to all of them, remained exactly the same.

'Douglas is here somewhere,' Wendy was continuing. Birdie found she had to lean forward to hear. Wendy's low-pitched voice varied very little in tone. She spoke fast, and at length, without any apparent pause, or rise and fall. The roar of conversation around them swallowed up every second word. 'He came over from Perth especially for this. He's been here a few days and he's staying with me, but I've hardly seen him yet. Not for a good long talk, anyway. He's been rushing around everywhere, catching up with people. Well, you can understand that, can't you? Old school friends. It's nice to get back in touch. He'll be so thrilled to see you. It's been ages, hasn't it? Remember how you two used to play hidings in the garden, and climb round the rocks to the beach and scare me to death? Oh, you were terrible. Weren't they terrible, Mr Birdwood?'

Birdie smiled weakly.

'Max tells me you've been away,' countered Angus Birdwood. 'England?'

Wendy rolled her eyes. 'I had the most marvellous time. Dad sent me. My birthday present. I'm so spoilt. I only got back last week. Two months away. Can you imagine?' She clasped her hands. 'I felt terrible leaving Dad all that time. He gets lonely all the way out here, I think, now he's getting on. He's got his work, and the housekeeper is a real treasure—looks after him beautifully but that's not family, is it, and with Douglas in WA and Berwyn in the Mountains . . . but anyway he said he'd be fine and he gave me the tickets and of course I'd never been overseas, except for Fiji on my honeymoon. Mind you, I'd never left my house for so long before. I was worried about that. But a neighbour fed the cat and watered the garden and everything. I thought I might be burgled, that often happens, doesn't it? But I wasn't. I stayed with an old school friend who lives in London now. She was marvellous. We saw everything. I nearly walked my feet off for two months. And of course I haunted the V and A . . .' She darted a quick look at them. '. . . The Victoria and Albert Museum, I mean,' she explained carefully. 'They call it the V and A. It was my home away from home. Well, there was so much there I just had to have. I bought lots of postcards and so on, of course, but then there were lots of things not on cards, so I'd take pencil and paper and work away . . .'

'What for, Wendy?' Birdie broke in, stemming the flow out of a growing fear that she was losing both the thread of the conversation and her mind. Out of the corner of her eye she saw her father being pounced upon by a shrieking, twinkling-eyed creature with impossibly long false eyelashes, pink lipstick and a mass of curling red hair. Weatherbeaten arms jingling with bracelets, brown, wrinkled hands tipped with sharp red claws, gesticulated beneath the flowing sleeves of a bright pink fringed garment that fell to the floor in silky folds. It was Isa Truby, in party mode. Max's attempted depredations on her feline family didn't seem to be suppressing her spirits tonight, at least. Laughing and talking at the top of her voice, she was in fine fettle, and very much at home. Beneath the theatrical make-up, false fingernails and wig lurked the sweet, wholesome old lady features of Auntie Dora, Springdale margarine saleswoman supreme. But you'd have to look hard to find them now. Wrinkles and grey hair had brought to Isa the fortune that talent, wit, youth and beauty had not. But Auntie Dora was a part Isa played, to be put firmly aside in private time. The real Isa, paint, powder and all, was with them now.

'Darling, it's been forever! How the hell are you? Can you believe Max is seventy! My God, and I'm sixty-nine next August. I can't bear it!' Isa was bawling in Angus Birdwood's ear, as she embraced him, enveloping his dumpy, conservative figure in flapping pink silk and tangled curls. Birdie watched her father calmly disengage himself, removing a red hair from his mouth as he did so. He handed it back to Isa. 'Sixty-nine's not so bad, Isa. Think of it as *soixante-neuf*. You always liked that.' Birdie was slightly shocked. She hadn't thought of her father as someone capable of even the mildest ribaldry. It wasn't his usual style. But here, it was obviously the way to go. Isa screeched with delighted laughter, preened, and began chattering. It was like watching an owl and a macaw holding a conversation. But they saw nothing odd in it. They'd known each other for forty years, and through their separate relationships with Max Tully, had grown to think of themselves as friends.

Wendy was answering. Birdie squinted and leaned forward, straining to hear. 'Patters,' Wendy was droning. 'For my dogs.'

'Dogs?' The word escaped Birdie's lips involuntarily. Nothing should surprise her, she knew that. But—

Wendy flapped her hands and smiled. 'Not dogs. Dolls.' She cradled her arms and made a rocking motion. 'Dolls. Patterns for my dolls' clothes. Sorry. Of course you wouldn't know. It's not the sort of thing Dad would mention. I make dolls. It's my passion. I've been doing it for years. But since—since Roger passed away—' Her mouth quivered and her eyes brimmed with tears. 'Oh, sorry! Silly—after all this time I still . . .' Her voice blended once again with the roar of the crowd, and was lost.

Birdie fiddled with the stem of her glass, and watched Wendy's lips move. Behind her she could hear Isa's laughter. Maybe she could attract her father's attention if she turned slightly to one side. She began to move her shoulders casually.

'Here he is! Douglas! Here!' Wendy's voice had risen. She was waving. She seized Birdie's arm. 'Look who I have here!'

'Verity!' Douglas Tully smiled pleasantly at Birdie as he edged towards them. He was a tall, well-built man, conventionally handsome and very clean cut in a spotless white shirt and yellow tie. So this was how little Douglas had grown up. He was some sort of salesman, Birdie remembered. Anyone less like Max it was difficult to imagine. No wonder they didn't get on. Douglas must be in his late twenties now. He'd been—what—twelve or thirteen when she'd last seen him? On special leave from boarding school, for his father's wedding to Berwyn Kyte. She remembered little about him on that evening. He was of no interest to her. She was of no interest to him. He seemed to her another species. Inarticulate in public, loud-mouthed in private. Good-looking and aware of it. Slightly plump and blurry in the features, with downy cheeks and unformed mouth, blushing deeply when Isa Truby pinched his chin and told Max he'd be a heartbreaker one day.

As it happened he'd only been out of school a year or two when this was proved correct. The girl he'd 'got into trouble' was paid off by Max, the word went, and Douglas took to his heels overseas. Birdie remembered hearing about this. Some whisper at a party, perhaps. She remembered how distasteful she'd found the story. And how, in the arrogance of her own youth she had felt equal contempt for Douglas and for the girl who had been ignorant, stupid and gullible enough to get herself pregnant by an oaf like him.

TWO

—

Presently Birdie found her cheek being kissed by the oaf himself. His lips were warm. He smelt of soap and lemony cologne.

'Imagine us three here at "Third Wish" again. After all this time,' crowed Wendy, clutching both their arms. 'Douglas, doesn't Birdie look just the same? We were just talking about old times. The good old times, I mean, before Dad married Berwyn.'

'Always had it in for Berwyn, haven't you, Wendy?' Douglas grinned.

'Don't say that, Douglas. That's a terrible thing to say,' his sister retorted. 'I haven't got it in for Berwyn. I'm very fond of Berwyn. I think she's terribly talented. Roger always thought so too. Terribly talented. We just haven't got much in common, that's all. She's a bit—odd, I always think. Odd. I mean, look how she's treated poor old Dad. Leaving him to live all by himself here just because she wants to paint in the

Mountains. It doesn't seem fair. But still, that's their business, isn't it? If he doesn't mind I'm hardly in a position to comment. And Berwyn and I have always got on. I don't know how you can say we haven't. We've never had a cross word.'

'Sure.' Douglas drained his glass, and looked around for a waiter.

'No, I just meant—we did have lovely times here at "Third Wish", didn't we? In the old days?'

'Yeah.' Douglas jerked up his chin slightly, as if to loosen the choking grip of his impeccable collar. 'Lovely.' His voice roughened. 'I remember it well. Let out of that concentration camp they called a school to spend the summer watching crowds of assorted wankers getting drunk at Father's expense—sorry, Verity, your olds excluded—while Father mauls assorted floosies on the terrace. And meanwhile Mother flies round Europe with a stepfather who hates my guts, and calls every second Sunday. Lovely it was. Just the thing for a growing lad. I'm sure Verity enjoyed it too. No end. Ah, thank God.' He plumped his empty glass down on a passing waiter's tray, and secured a full one.

'Douglas—don't talk like that.' Wendy's face had fallen. 'You sound as if you were unhappy the whole time. But you weren't. You weren't.'

He glanced at her, and the bitter twist to his mouth softened. 'Oh, of course I wasn't. I'm only joking, sis. We had great times. Thanks to you. Thanks to the fact that our dear father used you mercilessly as a free babysitter, we had great times.'

Wendy smiled at him uncertainly. He drank thirstily, and made an obvious effort. 'The house is just the same. But the old man's let the garden go, as you said.'

'Isn't it awful?' Wendy agreed eagerly. 'I'm dying to get into it. Everything needs a good prune. A clear-out, you know? Then you could walk in it again. Look, it's so overgrown, Verity Jane. Full of spiders. And snakes, I'll bet. But Dad won't let a gardener anywhere near it. He says he likes it how it is. I'm hoping, though . . . after tonight . . .' She broke off, and looked mysterious.

'The famous surprise,' growled Douglas. 'So what if he's retiring? I don't see that makes any difference.'

'Douglas! Sshh!' Wendy looked aghast. 'Isa will hear you. And we don't even know that's it. I just said I thought—Verity, you won't say anything, will you?'

Birdie shrugged and shook her head.

'Why should she care, Wendy?' Douglas jerked his chin again. 'She's not obsessed by Max and his doings. Her old man's the one to care. He's the one whose station's losing its star. Still, he's got plenty of other irons in the fire, and he must have been expecting it. At Max's age.'

'I think he knows all about it,' said Birdie. 'Max must have told him.' A bored-looking waitress proferred a tray piled with the multicoloured, oddly-shaped morsels home economics teachers used to call 'hot suggestions'. Following Wendy's lead Birdie took a flaky pastry something-or-other and bit into it. It was warm and delicious and filled with some sort of sea-food so spiced as to be unrecognisable.

'These are luscious,' said Wendy, wiping her fingers delicately on a napkin. She turned to the waitress, who had brightened up considerably as she offered the tray to Douglas. 'Could you please tell the caterers to send the food around a bit faster, dear? We've been standing here some time and this is the first tray we've seen.' The waitress, put in her place, broke eye contact with Douglas, nodded and moved away. Douglas watched her as she retreated towards the kitchen. He raised his eyebrows and popped a meatball into his mouth. 'Nice arse,' he said with his mouth full. 'Mmm mmm.'

Birdie considered him carefully. There was something about him that didn't ring true. What was it?

'Oh, Douglas!' Wendy was laughing indulgently.

'Nothing on the little china doll though, Wendy. I have to tell you, your taste's improving.' Douglas was still looking in the direction of the kitchen. Birdie followed his eyes. The waitress of whose figure he appar-

ently approved was standing there speaking to a small,
delicate-looking Asian woman in a simply-cut white
dress. Douglas's china doll, presumably. Mai, the
housekeeper. She calmly dealt with the girl's enquiry
and sent her back into the kitchen.

'The housekeeper who was here before—Mrs
Kafoops with the plaits—had a face that'd curdle milk,'
Douglas went on. 'Little Mai is a beauty. What a body!'

'Poor Mrs Carstairs. Douglas, that was years ago.
Years! Heavens, Dad's been through a dozen since
then. I'm just tickled with Mai. I did wonder. You
know. Vietnamese. But she had very good references.
Not too expensive. And she's turned out to be a real
treasure. Very quiet. Frightened of her own shadow,
really. I think she hides things if they get broken. You
know the sort of thing. Scared of owning up. But she's
beautifully clean. And she'd been here six months. A
record! It's all very well for you, over there in Perth
out of harm's way, but I've got the responsibility of
looking after Dad and he's dreadful, honestly.'

Running on like a monotone brook, Wendy
turned to Birdie. 'It was all right when I was living
here. I used to deal with the housekeeper and the
other staff. We never had any real trouble at all. People stayed and stayed. But once Dad was dealing with
them on his own, it was hopeless. You know, he gets
me to hire these poor women and then he's so rude
to them they leave. Or he says they drive him crazy
and he sacks them, just like that. One only lasted five
hours!'

Birdie grinned. She couldn't imagine anyone
housekeeping for Max Tully for five minutes.

'Well, let's hope Mai lasts a bit longer—at least until I go,' leered Douglas.

'Now, a joke's a joke, but don't you go upsetting
Mai, Douglas,' said Wendy firmly. 'I think you frightened her when you met her before.'

'I'll fix that, Wendy. Just leave her to me.'

'Douglas don't be silly. She's very shy, like those
people are, and her English isn't very good. You keep

away from her. I'd die if she left us now. Later it won't matter so much.'

'Why not?' Douglas went on staring at the woman called Mai.

'Well . . .' Wendy looked slightly coy. 'Well, I think Dad's got this little scheme in mind, you see. I think— well, it doesn't hurt to say to you, does it? I think that now he's retiring he's going to try to persuade me to come back here to live. To look after things for him. Handle the paperwork again, and run the house. Then I can handle the housekeeper or cleaners or whatever, like I used to before. He's thrown out a few hints.' She sighed. 'It would be a wrench, to leave my own home, but there you are. It's empty for me now Roger's gone. And Dad's been very good to me. If he needs me now, it's the least I can do.'

Douglas opened his mouth to speak, but a piercing whistle forestalled him. Silence abruptly fell, and then a low murmur began. All eyes turned to Max Tully, standing in his glaring shirt by the grand piano. He grinned, and his fingers dropped from his lips. He picked up his glass from the piano stool. Waiters began to move around the room with trays of fresh champagne.

'Here it comes!' whispered Isa Truby unnecessarily. 'Openers, please!' Wendy turned and darted her a reproving look. Isa tittered. 'Pardon me, I'm sure,' she said, and drained her glass.

'Comrades,' Max began. 'I'll be brief.'

'Hear, hear,' yelled someone from the back.

'I'll ignore that. First, thank you for coming. Thank you for the birthday wishes, and the presents. Especially for the presents. For those of you who forgot, I take cheques, Diners and American Express. See Wendy at the door on your way out.'

Laughter.

'I'm seventy today. The big seven-oh. When a man gets to be seventy, he knows who his friends are. I do, anyway.' Max's small eyes swept the room, soft behind his glasses. 'And my friends are here. I love you all.

We've all had lots of good times in this very room over
the years. I've been very lucky.'

'We're the lucky ones, Max,' called Isa.

'Thank you, Isa.' Max's voice was gentle. He
looked down at his glass for a moment. Then he
looked up again, and smiled. 'Enough of the mushy
stuff, then,' he said. 'I've got an announcement to
make. Two announcements, as a matter of fact. First,
I've decided, at long last, to make an honest woman
out of Miss Claudia Budd, and do what her magazine
has said I'm going to do every year for as long as I can
remember. I'm going to retire. Friday will be the last
Max's Morning Radio Show.'

A shout of surprise. A chorus of no, no Max.
Birdie felt Wendy's hand grip her arm. 'I told you,'
whispered Wendy with tears in her eyes. 'I knew that
was what he was going to do. Poor old Dad. What a
break for him. Still, it's for the best, Verity Jane. It's
for the best. He's getting very tired.'

Birdie twisted around to look at her father. He returned her look with a grimace. Had to happen sometime, I guess, kid, his expression said. We're all getting
on. Then he jerked his head and Birdie turned back
to face the front. She saw Berwyn standing near Max,
looking rather surprised. It was as if she hadn't been
expecting this. Maybe she hadn't thought Max would
go through with it, for all his plans.

Max was holding up a hand to beat back the noise
and ask for silence. 'Frankly, the daily grind is something I'm a bit sick of now. I'm too old for it. There
are younger blokes than me to carry on. With more
presentable accents, prettier faces and broader backs.
Not that that would be hard.'

Laughter.

'And I've got better things to do with the rest of
my life. One of them, thanks to my old friend Angus
Birdwood, who's been in on this for a month, is a
weekday ten-minute opinion piece before the six
o'clock news. So you see the airwaves aren't going to
be completely unpolluted by Max Tully's uninformed,
bigoted egomania, as someone put it last week.'

Frenzied cheers.

Max was holding up his hand again. 'Now,' he said, his eyes glittering behind his glasses. 'I've saved the best till last. I decided to make this announcement tonight, because you're all here, and I wanted you all to know, and to be happy with me.'

'Now what?' Douglas muttered, shifting impatiently. 'He's going to go into politics? Going to join an expedition to the Antarctic? Giving a million dollars to cancer research? Entering the Mr Universe quest?'

'Sshhh!' Wendy frowned at him and leaned forward, listening intently.

'I'm going to get married,' said Max. He grinned at the shouts of surprise, gold glinting, eyes sparkling. He raised his voice over the hubbub. 'Please meet the young lady who has consented to be my wife. Miss Mai Tran.' He held out his hand. And Wendy's treasure, seductive and very young in her simple, white dress moved up to join him.

There was an instant's dead silence. Birdie looked out around her. Amazement was writ large on all the faces in sight. She heard her father swear softly, and Isa respond. Felt Wendy's hand drop from her arm. Saw Berwyn, the only guest not to be surprised, turn away. Then the moment passed in a storm of sound. Exclamations, shouted congratulations, the hum of tongues as people turned to each other to discuss the latest Max Tully sensation. People crowded up to Max and Mai, talking, talking. Max beamed, his arm around his bride to be, who might have been made of porcelain, so perfectly still and cool she stood there.

'I don't understand this,' Wendy was stammering, forgetting to keep her voice down. 'What's Dad doing? Is he joking?'

'Doesn't look like it,' sneered Douglas, gesturing in the direction of Max, now posing with Mai for the photographer rapidly pushed forward by the positively slavering Claudia Budd.

'Douglas!' Wendy was panicking now. 'They're taking pictures. We've got to stop it! Dad's not well. The girl's his housekeeper! She's—she's young enough to be his grand-daughter. And—she's—Vietnamese!'

'Half his luck,' spat Douglas. 'He can afford it, can't he? A hobby for his retirement?'

'Douglas! What do you mean? He's married already! To Berwyn. What's he thinking of?' Wendy craned her neck, searching the crowd. She found who she was looking for and beckoned urgently. Birdie saw Berwyn Kyte shake her head slightly, then shrug and begin sidling towards them. Her eyes were lowered, the better to avoid meeting the fascinated gaze of the curious who followed her progress.

As soon as she was within grasping distance, Wendy reached for her and pulled her into the safety of their circle. 'Berwyn, Berwyn I don't know what to say!' she began. 'Dad—he must be mad!'

Berwyn's mouth twisted in a wry smile. 'Not mad. Just Max,' she said. She raised her eyebrows at Birdie. 'I didn't know about the retirement,' she said. 'And Angus obviously didn't know . . . oh, there he is.' She lifted a hand to Angus over Birdie's head. 'So Max kept us both half in the dark. Retiring! He didn't say a word about it to me.'

Angus shook his head. 'I'm speechless,' he said. 'Marrying again! That's one thing I never thought he'd do.'

Beside him Isa Truby laughed shrilly. 'Why not? He's had plenty of practice. Three wives to date. Why not make it four? Uh-oh, look at that!' She pointed.

Max had clasped a necklace around his intended's throat, and was now fumbling with earrings. She stood passive under his hands. The jewellery glittered green and gold as the photographer's camera flashed.

'Emeralds,' murmured Angus. 'Oh, dear.'

'Emeralds! But listen—I don't understand.' Wendy seemed close to tears. 'Berwyn, Dad's married to you. He can't marry—that girl.'

'Well, not till after the divorce,' said Berwyn calmly. 'But that's underway. He spoke to me about it last week. There won't be any problem. After all,

Wendy, we've been separated for something like thirteen years.'

Wendy blinked. She looked up to where her father stood, one hand resting possessively on Mai's smooth, golden shoulder, the other around her tiny waist. 'But what's Dad doing it for? I mean, I can understand her—a lovely house and security and so on. But what on earth's Dad getting out of it? What can a girl like that offer him?'

They stared at her. She stared back, honestly bewildered. Berwyn turned away and Isa snorted with laughter.

'Come off it, Wendy,' said Douglas roughly. 'What d'you think? Look at him. He can't take his hands off her.'

Wendy's cheeks abruptly stained red. 'Douglas! That's disgusting! He's seventy years old!'

Douglas shook his head. 'Face it, you were a bloody goose to hire her, Wendy. A tasty piece like that with her eye on the main chance, and an old lech like Dad? What did you think would happen? No one except you'd be surprised.' He slapped his forehead in mock dismay. 'Bang goes the loot. Berwyn would have shelled out. We both know that. But this one's a different kettle of fish. She'll get the lot when the old man pops off, and she'll be bloody keeping every penny, I'd say. Thanks a lot, sis.'

'Douglas! Don't say things like . . .' Wendy's voice trailed off, as though she didn't have the heart to go on.

Birdie felt a pang of sympathy for her. One minute revelling in the party, a pastel picture of the future shimmering before her: Max in his dotage—gentle, grateful, safe; Wendy tending him—dutiful, managing, caring. Then, in a single, shocking instant, the picture shattered by Max himself, springing without warning, grinning and nodding, from the box in which she thought he was secured, socking her between the eyes with a new plan, a new life, a new stepmother. A stepmother half her own age. A girl she herself had brought into his house. Birdie watched Wendy's face as she struggled to digest what had happened, and adjust herself to it. Which way would she jump? Then she saw the lips begin to thin and the eyes to narrow. So that was how it was going to be.

'The sly little piece,' breathed Wendy. She looked around at them. 'She must have been working away at him for months, getting round him. All the time I was away, and he was lonely. I've heard of this sort of thing happening. These girls will do anything for security. She must have planned it from the start.'

'Probably,' laughed Isa Truby. 'But look, worry not kids. Take my word for it. She'll be in and out of this place like a hooker through a revolving door. Believe me. I know Max. He'll get bored. He will. He always does. He'll have his fun playing King Dick with naked slave-girl peeling his grapes and sucking his cock on demand for six months, and then it'll be all over.'

Douglas guffawed. Wendy's blush deepened.

'You're right,' said Berwyn. Her face was closed. 'And that's really what makes it so—I don't know—so *silly*. I can't think what's got into him. He told me . . .' she hesitated, then cleared her throat slightly and went on. 'He told me they planned to have a family. That's why he wanted to get married.'

'*Children?*' Isa's face sharpened and tightened under the mask of make-up. 'You're joking!'

'That's what he said. He was quite serious, I think.'

'Oh, great!' Douglas Tully gritted his teeth. For the first time he seemed genuinely angry. 'He takes the bun, doesn't he? Selfish, arrogant old bastard. Another lot of kids now. Just to show he can have everything. Do any bloody thing. Because he's got money, and success, and he's bloody wonderful Max Tully. While the rest of us—'

'Hello, hello!' sang Claudia Budd, swirling in upon them in a gust of musky perfume and a jingle of bracelets and chains. 'The family of the moment! Isa! You look marvelous. Hello, Birdie. Well! What amazing news! I can't believe it! It must have been such a shock, Berwyn darling!'

'Oh, no,' said Berwyn stiffly. 'Not at all.'

'Really?' Claudia's black-fringed eyes widened in innocent surprise. She shook her bracelets back on her arms and picked casually at her sleeve. 'Max discussed it with you, then?'

'Looking for some free quotes, are you, Claudia?' Birdie intervened. Berwyn wasn't good at this sort of thing. And Birdie knew Claudia of old.

'Don't be silly, Birdie!' Claudia dismissed her with an irritated curve of her thin lips. 'I've got everything I need from Max. And Mai. What a dear little thing she is, Wendy. Sweet! She was his housekeeper, I gather.'

'You took some pictures,' Wendy said.

'Yes we did! So lucky I had Daryl here. We're on deadline but we can still squeeze this in for the next issue. Isn't *that* lucky!'

'Lucky all round,' muttered Douglas, and earned another wide-eyed stare.

'I'll get Daryl to get some family shots for you while we're here, if you like,' Claudia went on, looking brightly around the room. 'You might like them to keep. Why don't you come over? Happy snaps with Max and Mai to keep? Wendy, Douglas—and even you, Isa?'

'Oh—yes, that would be lovely,' said Wendy, rising to the occasion gamely. 'Come on, Douglas.'

'And Berwyn, of course,' added Claudia casually. 'I hear you're going to do a portrait of Mai, Berwyn? As a birthday present for Max, he tells me. Aren't you wonderful?'

'Not particularly. I have to go now. Bye.' Berwyn backed away from Claudia and slipped away, nodding to Angus as she passed him.

'Is she offended?' Claudia's eyes were wide again. 'I don't think I said anything, did I? She's taking this badly, isn't she? That's it, isn't it? Well, you can understand that. And obviously she doesn't want her picture taken. Well, she only had to say so. Why should I mind? She's the loser. She should be taking every chance she can to get publicity. The galleries are all going bad. And people soon forget . . .' She broke off, suddenly aware that in her pique at Berwyn's departure she'd made an uncharacteristic blunder. Her eyes went blank, while her mouth went on smiling broadly. Birdie watched with amusement as Wendy slowly got the point.

'Oh, I didn't realise you'd be using the pictures of us in the *magazine*,' she said. 'I thought they were just for us to keep. Oh, I really couldn't . . .'

'Oh,' Claudia tossed her head and waggled her fingers. 'We might have used one or two, if we had room. Anyway . . . It doesn't *matter* at all.'

'Much,' Birdie heard Isa stage-whisper to Angus. 'Berwyn, Maxie and Mai. Lordy what a trio. The man, the wife and the fiancée. *Charmant, n'est-ce-pas?*'

'Oh, Wendy,' gushed Claudia, ignoring Isa completely. 'It must be so *odd* to have a prospective stepmother who's only twenty-five! Does it seem odd to you?'

'Is that how old she is?' Things were moving too fast for Wendy.

'Hey!' Max was pushing his way towards them, roaring. 'Hey, Budd, leave my family alone, you tricky old tart! Berwyn's told me what your game is. On her way out, thanks to you. You know what she's like. She hates publicity. You've scared her off. Now play fair. I've given you the goss. If you're a good girl I'll give you the wedding. And the first baby. If you're bad, I'll be on to the opposition before you can say circulation. If you can without choking.'

'Can't blame a girl for trying!' Caught out, Claudia was kittenish. 'A baby? Expected when?'

'Come off it,' grinned Max. He caught Angus's eye and raised an eyebrow at him. 'She dies, she dies,' he said. It was an old joke.

'Happy days, Max!' called Isa, carrying it all off beautifully.

'Dad—' Wendy was in torment.

'Pleased?' Max patted her on the back. 'Knew you

would be, lovey. Don't have to worry about me any more now, do you?'

He really believes that. He's got no *idea* thought Birdie. Or has he? Maybe he's just brazening it out.

'Now, excuse me while I eject this scandalmonger,' Max was shouting. 'Come on, Budd. Consider yourself nipped. You and your snap-happy mate have had your lot.'

'I need the phone, Max.'

'In my study. I'll see you right, Claudia. Come on.' Max began bustling her off. He looked back over his shoulder. I'll be back, he mouthed silently then turned away again and went on, talking and laughing as well-wishers slapped him on the back, called out and kissed him as he passed.

Marooned alone beside the grand piano, Miss Mai Tran watched Max's progress. Then she cast down her eyes and went on murmuring what she hoped were sensible, appropriate answers to the questions flung by the excited, chattering throng around her. Her tiny feet were aching in the high, white sandals she knew Max favoured. Her head thumped with the cigarette smoke and the noise, and the jewelled comb that held her mass of glossy black hair on her head. Her figure-hugging white dress was binding her around the waist and diaphragm, making her breathless. The emerald necklace was like a collar, the earrings, fastened too tightly by Max in his enthusiasm, pinched her ears. But her smooth, pretty face was as calm and cool as a doll's. No one at all could have guessed what she was thinking.

THREE

A little over two weeks later, at 9 a.m. precisely, the phone rang in the tiny, cluttered front room Birdie called her office. Clutching a mug of tea, she padded from the kitchen at the back of the house to answer it.

'Birdie!' The familiar, rich voice that always seemed so at odds with the wiry little man from whom it emanated, boomed in her ear.

'Max?' Who else could it be? But why on earth was he ringing her? Then Birdie's heart thudded. Dad! Had something happened to—

'Angus gave me your phone number, lovey. Hope you don't mind. I need something. Actually, I've got a job for you.'

'Yeah?' Birdie lowered herself into the chair behind her desk, her heart still racing. She felt almost angry. With Max, for frightening her, and with herself, for being frightened. There was no reason for it whatever. Nothing at all was wrong with her father, or likely to be. He was strong as a horse. It was that party that had done it, she thought. Seeing all those people so much older. That sudden realisation of how quickly time was passing. Probably she was still thrown off balance by not going to work every day too. And not having enough to do. Freelancing was all very well. But when you weren't busy you had too much time to think. And jobs were rather thin on the ground at the moment. Time of year, she'd told herself. Kids on holidays. Hot weather. Whatever, the fact remained she'd been reduced to tidying up her files this week. In her view this meant things were grim.

Max was talking again. Hell, she hadn't been listening. Pull yourself together Birdwood, she scolded herself. He said he had a job for you. She took a sip of tea.

'Sorry, Max. Could you say that again?'

'I said, it's a bit tricky, Birdie. Fact is . . .' Max hesitated for a moment. He cleared his throat. 'Fact is, some funny things have been going on. Here, at "Third Wish". I want you to come out and clear them up.'

'Me?'

'Angus told me at the party you'd set yourself up as a private investigator. About time, I reckon. As I said to him, why should you be doing the cops' work for them and not being paid for it? Anyhow—'

'What's the problem, Max?' Birdie picked up a pencil and began nibbling it. How interesting. She couldn't begin to think what she could do for Max Tully that he couldn't do for himself, with his connections.

'I'll explain to you when you come. All right? It'll be much easier in person. You just come. Can you come now?'

'Oh—well . . .' Birdie didn't want to be too easy to get. It didn't look good for a detective to be able to drop everything and just come on over. How could you have confidence in someone like that? 'I'll see what I can do,' she said. 'I'll call you back,' she said. 'Five minutes.'

As she hung up she glanced across at the filing cabinets in the corner of the room. Untidy piles of paper massed on the floor around them. Even as she watched, one folder tilted and slipped from the top of its pile, spewing its contents onto the rug. It was like a sign. She made up her mind, waited while three minutes dragged by, and then rang Max's number.

'Greetings,' said Max's voice. 'If you're selling something, hang up now. If you're Ian Freedom in particular don't call again or I'll have you run in. Otherwise, could you please leave your name and number after the tone? Thanks.'

Birdie waited obediently for the electronic beep, smiling to herself. 'It's Birdie,' she began, and broke off as the receiver was snatched up at the other end.

'Birdie?' Max barked. 'What's the story?'

'I'll be with you at midday,' Birdie reported crisply. 'My rates are . . .'

'Oh, God, don't worry about that. I'll pay whatever they are. Now, look. I want you to come with enough clothes to last you a few days. I want you to stay here two, maybe three nights. Maybe even longer. You can have the housekeeper's quarters. Quite self-contained. All right?'

Birdie shrugged to herself. All right? 'All right,' she said into the phone.

'Good. And one more thing. Now this is going to sound a bit strange, Birdie, but trust me. Wendy and Douglas are staying. And Berwyn's here too—for the portrait of Mai. She's working in her old studio. I—don't want them—or anyone—to know—ah—why you're here. I want you to say that you're going to work on my book with me. The autobiography.'

'I didn't know you were writing an autobiography, Max.'

'I'm not.'

'Oh. OK.'

'Right. Good girl. See you at twelve then. Cheers!'

'Bye, Max.' Birdie hung up the phone, pushed her glasses back on her nose and removed the pencil from behind her ear. Ultra discretion required. *Very* interesting.

After a moment's thought she picked up the phone again and dialled her father's private office number. Madeline, his secretary, answered on the second ring with her usual seductive crispness. 'Mr Birdwood's office.'

'Madeline, it's Verity Birdwood here. Is my father there?'

'Putting you through.' The line clicked and went dead. Madeline wasn't one for light-hearted chit-chat. For her the world, apparently bounded as far as she was concerned by the four walls of the vast, busy building of which her hushed inner sanctum was the heart, was a serious place.

'What's up, kid?' The mild voice of Angus Birdwood cut into the silence.

'Hi. I'm just ringing to let you know I'm going to be away for a few days. At Max's. In case you need to get in touch.'

'Ah, he got on to you. Didn't waste any time. I only spoke to him about half an hour ago.' Silence. That's so like Dad, thought Birdie. No questions. No interference. Therefore no need for prevarication.

'He's got a job he wants me to do,' she said. 'It'll take a couple of days.'

'Right, kid.'

'I'll call you when I get back.'

'Fine.'

'Bye, then.'

'Birdie?' Her father's voice cut in abruptly. 'Take care, now.'

'I will.'

The line went dead. For good, this time. Birdie stared at the phone for a moment before putting it down. Take care?

Thoughtfully she switched on her own answering machine and left the room, bound for the kitchen. By the time she got there she was planning. A fresh cup of tea. Or coffee this time, maybe. A piece of toast. Then shower, change, pack. A few bills to pay. Petrol,

the bank, the post office. It would take about an hour
to drive from here to 'Third Wish' in the middle of
the morning. Ah, well, what with one thing and another there was no time now to finish the filing. It
would have to wait until she came back. Bad luck.

It was hot and sultry. Uncomfortable driving, even
with the windows down. Perhaps it would storm later,
Birdie thought. The beachside suburbs through which
she was passing now were teeming with people. School
holidays. Hot weather. Up the hill from Martin's
Beach. Around the hairpin bend where waves crashed
below you. Down the hill to the last beach before the
turn-off to Max's house. 'You are entering Paradise,'
the sign proclaimed. 'Please drive carefully.' Not much
of a problem there, Birdie thought glumly as the traffic built up and slowed to a crawl up Paradise Parade.
It was like a heat tunnel. Heat bounced and radiated
from the glass, metal and tiles of the shopfronts that
lined the road on both sides, heat rose from the black
road itself, heat spilled inwards from the enormous bitumen car park that ran along the hidden beach from
end to end.

It had been years since she had driven this way in
the daytime, Birdie realised. Paradise, it seemed, had
changed a lot since she was a child. The two takeaway
food shops had become two dozen. The cinema where
Wendy had taken them to Saturday movies in the old
days had become a supermarket. There were bou-
tiques now. Gift shops. Chemists. Butchers. Two fish
shops. A tennis shop. A board shop. A McDonald's. A
craft shop. A pet shop. A computer shop. Banks.
Video shops. A Milly's Bakehouse hot bread shop. Del-
icatessens that looked as if they sold more than devon,
ham and corned beef. Two dark little arcades with
signs outside wildly proclaiming the existence within
of occupants whose wares were hidden from the view
of the passing trade. The old Paradise Hotel was still
there though, she noted. She could see it in the distance, right at the far end of the beach, where the

road began to curve upwards to snake around the
headland. It looked just the same. Nice old two-storey
building with a verandah all around.

Groaning to herself, she pulled up at a pedestrian
crossing. Sweltering, she watched the hordes jostling
their way across the burning bitumen. From food
shops to beach. From beach to food shops. Brown-
limbed girls in bikini tops with towels wrapped around
their waists. Rowdy teenage boys sparring barefoot in
board shorts. Mug lairs with hairy backs strutting in
reveal-all Speedos. Harried sun-hatted mothers wheel-
ing strollers in which plump, sticky babies in frilly
knickers screwed up their eyes against the glare and
kicked bare toes against the towels, carry bags and
thermos flasks that shared their transport. Kids, dozens of kids, their noses smeared with multicoloured
zinc cream, their swimsuits filled with sand, their
hands filled with ice-creams, drinks, hot potato chips,
hamburgers, doughnuts, thick shakes. Paradise. More
like hell, thought Birdie. She gripped the slippery
wheel, waiting till the crowd dispersed and the last am-
blers reached the safety of the kerb. She felt sweat
breaking out on her forehead. It wasn't just the heat.

At last, the traffic was moving again. Crawl. Stop.
Crawl. Stop. Two cars went for the same parking spot
outside the supermarket. Stop. Come on! begged
Birdie, too proud to lean on her horn, but gratified
when the man behind her did. A moment later she
saw Douglas Tully, walking rapidly along the footpath
so as to keep up with a pretty, ponytailed young
woman in jeans. He was talking nineteen to the
dozen, and smiling like a shark. Chatting her up, obviously. He didn't believe in wasting any time, lady-
killer Douglas. Birdie turned her head away and
slumped down in her seat. She didn't want him to see
her. Crawl. Stop. Crawl. Stop. A line of cars, bumper
to bumper, trying to turn right across the traffic into
the only entrance to the car park. And then, suddenly,
clear road. Freedom.

Past the Paradise Hotel, the sea breeze once more
whistling in through the car windows. Up the hill,

around the headland, along the flat ribbon of road
that for a short while hugged the cliff edge, and then
a turn left. The main road plunged inland for a while,
now. Daytrippers were regretful, as the coastal views
were lost. But to get to Max's you went with the main
road and the hoi polloi only so far, then veered off,
with a feeling of superiority, to the right. There, a little winding street curved and then began to climb
slowly, dimmed and sheltered by the interlocked trees
that hummed with cicadas along its margins. The
street had no kerb or gutter. Deserted laneways mean-
dered casually off to left and right, dotted with muddy
No Through Road signs. You would think there were
no people here at all. But every now and then a gate
and a driveway would proclaim a dwelling hidden
from view.

At its highest point, the street levelled. Now you
could hear the sound of the sea, crashing on rocks.
Two houses crowned the cliff here. Isa Truby's modest
cottage, half-hidden in the trees, and beside and
above it, the rearing bulk of 'Third Wish'. Birdie
parked her car on the strip of sandy earth outside
Max Tully's high stone wall and got out. The smell of
salt spray, heat and rotting fruit filled her nose. Parrots shrieked. Behind the wall the palm trees stirred
faintly. She went to the door in the wall and pushed
the security button, as directed by the discreet notice
beside the letterbox. The speaker barked something
in a burst of static. 'Verity Birdwood,' she said to the
air. 'To see Max.' The gate clicked and she pushed it
open. For the second time in a fortnight she climbed
the stone steps, heaving her overnight bag along with
her, cursing as cats leapt, hissing, across her path and
bushes tickled her face.

Max was standing at the top of the steps, waiting
for her. 'Right on time,' he shouted. His glasses
glinted in the sunlight. As Birdie climbed towards him
she could see that he was in one of his hyperactive
moods. He was wearing a yellow shirt covered in
squiggles of black that danced before the eyes. His
welcoming grin was a little too broad, and from the

outstretched hand that clasped her own electricity seemed to flow.

'Come in. Muggy, isn't it? Are you thirsty? Iced tea?' He bustled her into the air-conditioned coolness of the house, glanced rapidly around and pulled out a bunch of keys. 'We'll settle in the study,' he said, jerking his head at the closed door on his right. 'Bloody house is crawling with people.' It seemed silent as the tomb to Birdie, but she said nothing. Max unlocked the study door, pushed her gently inside the room beyond, and left her standing.

Birdie looked around curiously. She'd never been in the study before. It had always been securely locked when she came to the house. Very much out of bounds, especially to children. Wendy had always appeared to regard it with almost superstitious awe. It was a very pleasant room, she thought. Soft browns and creams. Big desk with two phones, answering machine, fax, and every other high-tech convenience at one end, comfortable-looking couches and glass coffee table at the other. Huge windows looked out over the side of the headland. Bookshelves and framed photographs and cartoons covered the walls.

She heard the refrigerator opening and closing in the kitchen opposite, the chink of ice on crystal, a dull clunk. Then footsteps and a light clinking and Max was with her again, bearing a loaded tray. He'd had everything ready and waiting.

'Right. We're in business,' he said. He nudged at the study door with his foot and it swung shut with a decisive click. Then he carried the tray across the room and put it down on the table by the windows. 'Don't just stand there, lovey,' he urged, turning round to face her and beckoning impatiently. 'Come and take the weight off your feet.'

Birdie belatedly dropped her overnight bag and joined him, sinking gratefully into the cool embrace of a soft brown leather couch facing the view. The air-conditioning was blissful. The stillness was blissful. Green nodded outside the windows. Paradise Parade seemed a world away. As it was.

Max sat down opposite her and began pouring iced tea into long glasses. 'Mint? Lemon?' For a moment he was the perfect host. He handed her her glass and raised his own to her, watching with satisfaction as she drank. She licked her lips appreciatively. 'Oh, that's good,' she said, and drank again. She glanced at the answering machine on the big desk near the door. 'I've been meaning to ask you,' she said. 'Who's Ian Freedom?'

Max sneered. 'Bloody insurance agent. Got my number from somewhere. And persistent! "Getting married and retired, Mr Tully? Changing circumstances. You know what we always say. Changed circumstances, changed insurance needs . . ." Oh, yes. Can you imagine what it costs a seventy-year-old to get insurance? Nice bit of commission for somebody. Ian Freedom, for example. I told him, twice! I never had insurance, I don't believe in it, and I don't want it now. There's enough cash in the kick to take care of a small army for ten years after I'm pushing up daisies. So piss off. But he won't. So I'll leave that message on the machine for a week or so. That should put him off. If Wendy can't stand leaving it to the machine and answers, that's her look-out. She knows I won't talk to him.'

The rules of conversation and hospitality satisfied, Max obviously felt he could decently turn to business. He put his own glass down untasted, burrowed into his trouser pocket and pulled out three envelopes. He took sheets of paper from the first two, glanced at them briefly and then bent forward and lined them up on the table in front of Birdie.

'What do you reckon?' he said, and sat back, watching her read. 'They came yesterday and the day before.'

Cheap ruled paper from a chain-store pad, still with little threads of red gummed plastic clinging to the top edge. Two lines of laborious, cramped printing per message.

Birdie read the first:

Your being taken in granpa. Ask your Girlfriend about it. She's a cheat and a lieing
bitch. You should throw her out. If you dont
you'll be sorry.

The second was similar:

You think your smart Max Tully but your a
silly old git. Get rid of the slope bitch or I'll
tell the papers about you.

Birdie turned the sheets of paper over. Nothing more.
She sighed and shrugged. 'Nasty,' she said. 'Could I
see the envelopes?'

He passed them across. They were identical.
Standard size, press-seal. No stamps. Hand delivered,
then. Nothing on the front but the name Max Tully.

'This was in the letterbox early this morning. It's
exactly the same as the others. It's why I called you, really.' Max pushed the third envelope across the table.

Birdie raised her eyebrows as she looked at it. It
bore a single word—Mai—and contained a single
sheet of paper, folded twice.

'I didn't give it to her, of course,' said Max. 'Ever
since I got the second letter yesterday I've been scared
whoever it is might start on her, so I've been checking
the box every hour or so. There was nothing there last
night at ten-thirty. But this morning at six, there it
was. Read it.'

The same paper, same printing.

Your a sly bitch Mai. But you wont get away
with it. Granpa's going to throw you out. You
wait.

Max ran his hands through his thinning hair and
leaned forward. 'I think there might have been others,' he said. 'Others to Mai, that I don't know about.
Mai—poor little Mai's been upset all this week, Birdie.
She won't go out. Won't even walk in the garden—
and she's always loved that. She used to get out there

almost every afternoon. But she hasn't even been outside the front door since the weekend. She won't tell me why. Says she's tired. Says the cats in the garden scare her. She doesn't like them, that's a fact, but it's never kept her inside before.'

'Have you mentioned the letters to her at all?'

'God, no.' Max looked shocked. 'I haven't mentioned them to anyone, let alone Mai.'

Birdie sighed. 'Frankly I don't think even the cops could do much with these,' she said, flicking the flimsy papers before her, 'in the absence of any other action by the person responsible. But I still really believe you should take these to them anyhow. It's almost certain to be some nutter who saw that piece in *Hers* last week and knows where you live, don't you think?'

'Probably.' Max pressed his lips together. 'Probably. But—see, Birdie, it doesn't make sense. I've had lots of crank letters in my time. They'd come with the post as regularly as fan mail and PR handouts. God, I had a wall at the station papered with them at one time till I got sick of it. But think about it. Some crazy who saw our picture in *Hers* could easily find out where I live, I suppose. But why put a letter in the box in person? Why not send it through the mail? God, lovey, it's not as though we're on a bus route here. It's not as though we're easy to reach. And why make yourself conspicuous and put yourself in danger of getting sprung by hand delivering? Not just once, but three times and maybe more?' He fell silent and looked down at the three letters on the table, pushing them around with his fingertip.

'So. You think it could be someone from here,' said Birdie calmly. 'Someone close to you. In the house, or next door. That's it, isn't it?'

'That's about the size of it.' Max sighed. 'Sounds ridiculous, I know. Even more ridiculous now I say it to you than it seemed to me when I first thought about it. But—now I've got it into my head I can't get it out. It's a worry. And I've got to know, one way or the other. I suppose it's possible. Mai says Wendy and

Douglas don't like her. Says they're angry with her. Look—' he ran his hand through his hair again, 'I told her it was crazy when she first mentioned it after the party. I mean, why should they care? And if they do, bugger them I say. But it was worrying her. Still is, obviously. And then these bloody letters started arriving.'

'How long has everyone been here? And where are they all, anyway? I didn't see anyone when I came in.'

'No—the timing was good. I got them all upstairs and about their own affairs before you got here. Wendy's sewing some doll's dress in her room. She's been here since Sunday. Her living rooms are being painted, or something. She asked if she could come. Douglas too, since he's been staying with her. He's out at the moment. In his sister's car. As usual.'

'I saw him in Paradise, when I was driving up,' said Birdie, and watched Max grimace.

'You'd think he'd have the decency to spend a bit of time at home. Wendy hadn't laid eyes on him in years,' he growled. 'He can do what he likes, for mine, but she's disappointed. She was looking forward to seeing him.' He paused. 'Anyhow, as for the others, Berwyn came on Saturday. She's up in the studio. And I sent Mai up to the bedroom for a rest. She hasn't been sleeping. Poor little Mai.' A fond, gentle look passed over his face. 'What a doll she is,' he said softly, and then frowned. 'She doesn't deserve to be upset. I won't have it.'

'Max, who do you think's been writing the letters? Come on. You've obviously got someone in mind.'

'No I haven't.' Max set his mouth stubbornly. 'Well—put it this way. I can't see how it could be Berwyn. It's—well, it would be ludicrous to think she could produce such tacky twaddle, even if she wanted to. And I don't think it's Wendy. I don't think she'd be capable of using the word bitch, even in a poison-pen letter.' He grinned suddenly. 'It's beyond me how any child of mine could be so puritanical. Just shows.

Blood will tell. She's her mother reincarnated, as far as that goes.'

He paused. 'But Douglas, of course, has always been a bit of a problem—well, you know that.' He glanced at her sideways. 'When you were kids I always hoped you and he would get together, you know. He needed someone like you to keep him on the straight and narrow. A bit older, you know, with sense . . . No—' He held up his hand as Birdie moved uncomfortably. 'No, I don't mean to get off the point. Don't want to embarrass you. But the fact is Douglas started off badly, got mixed up with the wrong sort of people. And he's never come good since, as far as I can see. No telling what he'd be capable of. He's not too bright, but he'd be capable of thinking up a few misspellings I guess, and disguising his writing. And poor old Isa—God, I don't know if she *can* write—but anyhow she's mad as a meat-axe these days. You must have seen that the other night. Completely unpredictable. And she has said a few nasty things about Mai and me, since the party. Not that she can talk. She's been shacked up for days with some dumb-looking pretty boy she took on. She calls him her gardener. I ask you. Thinks she's Lady Chatterley, I think. Lady Chatterley gone wrong. She's got twenty-six cats in there, you know. Twenty-six of the things. God, I hate them.'

'Douglas or Isa, then,' Birdie summed up crisply. 'That's your theory, is it?'

'Well, if you bloody refuse to beat about the bush then, Birdwood, yes!' snapped Max. 'God, talk about blood telling. You're exactly like your old man!'

'Thank you,' said Birdie sincerely. She drank the rest of her tea. It had lost its chill, but was still refreshing. 'Now, I guess you want me to find out who it is for sure. Then you can either tell them to give over if it is a member of the family, or a friend, naming no names, or, conversely, report them to the cops if you don't know them from Adam. Right?'

'Right!' Max looked almost surprised, and then relieved. She'd understood. It stuck Birdie quite sud-

denly that he was used to dealing on an everyday basis
with people who were not nearly as quick-thinking as
he was. He was used to assuming a certain intellectual
superiority, and making allowances in his own mind
for other people as a result.

'You think the envelopes are put in the letterbox
at night.'

'Right.'

'You found one on Tuesday, one on Wednesday,
and the one to Mai today, Thursday.'

'That's it.'

'All right.' Birdie pushed her glasses back on her
nose. 'I'll keep watch on the box for a couple of
nights, and see if we get another delivery. OK by you?'

'Fine! Great!' Max rubbed his hands together; a
dry, rasping sound. He'd brightened up considerably
at the thought of action afoot. 'You'll hide. In the garden. You'll watch all night?'

'Of course. But tonight I'll stay out in the street.
If a stranger is involved in this they'll be putting the
letter in the box from that side, won't they? And Isa
would probably do that too, instead of battling her
way through your jungle. We may as well eliminate
those possibilities first, don't you think?' Rather than
setting up a watch on your family first up, she
thought. I do have some taste.

'Right! Good idea. Where will you station yourself?'

'Maybe I'll camp in my car. Anyway, leave it to me.
I'll work it out.'

'Let's suss it out now!' Max jumped to his feet.
'Let's have a look. Come down the driveway, bold as
brass. We'll pretend we're getting something from the
car.'

'Max, it'd be better if . . .'

But Max had reached the study door and
wrenched it open. He was beckoning furiously. 'Come
on!' he hissed in a piercing stage whisper. 'Coast's
clear.'

There was obviously no stopping him. Birdie followed him reluctantly as he bounded down the steep

driveway. Her own shoes skidded on the red gravel surface, and she dug in the balls of her feet to try to keep her balance.

'Oh, no! Get out of it, you *brute*!' Max's bellow was followed by a scuffle and a piercing yowl. Something black shot up the driveway, skidded to a halt in front of Birdie and plunged into the undergrowth.

'Filthy, sneaking, vicious brute!' Max was running back up the red gravel, panting, his face distorted with rage. He raced past Birdie and leapt up the stairs to the front door.

FOUR

———

'What is it?' But as she spoke, Birdie saw the green feather at her feet, and further down the driveway the sad little body, bright colours dimmed and matted with blood. She walked towards it. A rainbow lorikeet. A young one, by the look of it. Plump and small, with stubby-looking wings. She herself felt a tide of anger rise. If the black cat had been there at that moment she would have kicked it too.

Max reappeared at the door and walked slowly down the front stairs. He had something under his arm. His lips were set in a hard line. His narrowed eyes scanned the undergrowth on either side of Clive's stone steps. A miniature Rambo, thought Birdie, half amused, half appalled.

'Dad!' Wendy had followed him from the house. Her hands fluttered helplessly. 'Dad, don't! Isa's home. She'll hear you. Remember last time.'

Max ignored her. He bent and picked up a handful of gravel and threw it violently into the mass of green.

Again there was a scuffle, and suddenly a panicking blur of black leapt for the nearest palm tree, landing a few metres from the ground, in clear view. Yellow eyes glared out at them. Claws strained to climb on the slippery bark. Black, furry tail lashed. With a shout Max raised the air-rifle and fired. The cat's body jerked. It howled, and fell with a dull, final sounding thump.

'Got him!' roared Max, as much in shock, Birdie thought, as triumph. 'Got the black brute!'

'What's happening? No! Oh, no!' Isa Truby's shriek pierced the air from the garden next door. 'Don't! Max, don't! I'm coming!' There was a rush, a scuffle and a thump. They heard her cursing. 'Wait!' she yelled. She couldn't be seen, but shuddering bushes and the sound of cracking sticks marked her frenzied progress through the undergrowth and vines that clogged the way from the sagging wire boundary fence to the stone steps. Then she was standing there below them, leaves clinging to her grey hair, bright green shirt smeared with dirt. She was still wearing gardening gloves. Her eyes darted left and right. Her lips, painted bright red, were open, and she panted hard.

'Dad!' breathed poor Wendy. 'Oh, Dad!'

'One of your animals killed a lorikeet, Isa,' said Max calmly. His eyes glittered. 'I caught it in the act, this time. I disposed of it.'

'What?' Isa's gloved hand flew to her mouth.

Max pointed to the base of the big palm tree from which the cat had fallen. 'I'm sorry, but I did tell you. You keep your animals in, or I'll have to protect my property against them the only way I can.'

Isa ran wildly up the steps, then darted off them again to fight her way towards the tree. With an agonised cry she fell to her knees. 'Othello! Oh, God! Othello, no!' She stumbled to her feet, the limp body of the big black cat in her arms. She turned to face

Max, her mouth working, her face creased into a hundred lines of anguish.

'You murderer! You evil, vile murderer! You'll pay for this. I'll destroy you for this!'

Birdie, transfixed, heard Wendy's low moan from the front door to which she had retreated. But Max stood his ground.

'You're mad, Isa,' he snarled. 'You've bloody turned into a mad old woman, substituting cats for kids. It's not a kid, woman, it's a *cat*. An animal. Wake up to yourself.'

She stared at him with hatred. 'I am awake. Finally. I'm awake enough to see you for what you really are. And to know that if I'm mad I'm not the only one. Or the only one who's old, either. You're older than me. And you're using a little tart young enough to be your grand-daughter to pretend you're not, and selling out your friends and family because of it.'

'Get off my property, Isa!' Max turned on his heel and strode towards the house.

'She's only after your money!' screamed Isa after him. 'That's all she's after. What else could she possibly want from you, you stupid old man? You're seventy, and your dick's seventy too. Who do you think you're kidding?'

She was still shouting as the door closed, shutting her out.

Late that afternoon, Birdie crossed the red-gravelled terrace and began pacing down the stone steps into the garden. It had been too still in the house. Max was in his study, working on his broadcast for the night. This, she had discovered, was an unvarying routine at 'Third Wish' these days. From four to five he prepared and polished his radio piece. At five precisely the station rang on his specially installed private line and he read the piece to tape. At five-thirty they rang back and played it to him as it would go to air. Max trusted no one. At ten to six he listened to the broadcast. And woe betide producer, editor or technician who messed

it up. It was the routine of a man used to having his
own way. His time on air might be diminished, but he
wasn't going to drop his standards because of that. Or
make life easier for anyone. So Mondays to Fridays,
four to six, no exceptions, Max retreated into his own
small world, leaving 'Third Wish' and its inhabitants
to their own devices. And interestingly, the house
seemed to shut down in his absence.

In the studio upstairs, Berwyn was dutifully
sketching Mai. In her bedroom opposite, secure in the
knowledge that her troublesome father was safely controlled for two hours at least, Wendy stitched her
doll's clothes. Doll's clothes! Birdie had had some
vague vision of a Raggedy-Ann-type rag doll in spotted
frock and frilled pinafore when Wendy insisted on taking her up to see after lunch. She was unprepared for
the exquisite, china-faced creature in embroidered ba-
tiste petticoat sitting in a disturbingly lifelike manner
on the bedroom chair. Unprepared for the flounced
and tucked ball gown in palest blue silk lying on the
table beside it, the tiny ribbon roses, the painstaking
drawings of adornments still to come. Her face must
have shown her surprise, because Wendy had grown
animated, and with the delighted fervour of the true
enthusiast presented with a fresh audience, had shown
her how fine blue tulle would stiffen the silk when the
embroidery was finished, explained how the circlet of
roses would bind the curls of golden hair and told her
about the exhibition for which this doll was being prepared.

Birdie paced thoughtfully down the stone steps,
watching her feet. How strange were people's preoccu-
pations. And yet she had often thought that however
odd they seemed, they always filled some need of
which the hobbyists themselves were often unaware.
How many people, for example, displaying a range of
emotions varying from curiosity through amusement
to distaste, had made it clear that they regarded her
interest in murder as bizarre? And yet from her teenage years the subject had fascinated her. Why? It was
not an interest in violence in general. The beating up

of strangers in the street for drugs or money, the killing of householders and shopkeepers attacked during defence of their property, aroused in her simple, if rather distanced, sympathy for the victims. She was truly interested only when the murder was a personal crime. The deliberate destruction of one human being by another. Only then was the puzzle all-absorbing. Interesting. She, the most passionless of people, the most disengaged, liked to dissect other people's passions, lay bare their motives, make order out of the chaos of emotion, conflict and lies surrounding the crime, while she stood apart. And safe. The words came unbidden to her mind. She tossed her head slightly. Where had that come from? Silly.

A noise from Isa Truby's garden attracted her attention. She walked down another couple of steps and peered curiously through the trees. Someone was working there, under a giant magnolia near the boundary fence. Digging. A bare-chested man. As Birdie crouched slightly to obtain a clearer view she caught a flash of bright green. Isa was standing close by. She was clutching something in her arms. A box. Oh, God. Birdie suddenly realised that she was intruding upon the cat Othello's funeral. Holding her breath she turned and crept back up the garden steps, trying not to make a sound. The last thing she needed was for Isa to see her.

Reaching the top of the steps and therefore safely out of sight of the mourners, Birdie stopped. So the garden was a no go zone. What to do till Max emerged from his communion with the radio waves? She'd already decided on a place to wait out her vigil tonight. Her car was too risky, she'd decided. It was too close to the letterbox at present, and it would look odd if she moved it. But a group of bushes on the other side of the road would offer good cover, and give her a very direct view of anyone using the box from the outside.

She'd have to pretend to go to bed straight after dinner, and slip outside instead. She could rely on Max to keep the others busy while she did that. He

seemed to be able to organise them. The women, anyway. Douglas was obviously a different matter. Douglas
was out now, for example, and no one knew where he
was. He'd come home in time for lunch, stayed for an
hour or two, guffawing at Wendy's whispered account
of the cat incident, grown obviously restless and departed once more, mumbling something about being
home by six.

But he hadn't left before having a quiet word with
Birdie. He'd sidled up to her on the terrace after
lunch while Berwyn and Mai disappeared up the stairs
to the studio and Max attempted to jolly up Wendy
over the lunch dishes. 'You—ah—I gather you're
some sort of investigator or something,' he said with a
humorous dig in her ribs. 'When you're not writing
books with famous radio stars and hob-nobbing with
your rich dad.'

She'd looked at him with raised eyebrows, her
face impassive. Did he suspect something?

'It's just—look, to be straight with you,' Douglas
went on, his eyes darting everywhere, 'Wendy and I
think it might be a good idea to get someone—ah—to
have a bit of a look into her background. Her,'—he
jerked his head in the direction of the studio—
'upstairs.'

'Mai, you mean.'

'Yes.' He had the grace to look uncomfortable. 'I
mean, like Wendy says, we don't know anything about
her, do we?'

'She had references when Wendy hired her, didn't
she?'

'Oh, yes. References. But, I mean, her personal
life. And, like, what she did before. Before coming to
Australia. She could have been anything. Done anything.'

Been a hooker, for example. Birdie could read his
mind. She considered. If there were something like
this in Mai's past, would it worry Max? On the whole,
she thought not. But if Mai hadn't told him about it,
it might be a different story.

'I think it's really up to Max to worry about that

sort of thing, don't you?' she said primly. Oh, Lord, what a goody-two-shoes I sound, she thought.

Douglas sneered. 'Max can't see past a cute pair of tits, and doesn't want to.' He rubbed at his nose and stared off into the distance. 'Look, frankly it doesn't bother me one way or the other. The silly old fart can do what he likes and get himself into any mess he likes, as far as I'm concerned. But Wendy's worried. She's worried sick. She insisted on coming here to stay to try and keep an eye on things. She's not really having painting done. And—you know, poor old Wendy. She's only my half-sister but she's been good to me. Closest thing to a real mother I've ever had, really. So I said I'd talk to you.' He turned back to face her and gestured vaguely. 'Ask, if you might, you know, help us out. For old time's sake. And we'd pay your fees, of course.' He stuck a hand into his pocket and began nervously jingling his loose change.

The idea that perhaps she should encourage him flashed across Birdie's mind. If he thought she was working for him he might actually tell her if it were her or Wendy writing the anonymous letters. But reluctantly she dismissed the idea. It seemed altogether too perfidious, even for her. This was obviously one of the drawbacks in working for people whose lives were somehow entangled with one's own. She didn't like Douglas, and was more or less indifferent to Wendy, but they did have a long-term relationship, however lukewarm. Springing one of them on Max's behalf was one thing. Trapping them into confiding in her and then running to Max with the information was another.

She decided to bite the bullet. 'Sorry, Douglas,' she said, blinking at him through her thick glasses in what she hoped was an owlish manner. 'I'd like to help, but I'm working for Max on his book at the moment. It wouldn't seem right to take another job involving him so personally at the same time.'

Douglas's face flushed slightly at the rebuff. 'You never used to be such a prig,' he muttered, and turned away.

More priggish than you know, Birdie had thought. I've just thrown away the chance to solve this case in record time and get out of here.

Which I'd very much like to do, she said to herself now, looking down over the tangled garden with its rearing trees and hanging vines. There's something claustrophic about this place. Cliffs, waves and open sea one side. This jungle on the other. And an air-conditioned house filled with tension in the middle.

She glanced at her watch. Five o'clock. According to Max, Mai usually finished with Berwyn at about four-thirty. He'd suggested Birdie talk to her. 'She might confide in you,' he'd said hopefully. 'She might tell you what's worrying her. A friend. Another woman. From outside. You know. She like Berwyn a lot, and chats away to her while the sittings are on, I know that. But Berwyn hasn't said anything to me about any letters. And I reckon Mai might feel strange about telling her. Berwyn being my wife, and so on. She'd know Berwyn'd pass it on. Mai's such a soft, honest little thing, and she trusts me absolutely. But she mightn't want to worry me, if she's had one of those poisonous letters. Especially if she thinks someone in the house sent it.'

Well, now was as good a time as any to try to get Mai alone. Birdie wandered back into the house. The coolness of the air-conditioned atmosphere enfolded her as she shut the garden out, and she immediately felt more awake and on top of things. She stood in the vestibule and looked around. Max's study door was still firmly shut, of course. His portrait over the fireplace cockily surveyed the deserted living area. The sliding glass doors that led out to the pool were closed, and the pool beyond lay still and untroubled. But tiny noises emanated from the kitchen to the left of the vestibule. Someone was working there.

It was Mai. She had changed from the black outfit in which she modelled for Berwyn into soft green trousers and a white shirt. A simple plaited leather thong circled her golden throat. Her hair fell in a loose plait down her back. She looked exquisite, very tired, and very young. Twenty-five, Claudia Budd had said. And at the party that had seemed feasible. Today, dressed like this, she could have been fifteen. She was chopping vegetables at the huge granite island bench. Above her drooping head gleaming pots and pans hung. She gave a little start as Birdie entered.

'Sorry,' said Birdie breezily. 'I didn't mean to give you a fright.'

The girl said nothing and went back to her work. Her small hands moved another bunch of vegetables—some sort of spinach, Birdie thought—into place on the chopping board.

Birdie wandered to the bench and leaned on it in a friendly, ready-for-a-chat sort of way. Mai didn't look up. 'I've been in the garden,' Birdie said. She found she was speaking quietly, as if in the presence of some half-wild creature that might dash for cover if startled.

Mai again made no answer. The shining knife in her slim fingers hit the board with soft taps. Neat sections of spinach (if spinach it was) piled up in front of her. Birdie cleared her throat. 'They were burying the cat, next door,' she said, more loudly this time. 'The cat Max shot.'

Mai's fingers stilled. She looked up. 'The black cat,' she said. 'It is good Max shot it. I am glad it is dead.'

Oh. Birdie tried again. 'You're making dinner? Can I help? There are a lot of people staying, aren't there? Makes a lot of work.'

Mai shrugged. 'I am used to cooking for a crowd,' she said. 'Max likes my cooking. I like to cook for him.' She went back to her chopping, finished the spinach and went on to shallots.

'Vietnamese food?'

'Often Vietnamese. Max likes Asian food.' She looked up again. 'Wendy does not,' she added. Her face was expressionless.

I see, thought Birdie. She decided to try shock tactics. She watched Mai carefully as she began to work again. 'What time does the mail come, Mai?' she asked.

Mai's face remained untroubled. Her hands didn't
falter. 'Usually it comes just before lunch. Sometimes
a little later.'

'I like getting letters, don't you?' Birdie chattered.
She sounded idiotic even to herself, but Mai seemed
unsurprised. Possibly she was used to dealing with odd
people in Max's house.

'I do not have letters,' she said. 'I have no family
left, in Vietnam.' She finished the shallots. She began
heaping them into a bowl. 'I must do the fish now,'
she said.

Birdie had the distinct impression that this was
some sort of dismissal. Perhaps the fish needed more
concentration than the vegetables. Or the operation
was going to be unpleasant to watch. Whatever the
case, it was time to go. The conversation had hardly
been the girlish exchange of confidences that Max
had hoped for. But at least Birdie was now reasonably
sure of two things: Mai did not know Max had received anonymous letters about her. And she had not
received any herself. Otherwise she must surely have
betrayed herself by some flicker of anxiety, however
tiny, when letters and mail were mentioned.

Birdie wandered off into the living room and sat
herself down in one of the lounge chairs looking out
over the pool and the ocean beyond. Her fingers
tapped on the fine cream leather. The girl was worried, though. That was obvious. Perhaps it was simply
that she was more sensitive than Max to the awkwardness of her situation, and his family's disapproval of
the approaching marriage. Face it, it wouldn't be too
difficult to be more sensitive than Max on the matter.
It was extraordinary, really, that a man as cynical and
street-wise as he was could be so unaware of the way
others might view his actions, and be hurt by them.
Was it that he didn't see? Or that he didn't want to
see? Either way, the results were the same.

Birdie looked out to sea. It was so blue that it almost merged with the sky. The muffled sound of
waves crashing on the rocks below the pool reached

her ears, lulling her. She leaned back in her chair, thinking about Max ...

'Sleeping on the job, eh?' It was Max himself, grinning. He was barechested, and had a striped towel and a terry-towelling wrap over one shoulder. 'Want a swim? It'll wake you up.'

'No. No thanks.' Birdie struggled to sit upright, pushing her glasses back on her nose and feeling very much at a disadvantage. 'I had a late night,' she bleated, and immediately cursed herself. Never apologise, never explain.

'Mai's in the kitchen,' said Max meaningfully.

'I know. I've spoken to her.'

There was a creak from the stairs and both of them looked up. Berwyn was coming down, her face thoughtful.

'Ah, Berwyn,' Max called. 'Good! Mai's doing dinner. Will you help Birdie to a drink? I'm just going to have my swim. Just a couple of laps to freshen up. Then I'll be with you.' He winked conspiratorially at Birdie and went out onto the terrace, sliding the glass doors carefully shut behind him. He took off his glasses, put them on top of his towel and without hesitation dived into the pool.

The smooth mirror of its surface shattered, sparkled and came alive as the thin brown body in its multicoloured shorts thrashed through the transparency of the water. And at the same time, it seemed, the house came alive too. Berwyn began fossicking in the refrigerator behind the bar. Wendy, smiling in fresh lipstick, patting the back of her hair and straightening her belt, tripped down the stairs. Douglas let himself in the front door and strode towards them, calling greetings and professing a great thirst.

The three of them sat down with Birdie. Douglas sniffed the air. 'Dinner,' he said appreciatively. His afternoon's excursion, whatever it was, seemed to have restored his good humour.

'Asian food again.' Wendy grimaced. 'Honestly, she cooks beautifully but you get so sick of all those rich spices, don't you? I'd give anything for a nice chop or a sausage or something.'

Douglas laughed. Berwyn stood up restlessly, and began pacing around the big room. Wendy watched until she was out of earshot and then leaned forward to Douglas. 'Did you manage to say anything to Mai at all, Douglas?'

He looked uncomfortable. 'No. Not yet.' He drank a third of his beer in one swallow.

'I just think it would be better coming from you, because you're a man.'

'Yeah. Sure.'

Birdie looked at them enquiringly. Outside in the sun, Max churned through blue water.

'I—Douglas and I thought—well, it sounds terrible, Verity, but I thought that perhaps Mai had decided to marry Dad because she was, well, very short of money,' whispered Wendy.

'Wendy, for God's sake,' hissed Douglas. 'Don't go . . .'

But Wendy waved away his objections. 'It doesn't matter, Douglas. Not with Verity. She knows Dad. She knows how awful this is.' She nodded at Birdie. 'Anyway, I thought she might even be in trouble of some kind, and need money badly. Or she might have relatives she had to support. You know how Asian families are.' She drew breath. 'So I thought that if we offered her a little present—something from Douglas and me—she might decide that—well—' Her voice trailed off.

'She might decide to take herself off,' Douglas finished for her. He shook his head at her with a sort of irritated fondness. 'You don't seem to understand, sis, that there's no way we could offer her anything she'd accept. I'm just about skint. You'd have to mortgage your house, and you don't really want to do that, do you? Berwyn could do it, but she wouldn't. There's no way she'd cooperate. And even if she would, face it, the girl'd laugh at anything we could offer. It'd be pocket-money to her. She's after bigger stakes.'

They all jumped guiltily as the glass door behind

them rolled open and Max came in, securely wrapped in his white gown and rubbing at his hair. 'That's better,' he declared, looking around brightly. 'I'll get changed and be with you. Everybody happy? Good.' Whistling, he bounced up the stairs and disappeared into the master bedroom.

Douglas got up. 'More drinks anyone? Berwyn, come back and join us or you'll miss the next round.' He busied himself at the bar. 'Any more in the Isa and the cat saga while I was out?' he asked loudly over his shoulder. He was obviously determined to steer the conversation into more conventional channels.

'Not that I know of. Thank heavens,' sighed Wendy. 'What am I going to do with Dad? Poor Isa.' She made room for Berwyn on the couch, but with a slight smile, Berwyn shook her head and perched on the arm.

'Her gardener was burying the cat this afternoon,' Birdie volunteered. 'Down near the boundary fence, where that giant magnolia and the shed thing are on Isa's side.'

'Oh, yes. There's a little cat's graveyard there,' said Wendy. 'Under the tree. Poor Isa.'

'I wouldn't waste my sympathy, sis.' Douglas rolled his eyes as he put down the drinks. 'She's getting plenty of comfort, I'd say. Though it's beyond me how the guy can get it up. Even for three square a day I couldn't bonk an old hag like that.'

'Don't be disgusting, Douglas,' cried Wendy. 'Don't be ridiculous!' And for a moment Birdie saw the shadow of a stolid, disapproving, much younger Wendy, valiantly defending her view of what was and was not possible against the irrevocable evidence of her own eyes.

Max, overhearing on his way down the stairs, laughed. 'Bless your heart, Wendy,' he said, coming over and clapping her on the shoulder. 'Never change. What did you think of the piece tonight, by the way?'

'Oh, it was good. But I thought you were doing something about imports.'

Max chuckled. 'I was more in the mood for feral cats, as it happened. I threw out the import piece and wrote the new one in thirty minutes flat.'

'I hope Isa didn't listen.'

'She usually does. And I bloody hope she did. I wrote it specially for her.'

'Oh, Dad . . .'

Birdie turned her attention elsewhere.

'. . . In fact, Douglas,' Berwyn was saying loftily, 'you'd be surprised. Isa's still a wonderful-looking woman. I decided yesterday I'd like to paint her. I'm going to ask her, when she's calmed down. She's a great character.'

Max laughed. 'She's that all right. By God she was a knockout too, old Isa, when she was a girl.' He grinned reminiscently. 'A knockout, in every sense. Still and all, Berwyn, I reckon she should call it a day now, with the blokes. She's nearly seventy.'

'You, my friend, *are* seventy, and I haven't noticed you calling it a day.'

'But it's quite different for women, Berwyn,' Wendy objected. 'Women—well, for one thing they lose interest, don't they, as they get older? Especially after the change. And they lose their looks, where men don't, really. And an older woman wants to keep her dignity, doesn't she? It just isn't nice, at Isa's age.'

Berwyn's furious response to this was never voiced. For at that moment the doorbell rang.

'Oh God, speak of the devil,' groaned Max. 'She's come through the side fence. You answer it, Wendy. Protect me, like the angel you are.'

Wendy, her face puckered with anxiety, went obediently to the front door. They heard low murmuring and then Wendy's voice calling. 'Dad! Dad!' She sounded rather strained.

'Oh, spare me!' Max heaved himself to his feet and ambled to the door, his drink still clutched in his hand.

'Who is it?' whispered Berwyn. 'It doesn't sound like Isa.'

Birdie got up and peered after Max. 'It's the gardener from next door.'

'The boyfriend!' chortled Douglas. 'She must have sent him in to heavy Max. This I've got to see.'

'There's no point getting aggro with we, mate.' They heard Max's voice, hard and cold. 'The cat was on my property and . . .'

Berwyn and Douglas joined Birdie and they walked together towards the door. They saw Max, with Wendy fluttering behind him, facing a towering, slightly swaying male figure that nearly filled the doorway.

'I couldn't give a stuff about the cat!' The gardener's voice was thick with alcohol and rage. 'I couldn't give a stuff, so stop talking to me about it. Gave you a few nasty moments with those letters, didn't I? Made you think? Made her think too, I bet. But now I'm sick of mucking around. I want you to butt out of my life, grandpa. I want to see my wife. I've come for my wife. Mai.'

FIVE

———

'Didn't tell you she was married, did she?' snarled the man on the doorstep. 'Didn't tell you she had a husband. By God, I read in some filthy women's magazine that my wife ... my *wife* ... is marrying some other man. Some rich old geezer with more money than sense. So I come to find out, don't I? And I find her shacked up with—'

'Be quiet!' Max's voice was calm, but he was white and grim. He turned and called over his shoulder. 'Mai? Come here, will you?'

'That's right. Call her.' The man on the doorstep swayed. 'She didn't tell you, did she? I knew she hadn't. Sly, conniving bitch!'

'Shut up! Mai!' Max's voice rang out sharply now.

Birdie saw Mai glide from the kitchen into the vestibule. Her hands were clasped in front of her, the knuckles showing white. Her eyes were wide and startled. The muscles of her throat worked convulsively.

'Mai!' The man at the door started forward.

Max barred his path and glanced behind him at the quivering figure by the kitchen door. 'Mai, don't be frightened,' he said gently, holding out his arm to her. 'This man says he's your husband. Is that true?'

'Mai, darling, my God, it's me, Warren,' moaned the man. 'Why did you run away from me? What are you doing here with him? Mai?'

Mai Tran stood motionless. Her mouth was slightly open. Her hands were clutched against her chest. She didn't move.

'Mai!' Warren's voice had changed. Now it was high, and pleading. 'Come here. Come with me, now. You're my wife! You have to come.'

'She doesn't, you know,' said Max quietly.

'She does! She's my wife. She's mine!' Warren swayed, and bared his teeth. Saliva gathered at the corners of his mouth.

'Mai,' said Max softly, his hand still stretched out to her. 'Do you want to go with him? All you have to do is say yes. I'll understand. Do you want to?'

'No,' breathed Mai, and took his hand in both of hers, pressing it against her cheek.

With a howl Warren sprang, pushing Max aside, reaching for the shrinking girl. Wendy screamed. Douglas stepped forward. 'Piss off, mate!' he growled. 'Can't you see you're not wanted?'

For a split second the two big men faced one another in the doorway, sizing each other up. Then Douglas pushed Warren in the chest and sent him stumbling backwards. He followed him out the door. 'Get off this property,' he spat. 'And don't let me see you here again.'

Warren backed away. His lip curled. 'God, the old midget's got a bodyguard,' he sneered. 'What kind of job is that, you poofter?'

'I'm his son,' said Douglas levelly. 'Now fuck off.'

'His son? Oh, yeah? That what your mum told you? He's got a taste for whores, then. If you're his son I'm the queen of—'

Douglas's fist caught him squarely in the mouth. He fell to the ground.

'Ugh!' Berwyn shuddered and turned her head away.

Warren staggered to his feet, pressing the back of his hand against his bleeding mouth. He backed away from them, stumbling and nearly falling down the front steps and finally stopping on the red-gravelled terrace. 'You'll be sorry for this, you bastards,' he screamed. 'You'll be bloody sorry. I'll get the cops on to you. I'll tell the papers all about you. You won't get away with this. I'll never let Mai go. She's my wife. She'll always be my wife.'

Douglas moved forward menacingly and he turned and made for the stone steps, tripping over his own feet in his haste. He plunged down the steps, crying and swearing, then turned off into the undergrowth and disappeared from view. They heard him crashing through shrubs and vines for a few seconds. Then there was silence.

'Gone,' said Douglas to Max, returning to the house. For a moment his father stood rigidly staring into the garden, one hand still held imprisoned in both of Mai's, the other hanging by his side, fist clenched. Then he nodded and turned away as the door was slammed shut.

Wendy was trembling, clutching Douglas's arm. 'How awful! Oh, how awful! What a terrible man. Oh, Douglas, what would we have done if you hadn't been here? Oh, what if he does ring the papers? What will we do?'

'Calm down, Wendy.' But Max's voice lacked its usual authority. He had his arm around Mai now, but he didn't look at her. She had grown very still, her eyes downcast. Max stuck out his chin. He strode to the telephone in the living room, shepherding Mai along with him, punched a button and then dialled without picking up the receiver. They all heard someone pick up the phone at the other end. 'Hello?' Isa Truby's voice echoed through the room.

'Isa? Max. Are you aware that your so-called gardener has been in here blind drunk and violent?' Max spoke sharply at the phone. His eyes behind his shining glasses moved from face to face. Berwyn. Douglas. Wendy. Birdie. But still he didn't look at Mai.

Isa's laughter cackled through the speaker. 'So what if he's drunk? I'm drunk. We've been having a wake. And you know why, don't you?' Her voice wobbled for a moment, then strengthened again. 'You know why.'

Max gritted his teeth. 'Isa, this is serious. The man you've got in there's dangerous. Get rid of him.'

'You must be joking! Who do you think you are? He's done nothing any red-blooded man wouldn't do. You've got his wife in there. He brought her into this country. Paid her fare and all. Spent all his dough on her. Then when she found he wasn't as rich as she'd thought she just dropped him like a hot potato and went out looking for a better prospect. He told me all about it. Cried like a baby, poor boy.' She cackled again, a painful sound that was half a sob. 'So the little slut has turned out to be married already. What a laugh! She made a fool out of you. Serves you right, you arrogant prick. I'm just sorry you found out before you actually married a bigamist and made a *complete* arse of yourself!'

His face thunderous, Max cut the connection. He turned his face away from the other people in the room and swore softly.

'God,' breathed Birdie. She looked up and was astonished to see Berwyn smiling. Berwyn noticed her staring and leaned towards her. 'It's Max and Isa. Twas ever thus,' she murmured. 'Red in tooth and claw.'

Mai, drooping in the shelter of Max's arm, tears rolling down her cheeks, finally spoke. 'I am sorry, Max,' she said.

He turned back and looked at her for the first time. The lines of his face were hard but his voice was gentle. 'You *are* married to him, Mai? You're sure?'

'I am married to him,' said Mai flatly, as if repeating a lesson.

'Well—Mai, Mai, in God's name why didn't you *tell*

me?' Max burst out. He winced as she shrank away from him. 'No, no, don't be frightened,' he said, forcing his voice into a lower, calmer tone. 'I'm not angry with you, Mai. I'm not. I'm just trying to understand. Didn't you realise you couldn't marry me when you were already married to someone else?'

'Yes.' The words were scarcely audible.

'Then—'

She lifted her head and looked at him. Her eyes were tearless now. Her face was unreadable. 'In the beginning when you tell me we will marry I say to you over and over, "Max, I love you. I will stay with you. We do not need to marry." But you—you do not listen. So then I think you will be angry if I say more. So I say nothing. I listen and say nothing. I think—it does no harm to talk.'

Max stared at her, aghast. You could almost see him remembering. The tender conversations that had in fact been monologues. The passionate promises that had been unwanted, worrying intrusions. The silences that had been not shy acquiescence, but carefully judged expediency. He seemed to shrink and fade, dwarfed by the vast room in which he stood, overshadowed by the painting above his head.

'I did not know you would speak of it at your party. You do not say. You say it is your birthday party. You make a cake. Your friends will come. You do not say you will tell them—'

'It was a surprise. I thought you'd be pleased. Christ!' Max dropped his arm from Mai's shoulders and clapped a thin brown hand to his forehead. 'And then I let you be photographed for that bloody magazine. And you still didn't say anything. Not a word!' He shook his head, almost in wonder. 'Not a bloody word.'

'I could not tell you,' said Mai. Suddenly tears were rolling down her cheeks again.

Douglas murmured something under his breath.

'No.' Max took a breath, glanced at Douglas and at her and squared his shoulders. 'Don't cry,' he muttered. 'Don't cry, Mai. Look, why don't you go upstairs and have a lie down? I'll come up and talk to you later. All right?'

'Dad, what if he does ring the papers?' whispered Wendy. 'What will we do if . . . ?'

'Ah, sod the bloody papers!' snarled Max. 'They can print what they like. If they've got the guts to take me on.'

'I will go away,' breathed Mai, very softly. She touched Max's sleeve with quivering fingers. 'I will go, and then . . .'

'Mai, don't say anything now. You just go on up-stairs like a good girl. Please.' Max, thought Birdie, was at the end of his tether.

Mai looked at him once more, then cast her eyes down again and did as she was told. Her soft footsteps made no sound as she moved across the room and up the stairs. They heard the bedroom door click closed.

Max sank into a chair and put his head in his hands. 'God almighty,' he groaned.

The housekeeper's suite had a sitting room, a bed-room, a kitchenette and a bathroom, all in tones of beige and blue. Designed to suit all tastes, it was ut-terly characterless, but to Birdie, released at last from the welter of half-appalled, half-avid conjecture in which she'd been forced to participate by Wendy and Douglas once Max had gone upstairs to confront his disgraced intended and Berwyn had escaped to her studio, it was a haven. She surveyed her temporary do-main with pleasure. The apartment was entered from the 'Third Wish' kitchen, and fitted neatly into one corner of the house. The sitting room looked out onto the garden from one set of windows, and the nar-row side passage of the house from the other. That view featured Isa's trees and shrubs, a sagging wire fence, and a huge, wheeled garbage bin. Not so glam-orous. But even a palace like 'Third Wish', mused Birdie, had garbage. And garbage must go some-where.

The windows of the bedroom next door, with its

double bed, television set and wall of cupboards, also gave out onto the side passage. It would be dim in the daytime. But in this room especially, the sound of crashing waves was omnipresent. The tide must be rising. Birdie peered through the glass. A wind had blown up. There was no moon to be seen, and leaves and branches bending over the passage from Isa's side scratched on the windowpanes out in the blackness. Thank God there was no longer any need to keep watch through the night. The anonymous letter writer had been found. Or had declared himself.

Birdie drew the curtains, threw off her clothes and crawled into bed. This was the bed Mai had slept in, before she was promoted to the apartment upstairs. There now, presumably, the two key players in the drama of this evening were still discussing their next move. Or was one talking and one listening, eyes downcast, small hands folded?

The wind blew. The waves thundered. Birdie closed her eyes. Across the room twigs and leaves scratched on the windows. A cat yowled. Her eyes opened again. She thought of Mai's husband. An unbalanced character. An obsessive. Anyone could see that. Such men were dangerous. He could have a gun. He could be prowling out there. Or simply standing down in the thrashing garden, hidden, watching the darkened house. He could have been watching for hours. Could he be waiting his moment to—

Birdie turned over and burrowed under the covers, pulling the sheet over her ears. She willed herself to sleep. She forced herself to breath evenly. She thought of nothing. After a minute or two she got up. She'd decided to watch TV.

In the morning the wind had died, the waves were soft, the sea sparkled, and Birdie felt a fool. At a disadvantage, too, because thanks to her orgy of old movies in the night it was eight o'clock by the time she woke, and she knew Max was an early riser. He'd be up and breakfasted by now.

Up, breakfasted and gone as well, she found, as she let herself out of the housekeeper's apartment into the gleaming kitchen. A fluffy pile of big, fragrantly warm, glossy-topped currant buns lay on a rack by the oven. A note propped against the buns read: 'Good morning, all. Enjoy. Back soon. M.' He'd been cooking next door to her bedroom and she hadn't heard a thing. She regarded the confident, vigorous scrawl with interest. It plainly took a lot to keep Max down. She considered her own position. It would be best to go. And as soon as possible. But she didn't really feel she could leave until Max came back. She'd have to wait around till he did.

As she stood irresolute, wondering whether her need for coffee could overcome her boredom at the thought of finding the makings, she heard the stairs in the living area squeak. Good. Someone was coming down.

It was Wendy. She seemed to have recovered some of her equilibrium overnight. She was wearing a brightly-coloured sundress and sandals, and had put on lipstick. She smiled warmly at Birdie as she came into the kitchen. 'Seen Dad?' she asked immediately.

Birdie shook her head and pointed to the note. Wendy glanced at it and shook her head indulgently. 'He's incorrigible,' she said. 'Imagine him doing that, bless his heart.' She sighed. 'He probably didn't sleep too well.'

'Where would he be?' asked Birdie.

'He might have gone to Paradise for a surf. He does that sometimes, especially if he's had a bad night. He doesn't mind the beach if it's early and no one's there. Coffee or tea?' Humming to herself, Wendy filled an electric jug with water and began to pull coffee, tea and cups from various cupboards. Good, thought Birdie, and went to the refrigerator. She would get the milk. Who said she wasn't domesticated?

The buns were delicious. The coffee was excellent. Birdie felt strangely peaceful as she sat at the kitchen table eating and drinking. There was no doubt that for all her irritating ways Wendy was a comfortable companion in moments like this. She was practical and capable, and she liked looking after people. You could imagine her living peacefully with her husband and making his life very happy. But despite her long apprenticeship, Wendy wasn't suited to life with Max. What had he said? She was the image of her mother. She accepted his ways, and his friends, but would never be other than alien to them. Douglas was the same. How odd. Neither of Max's children seemed to have been affected either by his genes or his example. It was as though he was a sterile original, who could never reproduce himself.

Wendy poured herself another cup of tea from the round, brown pot and got up to boil more water. 'I might make some salmon rissoles for dinner,' she said. 'They're Douglas's favourite.' Then she sighed. 'Wasn't it terrible, last night, Verity?'

Birdie made a vague, soothing sound.

'Yes. I took a long time to get off to sleep,' Wendy went on. She added hot water to the pot and came back to the table. 'Thinking, you know. I'm so sorry for Dad. And I feel almost sorry for that girl. Being caught out like that, with everyone there. It must have been awful.'

'Mmm.' Birdie filled her mouth with currant bun and clasped her coffee cup firmly in both hands. She swayed slightly. Perhaps Wendy would take this as a sign that she was still only half-awake.

Wendy sipped tea. 'But it's all for the best, isn't it? You've got to be cruel to be kind sometimes. Like lancing a boil.'

Birdie stopped swaying. She started to feel sick. She swallowed the last of her bun hurriedly.

'I suppose she's upstairs packing her things,' mused Wendy. 'The bedroom door's shut. Actually, come to think of it, that's probably why Dad's gone out.' She sighed heavily. 'It really is for the best, isn't it, Verity? But poor Dad ...'

With relief, Birdie heard the stairs creak again and Berwyn entered the room, yawning and pushing her fingers through her short pepper and salt hair. She looked small and pale this morning, and the shadows under her eyes had deepened.

'There's still some tea in the pot, Berwyn,' offered Wendy rather diffidently. 'Or there's coffee.'

'Thanks.' Berwyn smiled briefly and sat down at the end of the table. She poured herself some tea and began to drink it. They watched her in silence. After a while she looked up. 'Seen Max?' she asked.

'No. He's gone out. We think he's—you know—giving Mai a bit of peace. To pack and so on,' said Wendy. 'He made currant buns, would you believe it? Will you have one?' She pushed the heaped plate down the table.

Berwyn shook her head. 'Not just now, thanks.' She met Birdie's eyes and then looked away.

Wendy drained her teacup and stood up. 'Well, look, I think I'll pop upstairs and tidy up while I have the chance,' she said. 'Will you be all right, Verity?'

'Oh, sure. I'll be fine.'

Wendy took her plate and cup to the sink and with a bright smile, bustled out of the room. Her heavy tread thumped on the stairs. The two at the table hunched over their cups until sounds from above their heads told them that Wendy had entered her room. Then Birdie looked up. 'How can a child know its father so little? Max won't let Mai go,' she said. 'It'll be a matter of pride with him, now, apart from anything else.'

'I don't know,' Berwyn again ran her fingers through her spiky hair. 'He might not be able to stop her.' She frowned. 'Anyway, maybe he won't try. That business with the husband rocked him. Knocked him sideways.'

Birdie flicked her finger towards the note that Wendy had propped beside the plate of buns. 'This sounds positive enough,' she commented.

'Oh, yes.' Berwyn dismissed the note with a shrug. 'He's good at putting up a front. He should be. He's been doing it all his life.'

'But surely . . .' Birdie frowned in her turn. 'Look,

Max is a man of the world. He can just help Mai get a divorce, and—'

'You don't understand. Of course he can. But will he want to? Look, I talked to him about her before the party. He was like a kid with a new toy. She was so soft and sweet and so trusting, he said. He wanted to look after her. Just wrap her up and keep her safe. She was transparent, he said. Open and honest as a child.' Berwyn grimaced. 'I wondered then what she could possibly be like. And when I met her at the party . . .'

'What did you think?' Birdie was honestly curious.

Berwyn gestured impatiently. 'I didn't know what to think. Well, I did, really. I thought it was dreadful. I mean, I couldn't see what on earth they could have in common.' She half-smiled. 'I don't mean to sound like Wendy. Of course she's a very pretty girl. Young and quite stunning to look at. Of course Max would be attracted to her. And someone he could look after—well, yes, that would suit him. Down to the ground.' She fell silent for a moment, then went on. 'But—like, I've been having terrible trouble painting her. She was a mystery to me. I couldn't penetrate. I was dithering. I guess now I can see why. She's been playing a part all along. More of a part than I'd thought. It's odd I didn't pick it. I'm usually—good with people.' She folded her hands together, and thoughtfully looked at the thin fingers with their short-clipped nails.

'I couldn't see why Max was so determined actually to marry her. God, he's had dozens of gorgeous girlfriends since I've known him,' she mused. 'They've never got under his skin at all.' She thought for a moment and then looked up. 'I've always admired him for that, in a funny sort of way, you know,' she said. 'It's something I'm incapable of. He has no moral sense, you might say, when it comes to light entertainment. But when it comes to deep attachments he's extremely discriminating. I must say I thought that this time he'd simply lost the plot. Decided to retire, got worried about being seventy, and got bowled over by a

helpless, trusting kitten image. That would be a powerful attractant, for Max. For a while, anyway.'

She stretched, and sighed. 'Thing is, now all that's
been blown apart. That's why I don't think he'll stay
keen enough to try to stop her going. For Max to find
out—not from Mai, even, but from someone else—
that she's been keeping a big secret all this time, that
she ran through some other bloke's money and left,
and that she'd been humouring Max himself, more or
less, and had no intention of marrying him after all—
well, I don't know ... Shot the image out of the sky,
didn't it?'

They made another pot of coffee and sat on at the
table, now a little island of crumbs, buttery plates and
used cups in the midst of Max's shining, empty
kitchen. They had made no inroads to speak of on the
pile of currant buns, which, neglected, cooled and
hardened on their plate making Birdie feel vaguely
guilty, as though by not forcing down another one she
was somehow rejecting Max's hospitality.

Eventually Berwyn took herself off upstairs and
Wendy came back, as if on cue. She began clearing
away the mess on the table, working quickly and almost automatically, as though her mind was on something else. She didn't seem to think it strange that it
had been left to her to do this work, and rejected
Birdie's half-hearted and belated offers of help. 'I'm
better on my own,' she said, rinsing and stacking
things into the dishwasher and wiping the sticky table
and already spotless benchtops with a cloth. 'I know
where everything goes.'

It was interesting, thought Birdie, that it was
Wendy, not Berwyn, who assumed responsibility as
hostess in this house, though Berwyn had lived here
with Max after Wendy had left, and presumably knew
the house well. Berwyn was very much the visitor here.
Perhaps she always had been. It was Wendy who was at
home.

Douglas came downstairs at ten-thirty, smoothly
shaven and impeccable as usual. He at least had lost

no sleep over his father's misfortune. On the contrary, he radiated well-being and satisfaction.

'Where's the unhappy couple?' he grinned.

'Oh, Douglas, how can you?' Wendy whispered reproachfully. 'Mai's still upstairs, packing. And poor old Dad's left her to it and gone out. You'll have to be nice to him, Douglas, when he comes back. He's had an awful shock.'

'Serves the silly old fart right,' beamed Douglas. He slapped his belly. 'Anything to eat round this joint?'

'I'll get you something,' Wendy said. 'If you promise to be good. Let's go and sit in the living room. We were just about to have a coffee anyway, Verity, weren't we?' She stared at Birdie with fierce concentration.

'Oh, yes,' said Birdie, whose body was by now so buzzing with caffeine and idleness that she felt quite light-headed.

In the living room Douglas plumped himself down into a chair and stared out at the view, still smiling. After a few minutes Wendy brought out a tray and set it down in front of him. She began chattering nervously. 'Douglas, we'll have to make some plans, before Dad gets home. When Mai's finished packing . . .'

Birdie felt she had to intervene. 'Wendy, we don't actually *know* she's packing, do we,' she said gently. 'You just thought she might be.'

'Oh . . .' Wendy hesitated. 'Oh, well . . .'

There was a low roar outside and a car horn sounded. Two short blasts and one long. Everyone looked up.

'Is that Max?' called Berwyn from upstairs.

A car door slammed. The front door opened. And then Max was striding towards them, thin and brown in red-flowered shirt and white trousers. He was beaming.

'G'day all,' he said. 'Beautiful day, isn't it?'

If this was keeping up appearances it was very effective. Max looked as if he didn't have a care in the world.

'Dad . . .' Wendy was screwed round in her chair, looking at him nervously.

He winked at her. 'All's well, lovey,' he said. He rubbed his hands together. 'Mai down yet? No? I'll go up then.' He made for the stairs then turned back to them impulsively, his hand on the banister. 'Don't look so worried, kids,' he said. 'Look, it's all right. Everything's all right. So there was a bit of a communication breakdown. Happens in the best of families. But Mai and I had a good talk last night, and we're all clear now.' He laughed. 'I'm fixing everything. As soon as the divorces are through we'll get married as planned. No more hitches.' His eyes sparkled. 'Then we'll have a bundle of kids. Three or four. Or five. Why not? Mai loves kids. And there's plenty of time. I plan to live till I'm a hundred and twenty. Now, nobody go nowhere. I'm making pizza for lunch.'

SIX

~~~~

Lunch, at twelve-thirty, was a frozen affair. Max's cele-
bratory pizza, rich with tomato, melting with cheese
and heaped with tiny shrimps was a gastronomic delight. At the head of the table Max himself was ebul-
lient, charming and determined. But the presence at
the other end of Mai, perfect, tiny and serene in her
soft black tunic and trousers and little bare sandals,
her leather band around her neck, her hair piled up
and fastened by her jewelled comb, rendered Wendy
stiff, Douglas sullen and Berwyn quiet and watchful.
Much was said, by Max, about marriage, happiness, babies and the need to hurry things along with all
speed. Also his plans for his book, which Birdie was
rather disconcerted to find had metamorphosed from
a convenient fiction to a genuine interest in twenty-
four hours. Nothing was said by anyone about Mai's
husband, though Birdie kept waiting for the pounding
on the door that would herald another round in the

battle for Mai's heart and mind. But it never came. And slowly, one by one, the parts of the machine that was going to drive this day to its inevitable conclusion began to slide smoothly and without sound, into place.

At one-thirty, Douglas pushed his chair back. He had to go out, he said. He was borrowing Wendy's car, as usual. But as usual he wouldn't say where he was going when she asked, volunteering only that he would be back at six. He stalked from the house without a word to Max. Without looking at Mai. Max laughed, winked at Birdie, and called him a pain in the arse. Wendy sighed.

At two, prompted quietly by Max, Berwyn and Mai rose from the table. Mai was dressed for a sitting. The portrait was, of course, to go ahead. Max escorted the two women to the stairs, bowed to Berwyn and kissed Mai gently, tipping her tender chin up with his crooked finger. *Fond, foolish old man.* The phrase slid into Birdie's mind like a snake. She tried to shake it out. But the picture of the hard, brown finger against soft, young skin stayed with her. And the flash of Mai's downcast eyes as she raised them to meet her lover's. Glowing, surely, with secret triumph.

At two-thirty, locked in the cream and brown study, Birdie sat in a sea of photographs. Hundreds of photographs. Max and the famous. Max and Isa clowning around in headphones, Max with Sonia, nervous, and Wendy, golden-haired and incredibly pretty at five, Max with men in suits, with beauty queens, with animals. Max with elegant Ingrid and porky baby Douglas in a christening robe. Max in nightclubs, on yachts, in trains, beside aircraft, on a camel. Max with her own mother and father. Max signing autographs, talking into microphones, walking down the street, laughing

with pie in his face. Max and Berwyn, arms entwined.
Max and dozens of people even he couldn't remember.

'Plenty of stuff here,' said Max, hyperactive, electric, tipping out yet another box. Clippings, fan mail,
cartoons, documents, business and personal mail
poured forth willy nilly, adding to the chaos. He
grinned. 'I've never bothered with a secretary. Wendy
did a bit while she was living here, but I fought her every inch of the way. I don't like being too organized.
Cramps my style. Makes me nervous. Tempts fate, I
reckon. I've always thought that if I ever got things in
order I'd probably drop dead the next day. It's too final. It's too depressing. Like making a will. Once you
start thinking that way, you're history.'

'You should make a will, Max. You're such a rich
man,' Birdie put in primly. Forbearing to add that his relationships were after all more than a little complicated.

'When Angus kicks the bucket you'll be rolling.
Have you made a will?'

No. Birdie hadn't. Who would she leave things to?
Her house. Her piano. Her books. Her sound system.
Her car. Her money, such as it was, and would be. To
her best (her only?) friend, Kate? To Kate's daughter,
Zoe? Even to Dan Toby, Detective-Sergeant Dan Toby,
with whom she had as close and ambiguous a relationship as Max had with Isa, without the steamy sexual past?

Birdie thought about Dan. She had cooperated
with him many times in the solving of crimes over the
years. And as time went by, they had fallen into the
habit of seeking each other out at other times, for
the sort of jokey comfort two loners can supply one
another when solitude palls. But she hadn't seen Dan
for a while now. Not since the night she told him she
was tired of amateur dabbling in crime, and that she
was going to go out on her own; to become a private
investigator.

She remembered his face, across the table at the
pub. He'd been laughing just before she told him.
And the laugh-lines were still deep around his eyes

when she self-consciously blurted out the news. Then suddenly the lines disappeared, his eyes flashed, his lips pressed together, making a straight, hard line. She realised he was shocked—and angry.

She'd been surprised about that. She'd expected ridicule. She'd thought he'd send her up. She'd thought he'd be sarcastic. But she hadn't thought he'd be angry.

He'd recovered quickly, of course. Twisted his angry expression into a sardonic one. Made a few jokes. Then he'd said it was late, got up and left, without finishing his beer. She'd never known him to do that before.

A couple of days later she'd seen her father. She found herself mentioning casually that she'd told Toby the news.

'Don't suppose it went down very well with him,' Angus had said.

She'd looked at him in surprise, and he'd shaken his head, smiling. 'He was the professional in the partnership, wasn't he?' he said. 'That was the deal, wasn't it? You've stepped outside your boundaries.'

'I don't see . . .' Birdie had protested, then stopped, bewildered.

Angus had shrugged. 'No one likes their mates setting up as competition, kid,' he said gently. 'You'll have to tread softly with him for a while.'

Suddenly Birdie felt terribly lonely. Her mouth drooped. She heard a sound, looked up, and found Max grinning wickedly at her. 'See?' he jeered. 'See?'

At three, by the window in her bedroom, Wendy was sewing pink ribbon roses to pale blue silk. She had to wear her glasses. The needle was as fine as a silver thread in her big, capable hand. Her stitches were minuscule. She breathed out softly with the pleasure of her work, letting her plump shoulders slump forward. Her mind was empty. She was utterly at peace. The doll she had made sat beside her, waiting to be

adorned. It would be beautiful and perfect when it
was done. Then she'd start another.

At three-thirty, at the Paradise Hotel, the man who was
Mai's husband, Isa's gardener and Max's enemy had
another drink. His head was beginning to swim. He
leaned against the bar and leered at the barmaid. She
giggled. Her name was Julie. She was blonde, with big,
plump breasts tied up tightly in a gingham halter top.
Her little denim shorts were cut very high. She was no
more than eighteen.

Julie thought he was nice. She laughed at his
jokes. Her big blue eyes, carefully outlined in black,
widened at the hundred dollar notes he flashed. Julie
was a casual. Three days a week. After work today, she
told him, she was going to the beach. He'd have to
come and watch, he said, his eyes on her cleavage. She
giggled.

By three-forty-five Max had become bored with mem-
orabilia, and anyway he was running out of time. He
was gathering the mess up into boxes again, as fren-
ziedly as previously he had scattered it. He'd had an
idea. 'I'll give this lot to Wendy,' he said. 'She'll get it
in rough order for you. She'll love it. She's got nothing else to do. I'll have to throw you out of here at
four anyway, Birdie. You can take the first box up to
her then. Tell her not to worry about dinner. Mai will
see to it.'

Birdie agreed rather regretfully. Like Douglas, she
was rather partial to salmon rissoles.

At four-thirty Birdie stood in the housekeeper's sitting
room, idly looking out at the garden. The sky was
overcast and heavy now. Not a leaf moved. Perhaps a
storm was brewing. A few cats were visible here and
there, pouncing at insects and lizards in the undergrowth, or sleeping on the warm stone steps. Fortu-

nately Max was locked in his study. Birdie felt relieved. Then she realised that now she was becoming obsessed with Max. She laughed, left the room and, to prove her independence, went up to see Mai.

Still dressed as she'd been for the sitting, the girl was perched on a chair by the dressing-table, slipping on soft, black shoes. The little sandals in which she modelled for Berwyn lay beside the chair, discarded. Her lips curved only enough for politeness when she saw Birdie at the door. 'Max is working,' she said. Her almond eyes flicked up and down, taking in Birdie's jeans, battered sneakers and blue t-shirt.

'I know,' said Birdie. She smiled, mimicking friendliness she didn't feel. 'I was just looking for someone to talk to.'

Mai turned back to fastening her shoes. She wasn't taken in. 'Wendy is in her room,' she said. 'Douglas is out.'

'He's always out,' said Birdie jovially. 'I wonder where he goes?'

'He has a woman,' shrugged Mai.

'Really?' Birdie was genuinely interested.

Mai yawned, quickly, like a cat. 'I think,' she said. She could be bored, or not. 'Max says no. But Max . . .' She shrugged again. 'Max thinks Douglas will marry you.' Her eyes flicked up and down again. This time the smile was real. She looked at her watch. 'Will you swim now?' she asked pointedly. She wanted Birdie to go. And, acutely uncomfortable, Birdie obliged.

She was halfway down the stairs when the phone rang. Wendy's voice called her. She went to Wendy's room and found her sitting on her bed surrounded by piles of photographs, the receiver in her hand. 'It's Isa. For you,' Wendy hissed, her hand cupped firmly over the receiver. 'She sounds all right. Do you want . . . ?'

Birdie did. She took the receiver and spoke.

Isa was nice as pie. Is this a good time to call? Ah, good, she thought so. Now, about the book. She had stacks of stuff about Max. Would Birdie like to come in and see? Now? It was a good time for her. She had fed the cats. Birdie shouldn't worry about Warren. He was shut up in the granny flat. Drinking, she thought. She thought Max could be right about Warren. She'd have to let him go. Would Birdie come? Yes, why not? Good. Just ring at the security door when she arrived. Isa would put the kettle on.

At ten to five, Birdie was sitting in Isa's living room with fourteen cats. Thirteen crouched like small sphinxes on floral-covered chairs, squashy footstools and beautiful old rugs, staring at her without blinking. The fourteenth, a huge, long-haired white, had taken to her for reasons of its own and had crawled onto her lap. It kneaded at her thighs with its paws, purring. It weighed a ton, and generated enormous heat.

'I'd love to have peacocks,' Isa was saying. 'But the cats might be a problem, don't you think?'

The cats were a problem all right. With or without peacocks, in Birdie's view. She shifted her legs, trying to make the white cat uncomfortable. But it simply re-adjusted its bulk to suit and purred on. It was so excessively big, fluffy, white and somnolent that it hardly seemed real, despite its activity. It reminded Birdie un-pleasantly of one of those fluffy animal pyjama cases that were popular when she was a child. In this case, a pyjama case filled with bricks.

'Twinkle! Lovely girl!' crooned Isa, in a weird fal-setto.

The cat blinked disdainfully.

The room was charming. Compared to the 'Third Wish' living room its view of the sea was severely re-stricted because the house was set too far back from the clifftop and the windows were small. But as the light slowly faded, its gentle, cluttered atmosphere lost none of its attractiveness. Photographs covered most available surfaces. Many of these featured Max. There were a couple of Douglas and Wendy, too, as children. And overwhelmingly there was Isa herself, at every age, in costumes ranging from the white robes of Ju-

liet ('a folly of my youth, darling,' giggled Isa. 'I was
appalling!') to the outrageous festoons of the title role
in *Auntie Mame.*

She really had been, thought Birdie, unusually,
sometimes ravishingly, beautiful. And Berwyn was
right. In her way, she still was. Springdale margarine
insisted Isa leave her hair untinted. There was to be
no embarrassment with wigs during Auntie Dora's personal appearances. And Isa had been too clever or too
poor to go in for facelifts. But she was still an
arresting-looking woman, however ravaged her sun-
soaked complexion.

On a low table stood a crystal vase filled with delphiniums and lilies.

'Max,' said Isa, nodding at it. 'They came this
morning. He always sends flowers after we've had a
fight.' Impulsively, she plucked a card from the side-
board and showed it to Birdie. *Isa. As always, Max.*

Isa smiled, kissed the card, and put it back. 'I've
kept them all, you know,' she whispered. 'I've got hundreds. But don't tell him that. Don't want him to
think I'm soft on him.' She winked, and a shadow of
the girl she had been peeped through the Auntie
Dora wrinkles familiar now to millions.

Birdie's astonishment must have showed, because
Isa laughed.

'We made it up. Of course we did. We always make
it up in the end. He didn't mean to shoot poor Othello,
you know. It was an accident. He couldn't hit a barn
door at twenty paces and he knows it. He was as
shocked as I was. I knew that once I cooled down. But
Christ, didn't I give him the rough end of my tongue
last night? Ah, poor Max!' Her eyes danced with pleasure. 'But he always comes back. Always comes back to
Isa, however I treat him, poor bugger. And I always take
him back, too. Whatever he's done. For forty years.' She
paused, her mouth drooping, her mind perhaps recalling other betrayals, other forgivenesses. 'Still, I met
him halfway this time. When I rang to thank him for the
flowers I told him I'd bell the cats. That should protect
his bloody birds. Mind you . . .' She lowered her voice as

if they could be overheard. 'It was the girlfriend, really, you know. She didn't like cats. But I ask you. How could anyone not like my darlings?' She bent forward, wrinkled up her nose and trilled lovingly to Twinkle the pyjama case, who ignored her. 'Anyway, my dear. Give me the goss. What's happening over yonder? I'm invited for dinner. I have to be worded up. Don't want to put my foot in it.'

Birdie grinned. She thought she now understood Isa's sudden desire to help on Max's book. She decided on discretion. 'Nothing much. Once Max said he was marrying Mai anyway as soon as the divorces came through, everyone went quiet.'

Isa laughed shrilly. 'I'll bet!'

The old clock on the mantelpiece began to chime. It was a sweet and mellow sound. 'Five o'clock!' carolled Isa. 'Good. We can skip the tea and have a drink. I loathe tea, don't you?'

'Well, no,' said Birdie. 'But I'd love a drink,' she added quickly.

'Goody!' Isa looked out the window. 'Going to rain,' she commented, and bustled out towards the kitchen at the back of the house. 'I never drink before five. And I *hate* to drink alone,' she called. 'Not that that's ever held me back in the past.' She popped her head back through the door. 'Has it sweetie-pies?' she sang to the cats, breaking again into the crooning falsetto she seemed to reserve for them. She disappeared again, and Birdie took the opportunity to give the white cat on her knees a vicious jab in the ribs. It looked at her reproachfully and jumped from her lap, stalking away angrily with its tail stuck up in the air.

A phone rang somewhere in the house, and was answered. Birdie strolled to the windows and stared out at the sea. It was grey and oily-looking and seagulls wheeled screaming in a heavy sky. A storm seemed indeed to be imminent. She considered making a dash for Max's while the going was good.

'Yoo hoo . . .' She became aware that Isa was calling her. 'Be with you in a minute . . . just need to take . . . this call . . .'

'OK,' she called back. Oh, well, why not? Drinks at Isa's, however cat-infested, seemed far more appealing at this point than silence at 'Third Wish', waiting for Max. The minutes ticked by. Birdie prowled around the room, looking at Isa's photographs and other displayed bits and pieces. A fanciful little corner cupboard, mounted on the wall and painted white to match the other woodwork in the room, caught her eye. It was obviously original. On impulse Birdie pulled it open. She gaped at the contents, shocked. Then she realised that the meticulously arranged objects she was looking at were not some sort of weird collection of bondage equipment, but collars, leads, rubber mice and all manner of other cat impedimenta. She was still snorting with occasional hysterical giggles when Isa came back.

The rain began at five-thirty. It pelted onto the metal roof of Isa's cottage, filling it with thunder. It beat into Max's jungle, ripping through the canopy, scattering white petals from the vines and soaking deep into the undergrowth and leaf litter below. Isa and Birdie had another drink, raised their voices and talked on. The cats, ears back, eyes wild, ran crouching for cover. Thousands of snails and slugs prepared to emerge from their hiding places and feast. At ten to six Max's voice boomed hollowly from Isa's radio, competing with the sound of the rain. A spirited defence of today's liberal divorce laws, under recent attack from groups who feared for the future of the family. It was Max's usual sort of thing, but lacked, Birdie thought, his usual flair. At ten past six, when the rain eased, she and Isa left the house and walked through the soft, sweet-smelling damp to 'Third Wish', warm with sherry and gossip. Birdie had decided Isa was very good value.

Douglas was waiting for them at the door. He had changed, and his hair was wet and sleekly combed. 'You got caught in the rain, too,' he commented unnecessarily, and stood back to let them in.

'Where is everyone? Still upstairs? The cheek of them, when I'm here for dinner. I'll fix them,' carolled Isa, making for the stairs. 'Lord, look at Max.' She pointed derisively through the glass doors to the pool where Max ploughed steadily through rain-spotted water. 'He's a lunatic, you know.'

Douglas watched her as she tripped up the stairs. 'Takes one to know one,' he grunted.

Max hauled himself out of the pool, shook his head like a wet dog and made for the doors. He slid one open, reached inside, grabbed his robe and glasses from the floor and put them on. He grinned benignly at Birdie and Douglas. 'Having a good chat, you two?' he said, coming in and closing the door behind him. 'Is Isa here? Where's everyone else?'

'Berwyn and Wendy are on their way,' called Isa from halfway down the stairs. 'But Mai isn't up here, Maxie.'

'Of course she's up there, you silly old tart,' laughed Max, rubbing at his wet hair. 'In the loo, probably. I'll see to her.' He padded upstairs in his white gown, very small and thin with his hair standing on end. 'Get out a couple of bottles of champagne, Douglas,' he shouted back over his shoulder.

They heard him calling Mai, but there was no reply, and then there was an exclamation and he was walking back down the stairs, his forehead wrinkled, a piece of paper clutched in his hand.

'Dad, what is it?' Wendy rushed to his side. The others simply looked.

The note was carefully written in a clear, rounded hand:

I have been trouble to you. Now I have brought more trouble to your house. My husband is a bad man. I see now that I must go. I am sorry. Mai

'She's gone,' breathed Isa. 'Oh, Max. I'm sorry.'
'Bullshit!' exclaimed Max. 'This is bullshit. Why

would she go? We went through it. She said she'd
stay.'

'Did she?' asked Berwyn quietly. 'Or did *you* say
that? And she say nothing? Like before?'

There was a deadly silence.

'Has she taken anything with her?' asked Birdie.

Max put his hand to his eyes as if the light hurt
them. 'The emeralds were on the dressing table.
They're gone. She wouldn't be wearing them. She always wore that leather neckpiece we got at the market.
She likes that. She's only had it a month. She said she
liked it better than—' His mouth trembled, and abruptly he rushed to the front door and flung it open.
'Mai!' he bellowed into the drifting rain. 'Mai!'

There was no reply. He turned back to them. His
face was white.

'I'll just change. Then I'm going to look for her,'
he said. 'I'll find her. Have dinner. Don't wait.'

After he'd gone, Isa went home. As she said, it seemed
more tasteful. The others looked at each other helplessly.

'Mai was all right when she left me after the sitting,' said Berwyn. 'Exactly the same as always, I would
have said. Whatever that implies.'

'I saw her after that, at four-thirty,' Birdie volunteered. 'In the bedroom. She was changing her shoes.
I actually got the impression she was trying to get rid
of me. As she would, if she was planning to leave.'

'Oh, I've just thought! Dad gave her a credit card
for the supermarket,' gasped Wendy. 'We'd better can-
cel it. Oh, but it's after five. We won't be able to get
on to them. Oh, if only . . .'

Douglas chuckled. 'Relax, Wendy. The old man
can afford it,' he drawled. 'If she costs him a few hundred now it'll be nothing to what she'd have cost him
if she'd stayed. Think of it that way.'

'Oh, Douglas!'

There was a banging on the front door. It was Isa
again. She came in talking, her mobile face agog.

'Warren's gone. Cleared out. He hasn't left a thing. He's gone.'

'Oh, yes. Mai said he had,' Berwyn put in. 'Didn't he say anything to you?'

'No!' Isa looked very put out. 'When did she tell you that?'

'During the sitting. Just in conversation. Such as it was.'

'But how did she know?' Isa looked around, pop-eyed. 'And do you mean he went before she did? That doesn't make sense.'

'I saw him at the pub this afternoon, when I called in for a quick one,' said Douglas. 'He was just drinking at the bar, on his own. Chatting up the barmaid.'

'We should do something. What will we do?' Isa's eyes were wide with excitement.

'Nothing,' said Berwyn flatly. 'There's nothing we can do. Except wait for Max.'

Max arrived home at seven, his face creased with anxiety, his mouth set in a hard line. He said nothing as Berwyn, Wendy, Douglas and Isa clustered around him, but brushed past them and went out on to the terrace where Birdie leaned against the railing watching the sea.

'No sign of her. Something's wrong. I'm going to call the cops,' he told her. 'Now look, you've got contacts. I want you to—'

'Max, they won't do anything. She's only been gone a couple of hours. But ...' Birdie shifted her feet uncomfortably. 'Apparently her husband's gone too.'

'Oh, I know that!' snapped Max impatiently. 'I paid him off, didn't I? Mai said he was always short. I knew he wouldn't be able to resist the cash. Gave him a bundle and promised him the same again if he stayed away. I took him to the main road myself. This morning.'

'You paid ...?'

'And Mai knew that. I told her. She knew he was

gone. There was no need for her to run. He was going to get a cab to town and piss off back to Queensland. She *knew* that, Birdie. She knew he was gone. Didn't she tell Berwyn at the sitting? I'd be surprised if she didn't.'

'Yes, she told Berwyn. But, Max, he didn't go. Not this morning, anyway. Douglas saw him at the pub this afternoon,' said Birdie slowly.

'*What?*' Max jerked his head around to look at her, his face a mask of dismay. 'Birdie, you've got to help me. Please—'

Against her better judgement, Birdie went with him to call Dan Toby. It took a while to track him down, but eventually she succeeded.

'Yes?' Toby sounded rushed and impatient. 'What is it? Better be good!'

Birdie explained the purpose of the call in a few hurried phrases, and passed the phone to Max before Toby could hang up. Their conversation was brief. In a bare two minutes Max was handing the receiver back to her, scowling furiously.

'What are you playing at, sooling your rich mates on to me, Birdwood?' snarled Toby's voice in her ear. 'We're bloody understaffed in here. Don't do it again!'

'Dan, I really think there might be a problem. This girl—'

'So she's done a bunk. Very likely with her husband, or fancy man, or whatever he is. The whole thing smells like a con to me. Work as a team, bluff the dough out of the old man and get out. It's been done before, it'll be done again. The victims never prosecute. Too bloody embarrassed at being taken down. Anyhow, whatever the story is, it's got nothing to do with us. We're a murder squad. You deal with it. You're the famous private dickess. Or should I say dickless?' Toby guffawed hollowly. 'Ring back when you've got a corpse for us. Otherwise, bite your bum.' He hung up.

Birdie lay in bed, wide awake. Far below the house, great waves crashed furiously against the cliff-face, filling the room with sound. Faces swam in the darkness. Max's face strained and worried as he went out the door to drive the streets again. The face of Mai's husband, twisted with rage and frustration. Mai herself: impassive, apparently serene, sitting in Max's beautiful bedroom, changing her shoes. Mai who had fled, sadly leaving a little note, prudently taking the emeralds.

It didn't make sense. Birdie sat up. None of it made sense. Again she thought about Mai. But this time she thought about her in a different way. Max's way. You've got to help me, Birdie, he'd said. She was happy. She wouldn't run, he'd said. Why should she?

All right. Accept Mai hasn't run. Accept Max's version of Mai: Mai honest, innocent, happy. Then where is she? What happened this afternoon?

Mai learns from Max that her ex-husband has taken money and left. She is free, at last. Free of him. Free of the guilt at not telling Max she was married. Free to marry Max, in due course. Reinforced against his family's disapproval by his obvious adoration and determination to have her despite everything. She is happy, peaceful, even quietly triumphant. She sits for Berwyn, discharging her last responsibility to Max for the day. Now she can do what she wishes. It is late afternoon. Dinner is not for hours. What would she do?

What she always did in the afternoons, before Warren came to spoil her peace. She'd change her shoes, and walk in the garden.

Birdie got up and threw on her clothes. She took her torch from her bag and let herself into the dark kitchen. The house was silent. Max had not returned, and everyone else, apparently, had gone to sleep. She tiptoed to the front door and opened it. Warm, moist air wrapped around her. Below her the garden lay, thick, black and dripping. Cats' eyes gleamed in the undergrowth.

Birdie moved away from the light of the house into the darkness. She began to walk down the stone steps, her torch beaming weakly ahead of her. The undergrowth on either side of her snapped and rustled with life. The back of her neck prickled. She hesitated. This was stupid. She should wait till tomorrow. But she knew she couldn't turn back now. She went on.

At the front gate she moved off the steps and began to search, calling softly. The undergrowth was thick, but a trail of broken ferns and bent shrub branches leading from the boundary of the house next door marked Isa's frenzied progress of the day before. Probably Mai's husband had come this way too, Birdie thought, pushing forward. She reached the wire fence, and shone her torch briefly into the silent garden beyond. The huge magnolia tree rose to the right. On the left was the hut where Isa had let her so-called gardener stay. It was empty and dark now, its door firmly closed.

Birdie turned and tramped back at an angle towards the steps. Now there were no broken ferns and mangled bushes to mark her way. Now she had to force her path, beating through wet overhanging leaves and branches, dodging dripping vines. Max's jungle rose up around her, impenetrable. She could see nothing but what was directly in front of her. She reached the steps again, and paused. This was absurd. Mai couldn't possibly have taken pleasure in this sort of thing. She came into the garden often, Max had said. She and the cats moved through this mass of darkness quietly and without fuss. They wouldn't battle against this undergrowth. They would follow familiar ways.

Then Birdie did what she should have done in the first place. Simply stood and looked, for minutes, letting her torch play over the dark mass of trees, bushes and vines, till her eyes grew accustomed to the shapes before her, and she was able to see the narrow gaps that separated them, and sense what was beyond. And then she was moving forward, bending and weaving, following the little tracks that wound, hidden, through the dense undergrowth. Cat tracks. Mai tracks, perhaps. Birdie slapped at mosquitoes. She tried not to think of snakes.

Spider webs gleamed in the light of the torch and brushed against her face. Her feet sank to the ankles in soaking leaves. Her nose was filled with the smell of rotting fruit, Chinese jasmine, and cats. She pushed on, her skin creeping as vines caught at her legs and arms. She could hear the sound of her own heart beating, and the panting of her own breath.

She reached a small clearing, and paused. Whispering darkness rose around her on all sides. The torch beam caught the eye of a cat. It gleamed, unblinking, fixed. Puzzled, she moved closer. Still no movement. She bent to investigate. No cat. A jewelled comb, flashing in the light, lying where it had fallen, half-hidden in the wet leaves. She skirted it and walked forward, holding her breath.

Mai was lying on her face, half-under a dark thicket of jasmine. Black hair spread out and gleaming like a silk shawl, black trousers, black shoes. Almost invisible. She was cool, wet, and quite dead.

SEVEN

—

Screwing up his eyes in the harsh whiteness of the floodlight, Dan Toby bent over the girl's body. 'Strangled,' he mumbled, more to himself than the young doctor kneeling beside him. 'Strangled from behind. Neck like a little chicken. Wouldn't have taken much. Then left where she fell.'

The doctor nodded, and cleared his throat nervously. He was good at his job, and in his quiet moments knew this. But Dan Toby made him nervous. 'The cord is still around her neck,' he said, wanting to prove his worth. 'It's unusual. A plaited leather thong, with knots at either end. The killer came prepared.'

"Mmm.' Toby bent lower, and made a great show of examining the thong. 'Made locally. Bought at a market—a month ago, maybe? That's what I'd say. What would you say?'

Behind him, Detective-Constable Milson sniffed in what could have been disgust, and glanced at Birdie.

The young doctor's head jerked up. Toby smiled nastily, but said nothing. He turned to the photographer. 'Finished?' he asked. 'Can we turn her over?' He stepped back and cursed as a bunch of flabby leaves bent and dripped water down the back of his neck.

The light body was turned onto its back. Toby put his fingers on the shallow depression that it had made in the leaves. 'Dry,' he noted. 'Photograph, please. Birdie, when did you say it started to rain?'

Birdie stared at Mai Tran, dead, and the knot in her stomach tightened. 'About five-thirty,' she said.

The camera flashed, again and again. The doctor bent to his work.

'Would you care to take a guess on the time of death?' Toby politely enquired, after a moment.

'Until—' the doctor began. But Toby held up a hand like a shovel and his face took on a pained expression.

'I know we have to do a PM, Gerard. I'm asking for a stab in the general direction. Just a stab. I'd value your expert opinion. It'd be such a help.'

You bastard, thought Birdie. It's me you're angry with. And yourself, for putting Max and me off this afternoon. Why take it out on him?

'All things being equal,' said the doctor with some dignity. 'I would say death occurred between four and six hours ago. It would be unlikely to have been longer. All things being equal.'

'Ah!' Toby squinted at his watch.' That would make it—all things being equal—between five and seven this evening that the murder occurred. And we know the rain started at five-thirty. Ergo, the murder occurred between five and five-thirty. Well, now. That wasn't so hard, was it?' A small sound attracted his attention. He looked up and jumped violently. 'Christ!'

Eerily lit by the floodlight, a face, mouth open, grey hair tangling, had appeared through a gap in the trees a few metres away. It seemed to be floating in blackness.

'It's Isa Truby, the next-door neighbour,' whispered Birdie. She'd had a shock herself. She hadn't realised the boundary fence was so near.

There was a slight scuffle, and the face bent and bobbed. Isa was coming over the wire. 'No!' barked Toby. 'Don't come this way!' The face turned up to him again, still open-mouthed.

'Why isn't there a proper fence at the side?' he hissed at Birdie. 'God knows, he's gone to enough trouble at the front.'

'There was some fight about the trees that'd have to go,' Birdie whispered back. 'In the end he put a security fence all round the two properties, at his own expense.'

'No trouble to some,' sniffed Toby.

'What's happening?' shrilled Isa from the leafy shadows.

'Police. We have a problem here, Madam,' said Milson crisply, moving a little towards her. 'We'd like to ask you a few questions. Could I ask you to come in—by the road?'

'I'm not dressed,' said Isa, finding her voice. 'Trouble? What's happened?' She blinked sightlessly into the light. 'Max? Are you there?'

'Max isn't home, Isa,' called Birdie. 'It's me, Birdie. I'm here. Could you come round?'

'Go and get her,' Toby muttered. 'Or we'll be here all night. I'll meet you up at the house. The troops can carry on here. Milson, you come with me. One big pair of feet less to trample down the evidence.' He pulled angrily at his tie. 'Shit, it's hot as hell. I can't breathe down here.'

'It's cooler in the house,' Birdie called over her shoulder as she began making her way to the steps.

He grunted. 'Not for long.'

Wendy, Douglas and Berwyn were sitting together on the couch near the pool doors. As far from the front door, and the garden, as they could get, Birdie thought, walking towards them with Isa, who seemed to have donned an extremely ladylike manner with her flowing cotton kaftan and elaborately twisted headscarf. Dan Toby was sitting opposite them, with Colin Milson perched on a straight-backed chair over to one side, notebook open on his thin, crossed knees.

Toby rose and greeted Isa with a brief baring of the teeth that was perhaps intended as a welcoming smile. Then he did a minor double-take. 'I think we've met before,' he said.

Isa inclined her head graciously. 'I don't think so,' she said. 'But you might have seen me on the stage. I'm an actress.' She looked into his eyes, awaiting a flash of recognition.

But Toby continued to look puzzled. 'No, it wouldn't be that. I don't have the time to get out to the theatre much.'

You don't go to the theatre at all, you old fraud, thought Birdie. You'd sooner make time for reruns of 'I Dream of Jeannie'.

Milson cleared his throat ostentatiously. The end of his pencil tapped softly on the pad.

Toby made no sign that he had heard. He gestured to an empty chair and Isa sank into it. 'Miss Birdwood has told you what's happened here?' he asked.

'I can't believe it!' Isa's eyes opened very wide. 'I just can't believe it? Can you, Wendy?'

'It's terrible!' Wendy was looking sick. 'And Dad's still out looking for her. What's he going to say when he comes home? Poor Dad.'

'Mai's the one who got done in, Wendy,' muttered Douglas, glancing at Toby. 'She's the one to feel sorry for. That bastard.'

'You're referring to the girl's husband, I presume,' said Toby. 'You feel he's the one responsible?'

'Oh, surely not!' exclaimed Isa.

'Well who else?' demanded Douglas. 'He's the one who was here yelling at her. He's the one who tracked her down and came looking. And she was scared of him, too. You could see that.'

Toby looked at him keenly and turned to Isa. 'You employed this man as a gardener, I gather. And allowed him to stay in the self-contained flat in your grounds. His name?'

'Warren. Warren Daley.' Isa was in obvious distress, but still very much the lady. 'He—well, I found him a very charming young man. I think—well—I started to think he might have a drinking problem, really. But there was no sign of anything like that when he arrived.'

'And when did he arrive?'

'Saturday. Last Saturday, just before lunch.'

'Less than a week ago.'

'Today's Friday, isn't it? Still Friday. Yes. It would have been a week tomorrow.'

'Did he give you an address? Show you any identification? References?'

'He just said he was from Queensland, and wanted casual work. I needed a gardener, so—I just took him on.' Isa hesitated as she sensed disapproval. 'Well, you don't usually ask people who are doing your garden the story of their lives, do you?' she said defensively.

Toby shrugged. 'Some people do. Description?'

'Tall—about as tall as Douglas. In his early thirties, I suppose. Very well built. Good-looking, in a fairly ordinary sort of way. Medium brown hair.'

'What was he wearing today?'

'Oh, I don't really know. But what does it matter, anyway? He could easily have changed. He took his bag with him when he left.'

'Can you describe that?'

'It was a soft carry bag. Black. With handles. And lots of zippers. You know that sort of bag. Look, really, he was quite respectable. I'm sure he wouldn't have done anything like this.'

'Mmm.' Toby glanced at Milson. 'Get them started on checking him out, will you?' he said. 'The first name, I gather, was confirmed by the wife, so that's genuine. The second could be an alias. Still, we may as well try. Ring from the study there. Then I'll need to have a word with all these good people individually. It'd be best to use the study for that, too, I think. If that's convenient?' His gaze swept the three on the lounge.

'Oh . . .' Wendy looked confused. 'Um, I'm not sure . . .' She glanced nervously at Douglas.

'Of course. That will be fine,' said Berwyn crisply.

Toby nodded to her. 'Thank you, Mrs Tully.'

Wendy jumped slightly, Isa looked amused and even Berwyn herself seemed startled to be addressed in this manner. She opened her mouth but then obviously thought better of whatever she was going to say, and shut it again.

'Could I ask why you need to talk to us on our own?' Douglas demanded. 'There's nothing we'd say on our own that we wouldn't say all together.'

'Just routine, sir,' said Toby blandly.

'I think we should wait till Dad gets home,' murmured Wendy. 'I don't think he'd like us—'

'Oh, Wendy for God's sake—' Douglas began. But Toby forestalled him.

'This is a case of murder, Mrs—' he consulted his notes, taking his time, '—Mrs Laidlaw. I'm afraid it can't wait. Now . . .'

'Well, I want a lawyer with me before I'll say a bloody word!' snapped Isa, her grande dame manner dropping from her like a silk negligee. 'If that boy did the little tart in I'll eat my toasting fork, but the fact is he was staying with me and I know what you cops are. Next you'll be blaming me for the whole bloody thing. And I can't afford any nasty publicity. Hear me? If I get any shit and it gets into the papers, I swear I'll sue the pants off you.'

'Auntie Dora!' Toby's jaded grey eyes brightened. 'You're Auntie Dora!'

Birdie put her face in her hands.

Toby saw Isa first. He took Milson with him into the study, leaving a stolid-looking uniformed policeman called Barassi in charge of the party in the living room. Birdie went to the study too. 'If you want a so-licitor, ma'am, Miss Birdwood will fill the bill,' Toby had told Isa solemnly. 'She's a woman of many parts. Newshound, private detective, solicitor, jill of all trades—and mistress of none.' He had sniggered unpleasantly at his own wit and Isa, to Birdie's chagrin, had sniggered along with him.

Isa's story was simple. Warren had called at her house last Saturday, saying he was looking for work and that a person further down the street had said she might be looking for someone to help in the garden. She was, in fact, and had welcomed him with open arms. He had said he'd been retrenched from his job in Queensland, and that his wife had got involved with another bloke, so he'd come to New South Wales to start again. She'd thought he seemed all right, and he was a nice, upstanding sort of a young man. Not grubby or long-haired or anything. And he had nice manners and knew a lady when he saw one. So she'd taken him on. When he asked if he could camp in a toolshed or something on her property till he got on his feet she'd been delighted to offer him the unoccupied flat in the garden to stay in. It meant she had to pay him much less, she admitted unblushingly. She was to pay him by the week. This meant that she hadn't paid at all, since he'd left before the week was up. Birdie got the distinct impression that she had a momentary gleam of satisfaction at this thought.

'Pretty good sort, was he?' asked Toby, who seemed to have taken on a rather roguish manner with Isa since realising the extent of her fame.

Isa shrugged, wagging her turbaned head. 'Not bad,' she answered, and then fixed Toby with a beady eye. 'Not that,' she said clearly, 'there was anything more between us than a totally professional relationship.'

'Oh, of *course* not,' said Toby, with such bewildered sincerity that Isa was clearly insulted.

'I wouldn't have been remotely interested in anything like *that*,' she said in a dismissive tone. 'He wasn't my type.'

Toby cleared his throat. He was getting out of his

depth. 'You had no idea that there was any relationship between this man and Mr Tully's fiancée?'

'None at all. He didn't say a word about it until
the day Max killed Othello.'

Toby's eyebrows shot up.

'Cat,' Birdie put in quickly. 'With an air-rifle. By
accident.'

Isa nodded, pressing her lips together. 'I was—
naturally—very upset.'

Toby nodded sympathetically. 'Bad luck,' he said.
'You'll have to get yourself another cat soon.'

'Isa has others, Dan.' Birdie put in dryly.

He smiled. 'Ah. How many do you have, Miss
Truby?'

'Only twenty-five, now.' Isa sighed, and dabbed at
her eyes.

'Ah.' Toby's smile had grown rather fixed. He
glanced at Birdie who returned his gaze impassively.
'So—your cat was killed and you were upset . . .'

'Yes, and Warren was very sweet to me, and
helped me bury poor Othello in a special place I keep
for my darlings who pass on—just near the flat, actually.'

'Nice for him,' muttered Toby.

'Yes it was,' said Isa, mishearing. 'And then he and
I had a drink together—well—' she tittered self-
consciously '—a few drinks, actually. And then he told
me about Mai, and how she'd run through all his
money and left him flat. After he'd brought her out to
Australia and everything, and paid for her tickets and
so on. And really, I felt very sorry for him. He was in
tears. He admitted then that he'd taken this job with
me so he could be near her.'

'How did he know she was here?'

Isa spread out her hands. 'Did you see *Hers* last
week? Mai and Max were plastered all over the front
cover. You couldn't pass a news stand without seeing
them leering out at you. Warren saw it, anyway. And
he said he dropped everything and just came to Sydney the next day.'

Toby looked thoughtfully at her. 'Strange that

she—the deceased—let herself be photographed under the circumstances, don't you think?'

Isa nodded vigorously. 'Strange isn't the word,' she agreed. 'But she was a strange girl.'

'Was she?' Toby rubbed his chin. 'And so, getting back to her husband for a minute, he lobbed into Sydney, and just made a bee-line for this house, did he? Knew exactly where it was?'

Isa stared at him, confused.

'"Third Wish" is a landmark, Dan,' Birdie reminded him quietly. 'Everybody knows where it is. It wouldn't be hard for anyone to track Max down. That's why he's got the security fence and everything.'

'Ah, yes. Thank you,' said Toby, without looking at her.

'I told Warren he should just forget all about her,' Isa burst out. 'She wasn't worth it. I knew she was no good the minute I saw her. Not that she wasn't clever with men. She was. Quite the professional, I'd say. She certainly had Max around her little finger. It wouldn't have lasted, of course. Max isn't a man to be taken in for long. But anyway Warren wouldn't listen. And in the end he went over to Max's and made a scene. Well, I couldn't blame him, really.'

'How did he seem when he came back?'

Isa spread out her hands. 'He didn't come back into the house. Went straight into his flat and shut the door. I didn't see him again, as it happened. I was a little unwell the next morning. I must have picked up some bug or other. Touch of the flu, perhaps.' She delicately touched her turbaned head, watching Toby's face. To his credit he preserved an expression of polite interest, so she went on. 'I stayed in bed way past my usual time. And when I did go out into the garden at about midday his door was shut and he was nowhere to be seen. I assumed he was in the flat. Now I think he may have already gone, because when I went to tell him Mai had disappeared—'

'What time was that?'

Isa looked at Birdie enquiringly.

'About seven? Quarter to seven? Something like

that anyway,' Birdie responded. 'We got here at about ten past six, I think. And you went home after Max left to look for her the first time.' She turned to Toby. 'And then Isa came back again to say the flat was empty and Warren had cleared out.'

'Right.' Toby peered up at them from under his eyebrows. 'So, going back a bit, until ten past six you two were . . .'

'At my place,' said Isa. She drew herself up slightly. 'I was helping Birdie with her research, actually. For Max's book.'

'I see. Research.'

'Well, a little chat.' Isa tittered. 'You know how it is. Max and I go back a long way.'

'Quite. And Miss Birdwood was at your place from, approximately . . . ?' Toby raised his eyebrows.

'From about a quarter to five until about five past six,' said Birdie promptly. She'd been thinking about that.

'You saw nothing at all out of the ordinary during that time?'

'My sitting room faces the sea, like Max's,' said Isa. 'We just sat there and watched the rain come down. Had a sherry. And listened to Max on the radio.'

'And you came back here together?'

'Yes. Isa was coming to dinner,' Birdie said.

'Despite the—ah—difficulty about the cat the day before?'

'Oh, yes.' Isa sighed. 'Max and I had words about it, of course. But then we made up. We always do. Max and I go back a long way.'

'Yes. You said. Well . . .' Toby got heavily to his feet. 'Thank you, Miss Truby. We'll need to have a look at the gardener's flat in due course, if that's all right.'

'I'll give you a key to the security door. I've got a spare. And the flat's not locked,' said Isa. 'Just go ahead any time and poke around. But you'll see—there's nothing there any more.' She allowed Toby to usher her to the door, then hesitated. 'I'll stay here for a while, if you don't mind. I'd like to be here for Max when he comes.'

'No problem,' said Toby, opening the door and holding out his arm to show her through to the living room. He nodded at Berwyn, Douglas and Wendy, still sitting together on the couch. 'I'm just going to have a word with Miss Birdwood. Be right with you,' he called. He pulled the door closed again and faced Birdie.

'Twenty-five bloody cats?' he exploded. 'My God, and she drinks like a fish by the sound of it, *and* fancies younger men. Auntie Dora! Mrs sweetness and light!'

'Well, she *is* an actress,' said Birdie, who found herself very pleased to see him. 'She can play a part like Auntie Dora on her ear. And anyway, she's no madder than anyone else, really. You know, the older I get the more I think ...'

Toby held up his hand with a pained expression. 'No philosophy, please. I've had a day like you wouldn't believe and being called out in the middle of the bloody night's all I needed to put the lid on it. Why don't these things ever happen in daylight?'

'This did,' Birdie pointed out. 'And Max and I called you not very long after, as it happened, to ask for help. But you didn't think it was important enough to investigate, then. You told me to ring back when I had a corpse.'

From his chair by the window Milson sniffed. Toby spun round to glare at him and then slowly turned back to Birdie.

She grinned at him. She couldn't help it. This conversation was so like exchanges they'd had at other times and in other places. Nothing had really changed. And in that moment, something in the atmosphere of the room shifted. Suddenly Toby seemed to relax. Not completely, but enough.

'You reported a disappearance, Birdwood. That is not reporting a death. It is nothing like reporting a death. Is that understood?'

'Yes, Dan.'

Toby glanced at her suspiciously, and pulled up his belt. 'Right,' he said. 'Now I'll have a word with the others out there. They might have seen something. God, the house is full of people. You'd think someone would have noticed a murder going on in their front garden.'

But of course, they hadn't.

Toby saw Wendy first. She talked fast and at length, but the upshot was that from the time Birdie brought Max's box of photographs to her at four, till she was called at six to come down for a drink, Wendy was working in her room. She had been keen to help her father, and had dropped her own work to do so. She'd had the photographs spread out on the bed, and therefore was not looking out the window. She had seen nothing.

Berwyn was next, nervous but composed. From the time Mai finished her sitting until Isa called her to come down just after six, Berwyn was in her studio, brooding over her portrait of Mai. This was common practice with her, particularly when the work was not going particularly well, as in this case. The studio faced the sea. She had seen nothing.

Douglas, slightly impatient at being kept till last, had gone out at one-thirty to meet a friend. A girlfriend, actually, he said, glancing at Birdie. Her name was Karen. No, he didn't know where she lived. He'd only met her the day before. Didn't even know her last name. They were to meet on the beach at a quarter to two, but she hadn't turned up. He shrugged, grinned ruefully at Toby, man to man. Win some, lose some. He gave her about forty-five minutes and then left. It was her loss. That's how he looked at it. He went over to the pub. By then it was about two-thirty. He saw Warren drinking in the public bar. To avoid any confrontation, Douglas had had his own drink in the beer garden which, as he said, he preferred anyway. He hadn't seen Warren leave. He had returned to 'Third Wish' at about six, when, as he put it, the old man came out of his cell and there was a bit of life about the place. His room was next to Wendy's, looking out over the garden. He'd gone there to change because his clothes were wet. But he, too, had seen nothing.

As he left the room, the phone rang. Milson picked it up, listened for a moment, and put it down again. 'Only three Warren Daleys so far traced in Queensland,' he said to Toby. 'One born last year. One who is eighteen. One who is eighty-two. We'll check them out. Might be relatives. Nothing from the airports, based on name or description. Nothing from the taxi companies either. As yet.'

'It's a phoney name, or I'll eat my hat,' growled Toby. 'Still. We'll get him in the end.' He looked at Birdie. 'Well?'

'Well what?'

'Aren't you going to tell me that Warren Daley or whatever his name is couldn't possibly be the murderer? That's your form, isn't it? Or have you got more conservative since you turned professional?'

Birdie raised her eyebrows. 'I don't know what you mean,' she said. 'Of course he's the most likely person to have killed poor Mai. I think he was obsessed with her. And crazy with jealousy. And impulsive. And stupid. I was surprised when Max said he'd let himself be bought off. I would have thought he was far too emotional for that. He could easily have drunk himself into a rage, come back to the house, hidden in the garden—'

'On the off-chance she'd turn up?'

'She often walked in the garden, before she knew he was around. He'd have known that. Isa would have told him, because Mai didn't like the cats and it was because of her that Max started making a real fuss about their being in his garden. And anyway, he'd probably spied on her.'

Toby twirled in Max's leather chair. 'How did the family feel about the new bride?'

'Well, none of them liked it much. As you can imagine. Would you?'

'Be glad to see the old man happy? Why not? Half

his luck, I say.' He got up and walked towards the door.

Birdie stared. *Why not? Half his luck.* That was exactly what her own father had said, on the way home in the car after Max's party. She remembered how startled she had been, to see him half-smile as he said it. She had never thought of her father as a sexual being. Never considered that he may have felt lonely or deprived during the many years since her beautiful, wayward mother's death. And above all never dreamt that he of all people would ever smile and envy his old friend a little pussy cat like Mai. She considered the proposition that Max Tully, Angus Birdwood and Dan Toby were in one way at least brothers under the skin. And found it alarming.

She followed Toby out into the living room and so was the first person Max Tully saw as he burst in the front door, shouting.

'Birdie! Have you found her? What's going on here? Where is she?'

Birdie looked at him steadily. 'It's not good news, Max. I'm sorry.'

'What do you mean? Where is she?' He looked haggard.

'In the garden. She's dead. I'm sorry.'

Max blinked. 'Dead?' His hand crept up to his face. He almost smiled. 'What do you mean, dead?'

There was a muffled sob from the other end of the room.

'Max, she's been killed. Murdered.'

Max stood very still, staring. Birdie glanced over at Berwyn, Wendy, Douglas and Isa. She needed help here, but they all seemed frozen to the spot.

Dan Toby stepped forward. 'Detective-Inspector Toby, sir,' he said firmly.

He's done this so many times before, thought Birdie. This is just a job to him. But I know Max. I've know him all my life. This is horrible.

'Could I have a word?' Toby was continuing smoothly. 'I'm very sorry to trouble you, but . . .'

Max waved him aside. 'I want to see her.'

'Max . . . she was strangled,' said Birdie gently.

'I want to see her.'

And of course, Max had his way.

In the garden, under the floodlights, he crouched down in the damp leaves and touched Mai's cheek. 'Poor little Mai,' he whispered. 'I'm sorry Mai.' He stroked the pale, cool skin. 'I told her she was safe,' he said. 'She believed me. She always believed me. And now look. Look at her poor little face. Her neck's all cut.'

'It was the leather necklet, sir,' Toby murmured. 'It was used to choke her.'

'Oh, God!' Max buried his face in his hands.

Birdie touched his shoulder. 'Max we'd better go in. Come on.'

He nodded, allowed himself to be helped up and led slowly back to the house. But once inside the brightly-lit living room he stopped. His shoulders were hunched, and his arms hung loosely by his sides. He looked around the room and the people standing there as if he'd never seen it or them before.

'Dad—' Wendy began.

But Isa ran over to him, tears streaming down her face. 'My dear,' she cried. 'My dear, I'm so sorry.'

'Isa!' Max clutched at her and at last broke down. She folded him in her arms and her hands patted and stroked his back while the terrible sobs shuddered through him. 'Not fair, is it?' she crooned, over and over. 'Not fair, Max.'

For a long minute they stood there, locked together. Then Max slowly straightened up. He wiped his eyes, and gently disengaged himself from Isa's arms. He turned to Toby. 'Sorry about that,' he said. 'It's been a shock. You understand.' He breathed deeply. Once, twice. Playing for time, thought Birdie. Trying to get his act together.

'You wanted to talk to me,' said Max. 'All right. I'm ready.'

EIGHT

Details first. Just routine. The settling process. Birdie watched Toby going through his paces, bulky in the armchair, Milson taking notes, a thin shadow in the corner. They weren't a happy team. But they were good, nonetheless. She'd seen them at it many times before. But she'd never imagined them here, in this house. Talking to Max.

'Now, Mr Tully,' murmured Toby. 'You talked to your fiancée last night, after her husband left. Could you tell me what was said?'

'She met him—' Max took a deep breath. 'She told me she met him in Vietnam. He was on a package tour.' His lip curled. 'She'd only known him two weeks when he asked her to marry him. But he said he loved her and wanted to look after her—all the usual malarky. She didn't have any family. She's—she was, an innocent. She thought he was good-looking, and kind . . .' He paused. His face was anguished.

'Go on, Mr Tully,' Toby prompted.

Max sighed, and went on, speaking fast now. 'He paid for her to come out here, they got married, and for a while, she said, he was good to her. Then he started getting angry, as she put it. Picking at her. Saying she was stupid, and her cooking made him sick, and she spent too much. Then he started beating her up.' His face tightened. 'It's hard to imagine what sort of pig would do that to a fragile little girl like Mai, but there you are. It happened. She cried when she told me. She was ashamed of it. *She* was ashamed. She made me promise I wouldn't tell the family—or anyone. But I guess it doesn't matter now.' He took a deep breath, and looked down at his hard, knotty-veined hands.

'She didn't speak much English then. He kept her passport and other papers with him. And she didn't have any money. She said—' he hesitated, swallowing, and then went on. 'She said she tried hard to be—to do—what he wanted. To be a good wife to him, as she put it. But he went on laying into her. Twice he pushed her down the stairs. He threatened to kill her. She thought he was going to.' His mouth trembled, and he firmed it with an effort. 'Afterwards he'd cry and say he loved her and wouldn't touch her again. He'd beg, and plead with her to forgive him. Carry on like he did at the door last night. The bastard! But in a few weeks it'd happen again. It's the classic story. We've all heard it a thousand times. That went on for three years. Three bloody years. He said she'd never get away from him. But in the end she did. Well—for a while.'

'How?' Birdie prompted. 'What did she do?'

'She listened to the radio, would you believe? Watched TV. Locked in the house most of the time it was all she had to do. Gradually she picked up more English. And one night when he was drunk she raided his wallet, found her passport and just left. Got herself to the airport, God knows how. And came to Sydney.'

'Why Sydney?' Birdie was still probing.

Max half-smiled. 'It was the only Australian place

she'd heard about in Vietnam. The Harbour Bridge, the Opera House, and Bondi Beach, she said. She'd always wanted to see them. But Warren hated Sydney. Said it stank. She thought he'd never come here. Thought that here she'd be safe.' He drew a shuddering breath. 'She got to Sydney, got a job under her maiden name, and just tried to forget all about him. Didn't tell anyone she had ever been married. Thought that way he'd never find her. Then after about a year she came here, and met me. And that finished that. Instead of looking after her, I ended up handing her to her killer on a plate.' He gritted his teeth. 'If only she'd told me,' he said. 'If only . . .'

'He wrote you threatening letters before coming to the door, I gather,' said Toby coolly. 'Do you still have those?'

'Oh, yes,' Max went over to the desk and pulled out the envelopes. He passed them to Toby, who looked at the three letters one by one, holding them gingerly by the edges.

'Mai never got hers, because I got to it first,' said Max. 'But she already knew Warren was next door. She saw him, when she was walking in the garden on Sunday afternoon. She was terrified. She didn't know what to do. So she did nothing. Just stayed inside the house and worried. I didn't know what was wrong with her. Thought the family was getting to her or something. Then when I started getting the letters I thought maybe she'd got one too. Finally I called Birdie.'

'Mmm.' Toby passed the letters and envelopes to Milson who put them carefully into a plastic bag. 'What do you think he had in mind when he wrote these?' he asked, jerking his head in their direction.

'Frankly I don't think he has a mind, in that sense,' muttered Max. 'I don't think he had the faintest idea what he was doing. He'd got here, and he'd found Mai. That's probably as far as he'd gone with a plan. The notes were just viciousness and spite. A cowardly bully's way of trying to stir up trouble, and make his presence felt. From what he said this morning he seemed to have had some woolly idea of scaring her so she'd run. Or upsetting her applecart with me, so I'd throw her out. I suppose he thought everyone was as paranoid and jealous as he was. He's a nasty customer, but thick as a brick. I'd say he turned up on the doorstep last night because he was drunk, and probably trying to impress Isa. She'd have egged him on. He'd told her some bullshit story about Mai dudding him and running off. When I spoke to him this morning he was just a sullen, ugly mass of rage, and hung over to boot. I gave him a wad of cash and told him to get out. And he went. Back to Queensland, he said. But . . .'

'He changed his mind,' Toby finished for him. He looked at Max keenly. 'How much money did you actually give him, Mr Tully?'

Max told him. Toby's eyes flickered. More than he earns in a year, thought Birdie.

'No point in mucking round,' said Max. 'I told him I'd give him the same again when the divorce was through, if he kept away.' He clenched his fists. 'What are you doing about finding him?' he demanded.

Toby was unruffled. It was interesting, thought Birdie, watching him, how unaffected he was by Max's money and fame. He had obviously been fascinated to meet Auntie Dora. But of course Max Tully's Morning had never been part of Toby's life. He'd been in the thick of things at work. He hadn't grown to depend on Max's company from morning tea till lunch. Whereas Auntie Dora came into his living room almost every night while he sat alone on his old pink couch, eating Chinese takeaway or fish and chips.

'Airlines, taxi companies and so on have been alerted,' Toby was droning. 'And now you've given us a description of the emeralds we can—'

'Ah—the emeralds. The emeralds.' Max looked at his hands again. 'He would be idiot enough to try to sell them, too. Wouldn't have any idea what they were worth, of course. They'll go to some shonky little dealer for a song.' He lifted his head, and his eyes were again glittering with tears. 'She loved them,' he said. 'She'd never in her life had anything like them. Poor little Mai.'

Toby shifted uncomfortably in his chair and rubbed at his nose. 'Mr Tully, I won't keep you much longer. As I said, we're trying to trace this man. But just to cover all other aspects—you haven't had any bad feeling with anyone else in the past few weeks? Seen any strangers hanging around? Parked cars you don't recognise?'

'No. Nothing like that.'

'The engagement was featured in a women's magazine. Have you had any indication that any of your fans—ah—object to your taking up with—such a young lady?' Toby paused, massively delicate. 'A young Asian lady?'

Max gestured impatiently. 'Just the usual nutters. The station knows about them. The letters'd be on file. No threats. Just abuse. Oh, and *Hers* probably got a few. You could check. The same sort of thing happened when I married Ingrid. And Berwyn, come to that.'

'You're still married to Berwyn Kyte, I gather.'

'The divorce is underway. It won't take long. We've been separated for years.'

'Does Miss Kyte object to the divorce?'

'Oh, no. Berwyn's not really the marrying kind. She didn't want to get married in the first place. I pushed her into it. And she left me after a couple of years.' Max's lips tightened and for a moment a shadow of old pain showed in his eyes, but he pushed on. 'She needed to be on her own. Her work. It's the most important thing in her life. I think living with me was too hard for her in those days. It was interfering.' He threw up his hands. 'Anyhow, that was years ago. Thirteen years ago. We just never bothered to cut the knot. A bit of protection for both of us, really.'

'Will you be going on with the divorce now, do you think?'

Max looked at him. 'I haven't thought about it. Oh, I don't know. Not much point is there? Now.'

'How did your children feel about the engagement, Mr Tully?'

'Look—what's ...?' Max gritted his teeth and broke off. 'I don't think they cared much for Mai,' he said levelly. 'They didn't know her, and they didn't understand her. But it was none of their business anyway, was it?'

'There is a lot of money involved, sir.'

'For God's sake, Toby! If they were worried about that and they felt like knocking someone off they'd kill *me*, wouldn't they? Not poor Mai. We weren't married yet, were we?'

'But you were going to be, sir. And children don't kill their parents lightly, in my experience. Whereas a stranger—an interloper ...'

'*What are you going on about!!*' Max exploded, pounding the table. Then he clutched at his head and breathed deeply. When his hands dropped, he was calm again. 'I'm sorry,' he said. 'I didn't mean to blow up. I'm upset.'

'Of course.' Toby was imperturbable.

'I just mean—if you knew Wendy and Douglas you'd see that this sort of stuff's just a waste of time. Wendy's got a nice little house and a small income from her late husband. And she knows she can always call on me if she needs to. Anyway, she's a good, decent woman who wouldn't hurt a fly. And Douglas is single, with no ties and no responsibilities. He isn't particularly flush, because he's spent up big over the years and hasn't put anything by. But on the whole he copes, and he's made it clear plenty of times that he doesn't want anything out of me. Look—Birdie's known them both all her life. Her dad and I are old mates. She'll tell you.'

Toby smiled briefly. 'All right,' he said. He planted his hands on his knees and levered himself to his feet. Max stood up to face him, pale now, and staggering slightly with exhaustion. He is seventy, thought Birdie. He's not a kid. God, what an ordeal for him. She thought suddenly of her father. She'd have to ring him. Let him know ...

'I'm going back outside now,' Toby was saying, slowly and clearly. 'We won't need to trouble you again tonight, Mr Tully. You get some rest. We'll talk again in the morning.'

Max wet his lips and looked away from him out at the darkness beyond the window. 'You'll have to do a postmortem,' he said.

'Yes, we will. You understand . . .'

'Of course I do.' He turned back to Toby. 'When did it happen? Any idea yet?'

'We know it was sometime between a quarter to five, when she was last seen, and five-thirty, when the rain started. Her watch had stopped at five minutes past five,' said Toby. Birdie looked up. This was new.

'We aren't taking the watch time as gospel, of course,' Toby was continuing. 'It could be a coincidence, or something the killer did to put us off the scent. But it's obviously worth noting.'

'Yes.' Max fell silent.

When Toby had left, Milson following him like a long shadow, Max turned to Birdie. 'She died while I was taping,' he said. His face was empty. 'Life and death go on. I talk on the radio.'

In the living room the family, and Isa, waited. Toby had obviously taken Constable Barassi back outside with him, for they were alone and unguarded. Max walked towards them, making an obvious effort to appear in control.

'You'd better get on home, Isa,' he said. 'Go to bed. You're all in, sweetheart.'

Isa did indeed look exhausted. Her usual sprightly manner was entirely absent, and her mouth drooped. 'Will you be all right?' she asked.

'As all right as I'll ever be,' he said, patting her hand.

She stood up, leaning on the arm of the couch, but hesitated, making no move to go. Her forehead was creased with fatigue and anxiety. 'You don't think—he—Warren, would be still hanging round, do you?' she said at last. 'I keep thinking about it.'

'Of course he wouldn't,' said Wendy, almost crossly. 'He'd have got as far away from here as he possibly could. And anyway, Isa, he's got no bone to pick with you. You're perfectly safe.'

'Plus the place is crawling with coppers,' drawled Douglas.

'I don't know,' Birdie put in. 'I think we ought to take care for a while, actually. He's not a rational person.'

'I agree,' said Max. He took Isa by the hand. 'Come on, lovey,' he said. 'I'll get a cop to take you home. Couldn't get safer than that, could you?'

He led her to the door, discovered Constable Barassi sitting on the front steps having a furtive cigarette, kissed his charge on the forehead and handed her over. Then he wandered back to the group by the windows and sat down, his hands hanging loosely over his knees.

'It's not your fault, Max,' Berwyn said quietly.

His head jerked up.

'Of *course* it's not Dad's fault!' Wendy exclaimed. 'Good heavens, what a strange thing to say, Berwyn.'

Berwyn didn't answer.

'You'd better go to bed, Dad,' said Douglas awkwardly. He leaned forward and touched his father's arm. Max flinched and pulled his arm away.

'I'm all right,' he muttered. 'Just leave me alone.'

Douglas stiffened.

'There's no question of it being Dad's fault,' Wendy blundered on, oblivious. 'The poor little girl brought it all on herself. If only she'd been honest with us. But she deceived Dad, and—'

'*Wendy! Shut up!*' Max's hand crashed on the table.

Wendy jumped as if she'd been struck. She blushed scarlet.

'There's no point in screaming at Wendy, Dad,' said Douglas coldly. 'Of course you're upset. But you can't bloody take it out on your family. You know Wendy's right. The girl was in a mess and she brought

her mess here with her, and now we're all mixed up in
it. She should have sorted her life out before she let
you get involved with her. She should have had the decency to—'

'You—you—' Max was stammering with rage. He
glared at Douglas with something like hatred. 'You
bloody keep out of this! What do you know about
what Mai went through? What would you bloody know
about sorting out a life? You've never bloody sorted
out your own. Leave me to handle my own affairs. I
couldn't make more of a muck of them than you.'

'Oh, Dad,' cried Wendy. 'Oh, Douglas! Don't—'

Douglas was white. 'If you'd have let me sort out
my life I would've. If you'd let Trish and me handle
our own affairs, maybe—'

'What bullshit!' sneered Max.

'Dad, Douglas, don't . . .' Wendy's face was anguished. 'Douglas, you mustn't say that to Dad. You
know you didn't want to get married. You were scared
stiff. You told me. And that girl—'

'What do you want?' snarled Max, crouched in his
armchair. 'You were only nineteen. Was I supposed to
let you marry some little pregnant floosy at nineteen?
Make the mistake I did? By God you'd have known it
then, mate. You with the blondes and the fast cars and
the flash mates. Stuck in some go-nowhere marriage
with a boring wife and a squalling kid dragging you
down like I was.'

Birdie heard Wendy's quick intake of breath, saw
the pain flash across her face. But the woman said
nothing, and Max and Douglas were far too involved
in their own troubles to think about hers.

'We should have got married. Or at least stayed together. We should have,' spat Douglas. 'Whether it
worked out or not. I loved Trish. She loved me. But
you and my mother and Wendy just pulled and
pushed and pushed at me till I didn't know what to
do. You packed me off overseas, made me abandon
her . . .'

'Ah, don't sentimentalise it, Douglas.' Max's
mouth curled contemptuously. 'She took the money

quick enough. And you weren't in love. You didn't
know what the word meant. You were thinking with
your cock. As usual.' He gripped the arms of the chair
and leaned forward, glasses flashing. 'And anyway, you
weren't in shackles. You were a grown man. You
agreed. You agreed to the whole thing. It's typical.
Take what you can get and then complain about it afterwards. I've paid out a fortune to get you off the
hook. I'm still paying. Every bloody month. Show
some bloody gratitude.'

'She agreed to take the money because she had
to!' shouted Douglas. 'I'd gone into smoke. She was
pregnant. Her folks had nothing at all. What did you
expect her to do? The money's nothing to you.'

'Douglas, all this was eight years ago,' sighed Max,
rubbing his eyes. Suddenly he seemed to have lost interest in the argument. 'What does it matter now?'

'What does it *matter*?' Douglas's heavy, handsome
face flushed from white to bright red. 'God, you're incredible. You robbed me of my *son*, you bastard! I've
never even seen him, in eight years. And I've got no
right to, either. You made her leave my name off the
birth certificate. I've got nothing and no one, thanks
to you. But you—you never stop. Grab, grab, grab.
This girl—you hardly knew her. But you were going to
marry her, just like that. Talk about thinking with your
cock! And kids, you were talking about. More kids for
yourself when you should be thinking about being a
grandfather. You make me sick!'

'Well if that's how you feel, it's mutual,' snarled
Max. '"Nothing and no one"—what a laugh. You've
had every bloody thing money can buy. You're like a
spoiled kid in a lolly shop, whingeing about one popsicle he missed out on. A popsicle he didn't want in
the first place. You had nothing in common with that
girl. Nothing. You'd have thrown your life away—'

'I wouldn't have thrown my life away. I'd have got
a life. Or at least the chance of one. God knows, I
haven't got one now. And what do you mean we had
nothing in common? We did. *You* had nothing in common with Trish. But I'm not like you. Not at all.'

Max turned his head away. His lip curled. 'As that murdering bastard next door said, that's hardly surprising, is it?'

'What?' Douglas lunged forward and grabbed his arm. 'What's that crack supposed to mean?'

'What do you think? Why don't you ask your mother about it?' hissed Max, and as Douglas stared at him, open-mouthed, he furiously shook off his hand, jumped to his feet and made for the study.

Douglas didn't turn to watch him go. Instead he raised his eyes to the portrait on the wall. It stared back at him: cocky, self absorbed, vibrating with life. It was impossible to guess what he might be thinking. For one long minute he stood motionless. Then he breathed out, as though he had been holding his breath for all that time. 'I'm off,' he said to Wendy. 'I'll be back for my clothes tomorrow.'

Wendy's face crumpled with anxiety. 'But Douglas, where will you go? The police . . .'

'I don't know yet. Out of here, anyway. I'll tell the cops. I'll be in touch.' He crossed the room to where she stood wringing her hands. He bent and kissed her on the cheek. 'Bye, sis. Don't worry.'

Wendy's lips trembled. He gently disengaged himself from her clutching hands, nodded to Berwyn and Birdie and strode to the front door without looking back. By the time it slammed behind him Wendy was in tears. 'I can't bear this. How could this have happened?' she wailed. 'How could this have happened to us? Oh, I curse the day that that girl came into this house. How could Dad say those things to Douglas?'

'For God's sake, Wendy,' snapped Berwyn. 'Just for once, focus on realities, can't you? Mai's dead! Max is half out of his mind. Douglas asked for everything he got. He's a fool.'

Wendy looked at her with dislike. 'He's not a fool,' she said. 'He's sad and lonely. And now Dad's driven him away. Again. For good this time, maybe.'

'Well, maybe that'd be the best thing for them both.'

Wendy stood up. 'I'm going to bed,' she said, her

voice shaking. 'And I think you should leave here to-morrow.'

After she had gone Birdie and Berwyn went into the kitchen and found some rice crackers and cheese and a bottle of soda water. They sat huddled at the table, nibbling like mice.

'Does Max really believe Douglas isn't his son?' asked Birdie after a while.

Berwyn shrugged. 'I think he's always thought so. Not that he's ever said it in so many words. But I always assumed it. Ingrid had her hooks into some man when Max threw her out. He told me that. Douglas was only two then, and the affair had been going on for at least three years.'

'This was Douglas's stepfather?'

'Oh, no. He came later. This was some wealthy, married man. Stockbroker, or something. Ingrid was trying to get him to leave his wife, Max said. Maybe she thought a pregnancy would do the trick. The guy wouldn't play, though. Never did leave his wife. He was a big, beefy type, Max said. Like Douglas. That's all he ever said about it.' Berwyn looked vaguely around the kitchen. Copper pans shone on their hooks, reflecting the room. The benchtops gleamed. 'Max isn't the fatherly type. Or he wasn't. He took responsibility for Douglas, but he's never liked him. Not once he found out about the other man. But lashing out like that's very uncharacteristic. Wendy's right about that, anyway. He'd never have used that particular weapon if he hadn't been knocked for six by this Mai thing. Douglas *is* a fool.' She paused. 'And sad and lonely,' she added. 'Wendy was right about that, too.'

Birdie woke suddenly, with no sense of how much time had passed, or what had woken her. She switched on the light and got up and went to the bedroom window, pulling the curtains aside. Darkness. The sound of the waves. Branches squeaking against glass. She could see nothing but her own reflection in the glass.

Suddenly she felt exposed, as though she was being watched. She quickly let the curtains fall back into place. She wondered whether the police were still working in the garden. Was Dan still there? Maybe she should go and see. It was while she was throwing on some clothes that she noticed the smell. Cinnamon.

She let herself into the kitchen. Max was standing there, taking a tray of pastries out of the oven. He shrugged at her surprised face. 'Will you make the coffee? Kettle's boiled,' he said.

'Max, what are you doing?' Birdie took the coffee he handed to her and put it into the pot.

'It keeps me calm,' he said, tipping the pastries onto a wire tray. 'I started out as a pastry-cook. I like cooking.'

'Yes, I know,' Birdie watched him. So thin. He rarely ate much of what he made. But he loved to see other people enjoying his food. He liked to tempt them, fill their mouths with sweetness, and see them smile. While needing nothing himself.

'I met Wendy's mother in a cake shop, you know,' Max went on, moving slowly to the refrigerator. He was subdued and quiet, as though all his vitality had somehow drained away. 'She was the softest, prettiest thing. I was bowled over. I'd never known a girl like her before.' He brought out butter, milk, sugar, and set them on the table. 'She died when Wendy was born.'

'What? But I thought—'

He smiled sadly. 'Metaphorically speaking. She . . . once we were married . . . once Wendy was born, she seemed to go into automatic. She changed so much. She had a lot to do, I know that. But she never laughed any more. Wouldn't have any fun. The soft little girl just disappeared. It was a sort of metamorphosis. She turned into a housewife. And she wanted me to change too. Into something. A husband who cooked barbecues and cleaned the car, maybe. I don't know. She got so angry when I couldn't—or wouldn't.

'She fought me tooth and nail to stop me going into radio. Hated the idea. Hated the people. Scared of the insecurity. She used to stand around at parties looking as if someone was going to hit her. Half scared, half aggro. Took everything anyone said the wrong way. And Isa—'

'You can hardly blame her for resenting Isa, Max.'

'Ah—Isa!' Max spread out his hand. 'Isa's always been there. Isa's no threat to anyone. Isa and me—we're just Isa and me.'

'Max,' Birdie brought the coffee pot over to the table. 'You couldn't expect Sonia to understand that. You couldn't expect any woman to. After all, it's not as though the relationship was—ah—platonic.'

'Hardly. At least in those days.' Max smiled reminiscently. 'What does that matter? Isa never wanted marriage. And Sonia wouldn't . . . Anyhow, the fact is I never loved my wives less because of Isa. I loved them less—or the first two, anyway—because of *them*. Isa was—just Isa.'

Still is Isa, thought Birdie. But it's different now. Because now Isa's old. Yet so are you, Max.

'Berwyn was different. I never wanted anyone else, with Berwyn. There wasn't the space. Isa understood that. She backed off. She entertained herself fine without me.' He was silent, for a long moment. 'But Berwyn's got her head screwed on. She understands me better than anyone. She knows I'm a dangerous bastard. Dangerous for her. So she keeps her distance.'

'And Mai?'

'Mai didn't care. Didn't care what I was or what I did. Accepted the whole package, good and bad. That was the beauty of Mai. I didn't threaten her. She didn't threaten me. We looked after each other. Safe harbour for both of us, I thought.' Max turned to the table, and started setting it, methodically, with plates, knives, cups. 'She trusted me,' he said. 'And so she died.'

'Max, that's not right!'

He didn't turn around. 'You should get a man, Birdie. You can't be alone all your life,' he said, without a change of tone.

'Why not? Frankly, I can't see much joy in partnerships. Look at Mai and that pig Warren. My mother and father. You and all your various spouses. Violence, lies, misery, games … The first three are untenable and I don't like playing games. Anyhow, I've never met a man I fancied for more than five minutes. Or vice versa. I get bored too easily.' Birdie knew she was being used to divert him. He was concentrating on her 'problem' to avoid confronting his own. That was all right with her.

'That's not the reason,' said Max. 'Sit down. Have a pastry.'

'What is the reason then?'

'You don't want to risk it, that's all. You don't want to let your guard down for a minute. If you watch from the sidelines, you're safe. Falling in love's a risk. Letting someone inside your shell. You could get hurt.'

'You're talking bullshit, Max. You don't let down your guard. You never have. All those women—and none of them really got under your skin, did they?'

'Oh, yes.' Max pushed the plate of sugar-frosted pastries towards her, and she took one. 'Berwyn did. And Mai. But Mai wouldn't have needed to run, like Berwyn did. Mai could have stayed with me forever.' His eyes had a faraway look, behind his glasses. 'But I'm an old man, Birdie. It doesn't matter what I've done or haven't done. I've done it tough. It's screwed me up. I admit it. You're different. You've got to take the risk. That's what life's all about. Living. Having it all.'

Birdie thought of Berwyn's words and watched him drain his coffee cup. To the last drop.

NINE

Max walked on the empty beach. Salt water foamed and hissed around his ankles, then withdrew. The wet sand gleamed in a bright, curving strip in front of him. It was very early. Soon he would go for a swim. Soon. Then this strange, unreal feeling in his head would clear. Then he'd be able to face this day.

Mai. Her face floated into his mind. Soft, trusting, sweet. Mai. Sitting on the floor by his feet, with her head leaning on his knee and his hand resting on her silken hair. Such peace. He closed his eyes. The edge of the sea swirled around him. So many years. So many women. She was to be his last. And now she had gone. Fear gripped him. It seemed to twist at his heart. And Mai's face dissolved, and changed . . .

Sonia. Where had she come from? Sonia, nine-teen, dimpling and giggling at the cake shop counter, in her fresh, white blouse. He'd never known a girl like Sonia before. She smelled so good. She wore soft,

fluffy cardigans her mother made. Her skin was like
milk. She went out sometimes with a boy from her
church. Max saw him once. Tall and skinny, with a big
Adam's apple, watery blue eyes and a fine speckling of
dandruff on the shoulders of his dark suit. A wimp. A
bore. A nice boy.

But Sonia ... At work he'd flirt with her, and
tease her, delighting in her excitement and the blush
he could raise on her softly-rounded cheeks. Away
from the shop he'd forget all about her. He'd drink
with his mates on Friday and Saturday nights, pick up
any girl he thought he could get to come across. And
he did quite well, really, considering his height and
plain looks. He'd learned early that making them
laugh was three-quarters of the battle.

Then one day Sonia had come into the shop early,
before opening time. She'd stood by the bench in the
back room as he kneaded dough. She'd giggled, and
then blushed and fallen silent and turned her head
away. He could feel her tension. He knew what she
wanted. And he'd touched her on her soft cheek with
his floury hand, and kissed her gently. Her lips were
soft and warm. 'You taste as good as you look,' he'd
said. It was a line he'd used many times, but as he felt
her tremble and burn against him he was startled and
moved, and that night, in his room in the boarding
house where he stayed, he kept thinking of her. And
the next day, she came early to the shop again.

The seduction of Sonia began as a dream-like
game. Her sweet softness fascinated him. Her curling
hair, her hands with their rounded pink nails and little pearl ring. The third time he kissed her he slid his
hand up to her breast, hearing her gasp with fear, feeling himself flush hot. They began going out, on Satur-
days. By mutual, unspoken consent they were discreet.
Her parents wouldn't have approved. His mates would
have laughed. They would travel out of the city in the
train, and picnic in the bush. They would eat sand-
wiches and drink warm lemonade. She would chatter.
He would think about her body. He would talk about
his ideas and schemes. She would gaze at him with

dark, liquid eyes. Conversations were just spaces between physical contact.

They'd kiss, lying on a rug he brought from the bed in his room. They played by her teenage virgin's rules, though he was twenty-four. Every time was like the first. He could take no intimacy for granted. He'd whisper that he loved her and after a while she'd relax, and let him slip his hands into her blouse, undo her buttons, loosen the white cotton bra so he could touch and kiss her breasts. Each time she'd let him go a little further. At last he would lie on top of her, his hand between her white thighs, delirious with desire, murmuring, 'Please, Sonia. Oh, I love you, oh, I want to ... please let me ... please ...' Then she'd stop him, pulling his hand away, trembling and straightening her clothes, and they'd fold up the rug and leave, to catch the train home with her flushed and dreamy and him aching, sweating and sticky. Next time, he'd tell himself. Next time. But he never thought beyond that.

When it finally happened, it happened so fast. He clung to her, and forgot everything he'd ever learned. She cried, and bled, and it was all over in two minutes. Tears rolled down her cheeks on the way home in the train. She was still crying when he kissed her goodbye. He felt a flash of irritation, then, as soon as she was gone, a rush of tenderness and pity. And by the evening he was aching for her again.

Sonia. Why was he thinking of Sonia now? Those hopes he'd had. Those feelings, when they were married, too young, too soon, with her belly already swelling with the baby visited on her by his lust. That miserable little flat. Sonia, soft in pink nylon nightdress in the heavy old double bed. A wife. A home. All the wanting of his twenty-four years pouring into one wave and sweeping him along in a sea of hope. For six months. A year. And then the stale, sour feeling of disenchantment creeping in. The boredom. The bafflement. The suppressed anger.

He felt the tears spill, stinging, from his eyes. In front of him sand shone in a gleaming ribbon. Behind him the blunt ruts his feet had made filled with foam and collapsed inwards.

Mai. He tried to recall her face. But now it kept drifting away from him, drifting at the corners of his mind, just out of reach. And other faces kept pushing it away. One especially. One he didn't want to see. Don't go, Mai.

He looked ahead and in the blurred, shining distance saw he was no longer alone on the beach. Small, dark, skinny, powerless, the boy stood looking out to sea. *Three wishes* . . . His heart swelled, his tongue grew thick in his mouth. *I can . . . I will . . . I swear . . .*

He turned, and ran.

'He went to the beach, just as I got here.' Toby paced beside Birdie. Into Isa's front gate, down the path, across to the neat shed near the sagging wire boundary fence. 'Said he'd be back in an hour. Funny sort of cove, isn't he?'

He pushed at the shed door with the backs of his fingers. The door squeaked and hung gaping open. They walked in. Nothing. An empty room, with a gas ring and sink. A used cake of pink soap. A few dead matches in a jar lid. A bed. A ruckled grey blanket. Beyond, a dark little bathroom. Toilet. Basin. Tiny shower cabinet, its flowered curtain still damp and slightly smelling of mildew. 'Milson went over it last night,' Toby said. 'He's right. There's nothing here.'

Outside again they breathed the early morning air. It was still and humid, tangy with salt. A huge tree covered in heavily scented white magnolias loomed close to the wire fence nearby. Wooden markers dotted the ground in the shadow of the tree's canopy. The cat graveyard.

Toby walked over to look. 'Crikey,' he muttered, screwing his head to one side to examine the markers. '"Lady: rest in peace". "Othello: my darling"—that's the new one, I gather. "Sweet dreams, little Sooty" . . . Shit a brick!'

Birdie wandered to the wire. 'You can see the house from here,' she said in surprise. 'Max's house.'

'I know.' Toby joined her. 'Look, but don't touch,' he said. He gestured towards the place behind the tree where the fence sagged low. Leaves and mud clung to the wire. 'That could be Isa, getting over the day before yesterday to save her puss-cat. Or it could be our man, getting over last night to kill his missus.'

Through small gaps in the shrubs and trees on Max's side you could just see flashes of the bright pink tape that now fenced in the spot where Mai had lain. The screened figures of uniformed police moved around it, flickering in and out of sight, oblivious of the watchers next door.

Birdie stared. From here you could peer undetected for as long as you liked. How many times, for how many hours, had the man who called himself Warren Daley waited here, watching the house where his runaway wife huddled, terrified and silent? Suddenly the atmosphere seemed stifling, the scent of the magnolias oppressive. It was as if brooding obsession had found a home under the great tree, and poisoned the air.

'Nasty,' Toby commented briefly. Birdie glanced at him. His face was set. He was feeling the same as she was. Somehow this increased her sense of dread.

'Let's go back,' she said.

'No bloody sign of Warren Daley, or whatever his name is,' said Toby as they went back through Isa's garden to the road. 'The barmaid at the Paradise, Julie Billings, remembers him, but doesn't know exactly when he left. Sometime around four-thirty, maybe. He paid for his first drink with a hundred dollar bill, he drank quite a lot, and he had a black bag with him. She remembers that, anyway.'

'He's got plenty of money, thanks to Max,' said Birdie. 'He could be holed up in a hotel. He could have bought a car and be driving back to Queensland. Anything.'

'The press are onto it,' growled Toby. 'Someone's opened their fat mouths. The story'll be headlines this afternoon. He's bound to see it. He'll know the body's been found. That'll put the wind up him and he'll be scared off trying to dispose of the jewellery or use the credit cards, worse luck.'

'Dan, why on earth would she have tried to run away when she thought her husband had been sent packing?' asked Birdie quietly.

'Oh, why do women do anything? I don't think that's a big issue, Birdwood. She knew her husband better than Max Tully did, presumably. Maybe she knew full well that he wouldn't go for good, and tried to make a break for it before he decided to come back. Who knows? She can't tell us now. And the fact is, the emeralds are gone, her handbag's gone, and the note was left and is genuine.'

'You've checked it out? Compared it with other things she wrote?'

Toby snorted. 'Of course we have. Think we're dills?'

'I just think we should keep open minds, that's all. This running away business seems funny to me.'

Toby pushed open Max's security door, now casually held ajar by half a brick, and nodded to the police constable on duty just inside. 'I always keep an open mind, dickess,' he rumbled. 'But thank you for your concern.'

Milson approached them. Unlike Toby he had shaved and was wearing a clean, ironed shirt. His thin lips were pressed together and turned down slightly at the corners.

'News,' muttered Toby. 'He's got news. I can always tell. It makes him look sour.' He raised his voice. 'What've you got, Milson?'

Milson stopped in front of them and looked meaningfully at Birdie. Toby beckoned impatiently. 'Don't worry about her. Give, will you? Found something?'

'Not yet,' said Milson. 'But we've started sifting the leaf litter. The rain's probably washed anything there is down below the surface.' He paused.

'Well? What is it then? Come on! This isn't Twenty Questions, you know.'

Milson flipped open his notebook. 'A local taxi driver reports driving a man answering Daley's description to this house from the Paradise Hotel. He believes they arrived here at almost exactly ten to five. He took a radio call immediately afterwards that confirms this.'

'Right!' Toby's tired eyes had brightened. He hitched at his belt. 'Now we're getting somewhere. Anything else?'

Milson flipped another page. 'A black bag answering the description was handed in at the Paradise police station about ten minutes ago. They haven't opened it. They're waiting for you. It was found last night under some scrub at the end of the beach.'

'Who found it?'

'A teenage girl who claimed she was jogging at the time.' Milson looked down his nose. 'In fact, the spot she indicated is a well-known local lover's lane. She was probably there with a boyfriend but doesn't want her parents to know.'

'Ah, well. At least she handed the stuff in. We've all done a bit of illicit snogging in our time, haven't we, Milson?' grinned Toby.

Milson sniffed. It was clear that he, at least, had not.

As Toby very well knew.

As they made their way back to the house up the steep stone steps, the driveway doors opened without apparent human intervention. Max's car appeared and began crawling up the drive. The gates swung shut behind it. Remote control, thought Birdie. Magic.

She waited with Toby on the red gravel terrace while Max parked in the garage, and looked at him anxiously as he came towards them, his leather scuffs flapping, shorts flaring over thin, brown legs. He looked dreadful. He was almost shuffling. He stopped in front of them, his hand on his forehead. 'You wanted me?' he asked.

Toby, briefly and without frills, told him the latest developments. He nodded, but seemed abstracted, and turned away without comment when Toby had finished.

'Mr Tully!' Toby's voice was insistent.

Max peered back over his shoulder, his brow wrinkled with strain.

'We still don't know where this man is, Mr Tully. He could be hundreds of kilometres away, or somewhere quite close,' Toby said. 'He might feel—violent towards you. I think it might be as well for you to take some care. I wouldn't make any more trips to the beach at odd hours on your own, for a while, for example. See what I mean?'

Max nodded without speaking.

'And I think the same applies to the other people in the house. Your son Douglas, in particular.'

'Douglas.' Max stood for a moment, his eyes vacant, as if trying to remember something. He wet his lips. 'Douglas isn't here.'

'Not for now, Mr Tully. He's at a motel in Paradise, apparently. He left his address. But if he comes back . . .'

Max turned away again. 'He won't come back,' he said, and began climbing the stairs to the house.

Toby and Birdie exchanged glances. 'He's in a bad way,' Birdie murmured. She looked at her watch. 'I'll ring my father. He'll be up by now. Maybe he could do Max some good. He'd want to know, anyway, before he sees it in the papers.'

'Go for it,' grunted Toby. 'The old man had a blue with his son last night, I gather.'

'Yes. Quite nasty, too. Douglas and Max have never really got on. But last night it all blew up.' Birdie hesitated, then decided there was no need to go into details. 'Both of them were uptight, I suppose,' she added. 'Anyway . . .'

'Anyway, you go and call your pa. And after that, you look out for Berwyn Kyte and the daughter and tell them not to go out without seeing the cop at the gate. I don't want any more trouble. I'll get down to Paradise and have a look at that bag. I won't be happy till we've traced Daley.'

Birdie nodded. She agreed. Of course she agreed. Everything was falling into place. But somehow she felt uncomfortable. Almost guilty. As though there was something she wasn't facing up to.

She followed Toby into the house. The front door was open, but there was no one to be seen on the ground floor. She rang her father from the living room phone and told him what had happened. He listened in silence. She imagined him sitting in his dressing-gown by the kitchen table, his glasses at the end of his nose, a cup of tea in his hand.

'How's Max?' he said when she'd finished.

'Not good, Dad. He's—shattered.' The word came to her out of the blue. It wasn't one she'd normally use. But it was, somehow, appropriate.

There was a moment's silence. 'I'll call him on the private line,' her father said at last. 'Thanks for letting me know, kid.'

'That's OK.'

'You won't be staying on there, will you?'

'No. It's time to go. Toby's here. And Wendy and Berwyn. There's nothing for me to do.'

'Good. Sooner the better, kid. OK?'

'OK.'

Birdie hung up, feeling unsettled. There was something about this situation that she didn't understand. Loose ends trailed around her everywhere. She rubbed her eyes under her glasses. Maybe she was just tired. Everything was out of proportion.

She climbed the stairs to Berwyn's studio. The door, for once, was open. Berwyn was there, packing away her painting things. The studio was a big, airy, beautiful room. Through the curving windows the early morning sea shimmered in the sun. No good for painting in the morning, Berwyn had told her. But then she never painted in the morning. The afternoon was her time, and the light was fine then.

Berwyn seemed to have just got up. The sheets on the divan bed in the corner were tumbled. Her hair stood up in spikes, and her eyes were still puffy with sleep.

The room was a mess. Pens, pencils, paints, jars and bottles and rags. Cardboard boxes. Clothes. Coffee cups, orange peels and empty plates. Torn and screwed up paper tossed on the floor. And Mai was everywhere. Charcoal sketches of her head and shoulders were pinned and stuck all over the walls and benches. A few lines only, some of them. A shape, a curve of the cheek. 'The spaces are as important as the lines,' Berwyn had said once, in an interview. 'What you don't know is as important as what you do.' Mai with her hair up, down and simply pulled back. Mai in profile. Mai with flowers in her hair. On the easel in the centre of the room Mai floated on bare canvas in her black top and plaited leather necklet, with her glossy black hair piled high. She was looking straight at the artist, half-smiling. It was a studio portrait. Characterless. Lifeless.

Berwyn saw Birdie looking. 'It's no good, is it?'

'Very self-contained,' said Birdie. 'No background. Is that how you saw her?'

'No . . . Yes, I suppose so. She was very beautiful. But hard to paint. Hard to penetrate. Everything I tried looked chocolate-boxy. I hadn't found a suitable background idea. She barely spoke to me. We had no relationship, despite Max's wishful thinking about our cosy chats. I couldn't work her out.' Berwyn firmed her lips. 'Anyway, I won't have to now. I won't ever have to solve the problem. An unfinished portrait. I'm glad.'

'You didn't like her.'

'That's strong. I just didn't have any feeling one way or another.' Berwyn began pulling sketches from the walls, her eyes on the portrait.

'Why did you agree to do it?'

Mai's painted eyes stared out at them.

Berwyn shrugged. 'Max asked me. It was his birthday.'

'Won't you finish the picture, for Max?'

'Oh, no. I couldn't finish it. Never. Not now.'

She turned abruptly, threw down the sketches and began stuffing debris from the floor into the empty rubbish bin. Birdie gazed around. Mai looked back at her from all angles. Sly. Peaceful. Knowing. Regal. Shallow. Shy. Smug. What were you really, Mai?

Max appeared at the door. He held on to the jamb, stared in, at the two women, the sketches, the painting on the easel. A bemused expression flitted across his face. 'You're packing up,' he said.

Berwyn jammed waste paper into the bin, punching the white mass down almost angrily. 'It's best, Max.'

'Don't go, Berwyn. I need you.' He looked grey and old. He cleared his throat. 'I mean, I need people around me. Please. Please stay. Just for a few more days. Birdie, you too.' His eyes flickered in Birdie's direction, almost unseeing. 'You stay too.'

At the sound of his voice Wendy had come out of her room opposite. Now she was hovering behind him, frowning anxiously. Berwyn glanced at her. 'Max—you don't think it would be better if you had a bit of peace and quiet?'

Max leaned more heavily on the door jamb. His knuckles were white. 'Good God, that'd be the finish of me. I need people and noise round me or I'll go nuts. You know that, Berwyn.' His hand rose trembling to his forehead. Berwyn stood stock still.

'Dad, you're not well,' gasped Wendy. She stepped forward quickly and put her arms around him. 'Come and lie down. Come on, please. Please lie down.' She tried to lead him away, but he resisted and shrugged off her arms fretfully.

'I'm perfectly all right, Wendy. I'm not a child. I don't need looking after.'

'Dad, honestly! You haven't been to bed. You're exhausted. You need rest. If you won't do it for yourself, please do it for me. I'm worried sick about you.' Wendy was almost in tears.

'Look, Wendy, if you can't stop fussing, you can go

home yourself. I'll be all right here with Birdie and Berwyn.'

'Oh, Dad!'

Max ignored her and looked directly at Berwyn. 'You will stay, won't you?' he pleaded.

She suddenly gave in. She gave a final punch to the papers in the bin and rubbed a hand over her forehead, leaving a smear of charcoal there. 'Of course I will. If you want me to.'

'Thank you.' Max closed his eyes. Poor Wendy was quite right, Birdie thought. He really didn't look well. Even worse than he had last night. His swim must have been too much for him. She looked at him more closely. If he's had a swim. His hair isn't even damp. The thought reminded her of her mission.

'Ah—Dan Toby asked me to tell you not to go anywhere alone, or without telling one of the cops. They've found Warren Daley's bag, at Paradise. They think he might still be in the area.'

'Nice,' muttered Berwyn. Her long, nervous fingers played with a paintbrush.

'Oh, good heavens! But what about Douglas?' worried Wendy. 'He doesn't know that. What if—?'

'He told the cops he was going to a motel in Paradise,' Birdie offered. 'He'll be all right. And as for Warren Daley, I've been thinking. I don't see—' She hesitated. No. There was nothing she could say. Nothing that made any sense, anyway. She became aware that the others were staring at her. She cleared her throat and went on. 'Anyhow, Wendy, Douglas'll be back here this morning to pick up his clothes. You can tell him what Toby said then, can't you?'

'Maybe we could persuade him to come back here.' Wendy brightened slightly. 'To look after us all, you know? With that man hanging around.'

'Forget it. I wouldn't have him, Wendy,' growled Max. 'Ungrateful bastard. I've been thinking, you know. He was out every single bloody day while he was staying here. Do you realise that? Every bloody day. Came in for meals, of course. Saving himself a quid. Then off again.'

'He's looking for a job,' Wendy burst out. She looked guilty and bit her lips. 'I wasn't supposed to say. He was embarrassed, Dad. But that place where he was in Perth retrenched thirty-five people. It was badly managed, Douglas said, and he—'

'Oh, yeah. Sure. He was just unlucky. Again.' Max sneered. 'Took away his fancy car and his expense account, did they? So he thought he'd come back and sponge off soft-touch Max again while he spent his time drinking at the pub and chasing women who'd make him feel like a big man. Kidding he came to see his dear old dad. Huh! The hypocritical bastard! But he didn't fool me. Not this time. Mai was on to him, for a start. She said he had a woman stashed somewhere.' His eyes strayed to the painting on the easel.

'Mai told me that, too,' said Birdie. She remembered Mai saying it. Sitting in the bedroom. Glancing at her watch. Her hair swept up and held by its jewelled comb. The leather thong that killed her bound around her fragile, white neck. Berwyn was painting her like that. Painting her with a Mona Lisa smile. No background. No body. Just a face. Unknowable.

'Yes.' Max grimaced, and turned away from the painting. 'Mai knew. Her instinct was good about those things. She knew men.' His lips curled. 'Douglas put the hard word on her, you know.'

'Did she tell you that?' Wendy was red with anger.

'Oh, yes. She had no guile, in matters like that. Just came right out and told me. She didn't think he was on the level, though. That's why she thought he was hung up on some other woman. She knew how attractive she was, all right, for all her innocence about other things. She reckoned she could tell he was forcing it. Putting it on. Saying he was mad about her, and wanted to look after her, and could do it much better than an old man like me.' Max's eyes narrowed and glittered behind his glasses. 'She thought he was probably trying to trap her into some indiscretion so he could tell me about it and I'd throw her out. She was right, of course.'

'She poisoned your mind against him!' cried Wendy.

'No, she didn't. She just told me the truth. It's Douglas's look-out if the truth put him in a bad light.'

Birdie thought about that. Fair enough. She had no doubt the story was true. It was exactly the sort of boneheaded plan Douglas would think of. But Mai could have kept quiet. And she didn't. She had enough guile, then, to know when the truth could benefit her. In one fell swoop she had protected herself against any future charge of unworthiness by Douglas, and at the same time put the knife in, to distance Max from him just a little more, and display her own transparent honesty. Clever, for a guileless innocent who typically hid broken plates instead of admitting to them. And managed to keep the fact that she was married a dead secret for months.

'Did she say when this happened, Max?' she asked.

He looked back at the portrait. 'I've lost track of time. Thursday. Yes. The day her husband turned up. She went up to the bedroom, remember, and I followed her. She was nearly hysterical by the time I got there. Crying and absolutely desperate, poor little thing. While I was calming her down so I could get the story straight about this marriage, she said the family was against her. Well, she'd said that before. But this time she said they hated her. Thought she was bad. And that just that morning Douglas had got her up to his room and made a pass at her. While I was off swimming or something. God!' He bared his teeth.

So it wasn't really a planned manoeuvre, thought Birdie. Mai had blurted it out when she was upset. Very upset. That put a different look on the thing again. That kept happening, with Mai.

Birdie left the others to it, and wandered downstairs again. Why did she keep thinking about Mai? What was nagging at her? She went to the front door and let herself out. It was still early but already the humidity was oppressive. There seemed to have been no sunrise. Thick, pale cloud covered the sky completely.

She stared down into the green, secret mass of the garden. It was because, somehow, Mai's personality was at the heart of this. Of course all murders were like that. You started with the victim. You had to. But this time it seemed even more important than usual to know, to put it crudely, if Mai was a goodie or a baddie. *Unfinished portrait.* She began to pace restlessly along the red gravel terrace, from one side to the other. Her shoes made scratching, crunching noises. The gardenias were yellowing, but their scent still hung heavy in the air. Like the giant magnolias at Isa's, they dominated the senses.

Mai. Isa's clever little tart? The girl in business for herself who'd found herself a good billet? Wendy's conniving gold-digger? Berwyn's smug, shallow young beauty—all surface and no substance? Douglas's woman of easy virtue with a shady past? Max's sweet innocent, with good instincts about human nature?

Birdie kicked at the red gravel. Who knew? Who would ever know, now. But why did it matter anyway? If Warren Daley, or whatever his name was, killed his wife, it didn't matter at all. It was irrelevant.

But she didn't think he had. Did she?

TEN

———

The question stopped her in her tracks. But the answer came quickly. No. The emeralds. The note. Signs of a runaway. If Warren Daley killed his wife he caught her trying to escape. Slipping out while Max was broadcasting and she knew the coast was clear. But whatever Toby chose to think, Birdie was sure that Max was right. Mai had no reason to run. Mai had believed there was nothing to run from any more.

And yet there was, because then came death. Down there, in the garden, where she loved to walk. A death that could easily have remained undiscovered, for no one walked in the garden but Mai and the cats. The jasmine vine would have covered her body. She would simply have disappeared, if Birdie had not intervened. Years from now a skeleton might have been found. Small and white, with a leather band around its neck, under the billowing vine. And by then, surely, her murderer would be safe.

Birdie could hear the waves crashing dully on the rocks of the headland. The tide was coming up again. The sun was climbing higher behind its veil of cloud. Another day.

The garden lay tangling below her, fecund and greedy for life. In the trees the parrots and fruit bats squabbled and swung. In the dark undergrowth cats lurked and pounced, lizards scuttled after moths, insects snatched at each other, snails and slugs tore at tender leaves. But little could be seen on the surface. The struggle went on, hidden and secret, below.

Birdie shivered. She turned her back on the garden and went back into the house. Wendy was in the kitchen, quietly cleaning out the refrigerator. Berwyn came down the stairs and passed the door, deep in thought, carrying her waste-paper basket and a cardboard box. Life went on. The shadows receded.

'Wicked waste,' sighed Wendy, tipping fastidiously chopped fish and vegetables into newspaper, and wrapping it up tightly. Intent upon her housekeeping she appeared not to register that this was the meal Mai had prepared but never cooked.

'Where's Birdie?' Max's voice sounded cracked and slightly impatient. They heard Berwyn's murmured reply and then her footsteps.

'Max says can you help him in the study,' she said to Birdie impassively. 'He wants to start work on his book again. Good idea, I think. He needs stimulation, not rest, in my opinion.' She took care not to look at Wendy.

Wendy ignored her, revealing the state of her feelings only by the violence with which she snatched at a tin from the bench and upended it. A cascade of hard, stale currant buns bounced out, some toppling to the floor, scattering crumbs where they fell. She bent to retrieve them, groaning as though the mess had been made by someone else.

Birdie found Max standing looking out at the headland. The coffee table and couches behind him were heaped with boxes and papers. He'd started ratting through his cupboards again. As he turned away from the window to face her she was again shocked by the change in him. Under the suntan his skin looked stretched and pale. Dark lines ran down from his nose to his mouth. His thin shoulders were hunched. He clutched a battered old cigarette tin in his hands. Perhaps he'd retrieved it from one of the cupboards. It was as though he had shrivelled up.

'Are you sure you want to do this, Max?' she asked.

'I've got to do something,' he said. 'No show till Monday.' He brooded for a moment, then gave a small start, and looked up. 'Ah, I was forgetting. No show at all worth talking about, eh?' He shuffled over to his desk, and sat down, putting the cigarette tin down in front of him. What was in it? Birdie wondered. Souvenirs, probably. Something special. Memories of Mai?

She stood and stared at the piles of paper. No useful work could be done like this. But she had to humour Max. Soon, she promised herself, she would find an excuse to go. Max didn't really want her here. Berwyn was the one he wanted. He'd only asked Birdie to stay so his need wouldn't be too obvious.

The phone rang. The white one. The private line used for the radio broadcasts. That would be Dad, Birdie thought, as Max picked up the receiver and listened.

'Hello, Angus.' Max's voice was flat. He glanced at Birdie, then back to the cigarette tin in front of him. He began pushing it around with a finger. 'Yes,' he said. 'Yes.'

Birdie slipped out of the room, closing the door behind her.

There was no one in sight downstairs now. She wandered aimlessly to the windows and looked out at the swimming pool, clear, pale blue in the sun. She jumped as the phone rang, and exclaimed to herself. She was getting edgy. She wondered if she should answer it, instead of leaving it to the answering machine, or Wendy. It could be Toby, ringing with news. About the contents of Warren Daley's bag, maybe. But as she stepped forward the electronic trilling stopped. Some-one upstairs had got it first. Damn! She waited impa-tiently.

Only a few moments had passed before Wendy came running down the stairs, her forehead creased with anxiety.

'What's up?' Birdie demanded. 'Was it Toby?'

'Oh no, no. It was Isa. She sounded—well, I don't know. Where's Dad? Is he on the other phone? I heard it ring in the studio.'

'Yes. He's talking to my dad. Listen, Wendy, what is it?'

'What's up?' called Berwyn from the top of the stairs. 'Any news?'

Wendy looked right and left as if she didn't quite know what to do. 'Isa,' she breathed. 'She sounded awful. As if she had something in her mouth. And she didn't talk properly. She just said "It's Isa. Come quickly." And then she just hung up before I could say anything. I hope she's all right.'

'Oh, of course she is. You know what a drama queen she is,' snorted Berwyn indulgently. 'She just wants some attention. Someone to talk to.' She sat down on the stairs, her hands full of half-squeezed tubes of paint.

'But I'll have to tell Dad,' Wendy fluttered. 'She'd be ringing for him. He'd expect me to tell him. And he's on the other phone. Oh, dear. Something's wrong. You didn't hear her, Berwyn. You don't know.'

'Oh, Wendy, honestly!' Berwyn stood up. 'What could Max do about it anyway? In the state he's in he can't go and check her out, can he? Let him have his phone call in peace. Look, I'll go myself if you're so worried, and tell him after the event.' She looked at the paint in her hands. 'Or Birdie can,' she suggested hopefully.

'I'm on my way,' Birdie had already started for the front door. Unlike Berwyn, she was eager to go. Her heart was thumping. There was a cop at the gate, she told herself. He'd have the key to Isa's security door. She'd take him with her. Isa was a drama queen all right. But Birdie wasn't as convinced as Berwyn seemed to be that this drama wasn't for real.

'Verity!' called Wendy. She looked worried out of her mind. 'Verity, be careful. Don't . . . Oh, Dad!'

Max was peering around the study door. 'Birdie, where are you going?' he demanded querulously. 'What about our—'

'Just popping over to Isa's. Back in a flash,' gabbled Birdie. She wrenched open the front door.

'It's Isa,' shrilled Wendy defiantly. 'She rang. Come quickly, she said. She sounded awful. I tried to say you couldn't, Dad, but she hung up. Berwyn thinks it's nothing but Verity's going to check and . . .'

'Isa?' Max's dull eyes sharpened and focused. 'What? Here, Birdie, hold it!' He hurried to the door. 'I'll see to this.'

'You idiot, Wendy!' snapped Berwyn. 'Now look what you've—'

'Dad, please . . .' whimpered Wendy at the same time.

Max ignored them both. He plunged past Birdie to the steps. She saw him run down the first two or three, saw him throw his arms up, heard him yell. And then saw him fall, clutching at empty air, pitching forward helplessly as the old, cold stone rose up to meet him. Saw him tumble slowly down to the place where the steps turned. And there lie still, legs sprawling, arms twisted beneath him, eyes closed.

'Tried to kill me.' Max was mumbling, tossing his head from side to side on the soft blue pillow case. He looked small under the bedclothes. Defenceless without his glasses. Berwyn sat beside him, gripping his hand, watching him with terrified eyes. 'It's all right, Max,' she murmured. 'Don't talk. Just rest. I'm here. Everyone's here.'

Wendy turned to the doctor. 'Are you sure he shouldn't have stayed in hospital?' she whispered.

'Oh, yes. He hasn't got any real problems. He's just shaken up,' said the doctor, snapping her old leather bag shut. 'X-rays were clear. He's much better off here. He'll just perform if we keep him in for nothing, knowing him.' She went over and patted Max's shoulder. 'Do as you're told and stop scaring your rels or we'll bung you into hospital for the duration, Max,' she said affectionately. 'Just take it easy. I'm going now. You got the gold-star treatment. But I do have other patients, you know.' She nodded to Berwyn and Birdie, patted her grey hair straight in the bedroom mirror and went out with Wendy. 'He was amazingly fortunate, actually,' they heard her say as they started to go down the stairs. 'He could have killed himself, pitching down those steps. Lucky he tripped in the middle of a flight, not at the top of one.'

Lucky. Birdie looked at Max. His left hand was bandaged and there were a few scratches on his face. But otherwise he was unscathed. The luck of the Irish. It could have been so much worse.

He could have been killed. They all knew that. They knew, too, that Max had been tricked into hurrying down the garden steps, for Isa had been still in bed when the police called, and blurrily denied having phoned 'Third Wish', to ask for help or for any other reason. And finally they knew that across the fourth step of the treacherous way down through the garden, where shrubs brushed across the stone, holding it in shadow, was a long, bare stick from a gum tree, jammed in place at ankle height. The most primitive sort of booby trap. But effective.

Isa could have been too fuddled to know if she'd made a call or not. The stick could have got itself into that position by terrible mischance. Or the whole thing could have been a set-up. By someone who knew Max wouldn't be able to resist a call from Isa. Who knew he would hurry to her. Who wanted him to fall to injury or death.

Yet the stick had not been there when Birdie had gone down to the garden to meet Toby at six-thirty. It had not been there when they climbed back up to the house at seven. There had been police in the garden till seven-thirty, and none of the officers on duty had seen anyone on the garden steps. So if the booby trap had been set up deliberately, by someone wishing Max ill, it had been done between seven-thirty and nine, when the phone call came through. And it had been done by someone already in the grounds, for the uniformed cop at the gate had seen no one arrive at Max's house, or Isa's.

And that someone couldn't be Warren Daley. He couldn't be here. The police would have found him. They'd combed the grounds. They'd searched Isa's property, too. And there'd been a cop watching the two gates ever since Mai's body was found.

'Birdie!' Max was calling to her. She went across to the bed. Berwyn moved quietly aside and Birdie took her place beside him. He held out his hand and she took it, feeling it hard and clammy in hers. 'Tell the cops, Birdie,' he muttered. He blinked vaguely at her. 'That bloke. He's here. He tried to kill me.'

'I'll tell them, Max. Don't worry. You're OK. Sleep.' *Warren Daley can't be here, Max. It wasn't him.*

His eyes darkened. 'No,' he said. 'Can't sleep. Can't stand . . . the faces . . . coming out at me.'

Her skin creeping, Birdie spun around to Wendy. 'Where are his spare glasses, Wendy? Get them for him. He can't see.'

'He should be resting,' said Wendy stubbornly. 'He doesn't need his glasses.'

'Yes, he does!' Birdie almost stamped her foot. 'I know. He can't *see*, Wendy. It's helping to make him disoriented. Look, just take my word for it.' As Wendy, looking hurt and confused, left the room, she pushed her own glasses back firmly on her nose. She well remembered the few times she'd been left without them for any length of time. The blurry, swimming world in front of her, the feeling of helplessness and panic . . .

Max's hand, with its big knuckles and raised, heavy veins, squeezed her own and let it go. 'You're a good kid,' he murmured. Then his head jerked up. 'Who's that?'

Birdie had heard nothing but when she looked

around she saw that Douglas was standing at the door
with Wendy. His face was sombre, but somehow, Birdie
thought, his demeanour had changed. The sullen,
heavy look had disappeared. Under the smoothly-
shaven, golden skin, the neat, clean blue shirt, he was
shimmering with excitement.

'It's Douglas, Max,' said Berwyn quietly.

'Douglas.' The old man on the bed seemed almost
to be talking to himself. He pushed his head back
onto the pillows, blinking at the ceiling. His son
walked over to him and stood looking down.

'You all right?' he asked gruffly.

'Well as can be expected,' said Max, with a travesty
of a smile. He licked his lips and made an obvious effort. 'Where were you when we needed you?'

'Skiving off. As usual.' Briefly, Douglas laid a hand
on Max's arm. It was a gentle touch. 'They'll get the
bastard,' he said.

Max licked his lips again. 'What I said about—
you—not being my . . . you know. I didn't mean it.'

'Yes you did.' Douglas looked down at him, and a
strange expression crossed his face. 'But it's all right.
I don't blame you. It made me understand a few
things. I'm glad you said it. We'll talk about it later, all
right?' He took the glasses Wendy silently placed in his
hand and gave them to Max. 'Here's your specs, you
poor, blind old bugger.'

Max fumbled to put the glasses on, and when he
had managed it lay back with relief. 'That's better,' he
muttered. 'Thanks.'

'Jeez, bumping him on the head makes him polite, doesn't it?' joked Douglas, his eyes still serious.
'We should make sure it happens more often.'

'Get out of it!' murmured Max. He closed his
eyes.

Birdie stood in the housekeeper's room, oppressed by
a feeling of dread she couldn't shake. This day had
seemed to go on forever, yet it was still only eleven
o'clock. Outside it could have been any time. Clouds

hid the sun, trapping the heat and humid air under their canopy. The light was eerie. It was like a steam bath outside. Sweating police swarmed the garden. The waves thundered against the headland. The tide was at its peak. Suddenly claustrophobic, she twitched back the curtains from the side windows. Extra daylight, even if it came with a view of the garbage bin, was preferable to their tasteful blue and cream closing her in. She stepped back and then stared, startled, at the windowpane she had just uncovered. Was she seeing things?

The handprints were very clear. Big, greasy and grey they marked the clear glass in textbook fashion, just above the garbage bin. They hadn't been there when she arrived. She knew that. She remembered particularly noting the sparkling clean windows when she first prowled round her temporary abode. And she hadn't registered any change yesterday. Surely she would have noticed. Yes. Yesterday, they had been clean. So the prints must have appeared last night, or even this morning. Someone had been looking in her window. Someone had stood in the narrow side passage, hidden from view of the garden by the garbage bin, and peered in. Warren Daley.

But there'd never been any question that the man was actually here. It was impossible. The place had been scoured. Every hiding place had been explored. Just in case, Toby had said, though he was sure the man, if he had any sense at all, had got clean away.

Birdie remembered Isa's nervousness, and their reassurances. She remembered her own feeling of being watched, and the noises in the night she'd explained away. She thought of the stick across the steps. The booby trap for Max, or for anyone else who hurried down through the garden. The trail that marked Warren Daley's progress from Isa's garden flat, to the Paradise Hotel and back to 'Third Wish' and then stopped dead. But there was nowhere for him to hide. Nowhere . . . she looked again at the handprints. And suddenly a memory floated to the top of her mind. Hiding from Wendy with Douglas, giggling with her hand over her mouth and nearly wetting her pants with tension as Wendy moved closer and her mother's high laugh floated in the air above them, mingling with the sound of music and the sea.

Her heart thudding violently in her chest Birdie backed slowly out of the room, never taking her eyes off the prints, half-terrified that a face would rise above the window ledge between them. She knew where Warren Daley was.

She ran to the front door and scanned the garden for Toby. There he was, standing on the red gravel with Milson. He looked up as she hurried towards him.

'Where've you been?' he enquired. 'Thought you'd be out here poking your nose in long ago.'

'Here,' she said, pulling at his arm. 'Come and see this.'

She led him to the side of the house where the garbage bin stood, massively squatting on its wheels and almost completely blocking the narrow passage between the house and the fence.

'We've looked around here, Birdwood,' growled Toby, obviously disappointed. 'There's nothing doing. It only leads to the cliff.' He watched as Birdie skirted the bin and slipped into the narrow opening beyond. 'Oh, Gawd! Wait here a second, Milson. I'll see what she's got in her bonnet.' Grunting, he squeezed past the bin.

'There.' Birdie was pointing. Toby whistled. The handprints on the windowpane were even more prominent on this side. The sill beneath them was smeared with dirt and something else—something dark and red that could have been blood. Deep ruts in the earth below the window showed where someone had stood, bracing himself, perhaps, against the bin to look inside.

'What's this room?' asked Toby after a moment.

'It's mine.' Birdie bit her lip and fell silent.

He glanced at her. She was looking towards the sea. The sound of the crashing waves filled the passage. They could taste salt on their tongues.

'Dan. I think he's out there,' whispered Birdie.

He looked at her for a long moment. 'There's nothing out there, mate,' he said finally. 'It's bare rock and then a sheer drop. He'd be dead.'

'No. There's a place ... When we were kids ... I've just remembered.'

Toby's hand flew up to quiet her. 'Milson!' he whispered urgently. 'You there?'

There was no reply. Toby cursed, and began to struggle past the bin. 'Milson!' he hissed. 'Where are you, for God's sake?'

And so it was only Birdie who saw the figure appear, looming, at the seaward entrance of the passage. Tall and thick-set, swaying slightly, it filled the narrow space. Hands raised to feel wall and fence on either side, it began to move forward in the sticky dimness. Hair matted with blood fell in thick strands over a nightmare face. A terrible gash ran down from forehead to cheek. One eye was black, puffy and closed, the other glazed and staring. The lips were bleeding.

'Dan!' Birdie breathed. She clutched at his shirt.

Toby twisted his neck to scowl at her. Saw what she was seeing. 'Christ!' he muttered.

The figure stopped. Bent forward, peering. Then abruptly it spun around and began blundering back the way it had come.

'Milson!' bawled Toby. 'Milson! Quick! He's here!'

Swearing, he pushed past Birdie and gave chase, his head and shoulders whipped by the leafy stems that poked through the fence.

'Dan, wait! Dan, he can't get away!' screamed Birdie. 'Dan, be careful!'

Her voice was almost drowned by the sound of the sea. She ran after him, her soft shoes slipping in the mud of the passage.

Toby was clambering across the cliff-face when she caught up with him. 'He's bloody gone!' he shouted. He blinked at her, his eyes streaming, his tie whipping over his shoulder. The glare of the sea was blinding. Waves crashed against the rocks below them. Above, the bottom of Max's pool hung like a great belly, supported by massive steel girders fixed to the rock.

Birdie grabbed his arm. 'He's there,' she shouted. She pointed to a narrow shelf of rock jutting out from the cliff-face fifty metres beyond and below them. 'There's a cave. A hole. You can hide in it. Dan, there's no hurry. The tide's up. He can't get away. He's trapped. For God's sake, be careful. Don't go down too far. Waves come up and—'

Toby moved, squinting down. Chips of rock broke away under his feet and bounced down the cliff, smashing into dust on the ledge below. 'Milson!' he roared. And as if on cue Milson appeared around the corner of the house with Barassi by his side. They began sidling gingerly towards the other two, pebbles showering down from under the soles of their slippery shoes.

'There he is!' Toby was pointing. And Birdie saw Warren Daley, twitching like a panicking animal, emerge from his hole in the cliff-face and begin climbing down, towards the wet rocks and the crashing waves, always edging to the right. 'He's going to try to get round the headland!' yelled Toby. He began slipping and sliding down the cliff himself.

'He can't!' Birdie grabbed his sleeve and held on. 'It's high tide. He can't get round. Oh, God! Stop!' She was calling to Warren Daley now. 'You can't do it! You can't! You'll be—'

And as the last words left her mouth and bounced uselessly back from the rocks they saw the sea draw back, saw the man on the cliff-face scramble forward. And then the gigantic wave was dashing forward, throwing tonnes of water and blinding spray on to the cliff, covering the man who clung there, and dragging him, screaming, down to the wicked rocks below.

'Police rescue's on its way, sir.' Barassi was looking rather sick. He kept his eyes on Toby's, so as not to let them fall to the base of the cliff where the broken body of Warren Daley, pinned between two jagged rocks, was being ruthlessly exposed as the sea sucked itself back, and pounded with water, foam and spray as each giant wave came in.

'He's dead as mutton you know, son,' said Toby casually. 'He can't feel a thing.'

Barassi swallowed, and nodded, then retreated as Milson approached, edging carefully towards them.

'Dawkins and Kee say the cave is deep enough to crouch in, out of sight of the sea,' he said crisply. 'They didn't touch anything, as ordered, but say that inside were . . .' he consulted his notebook '. . . an empty whisky bottle, three sweet-looking buns or rolls, some large sheets of paper crumpled and torn—they think drawing paper, signs of vomit, blood stains, and . . .' he raised his eyes from his pad, 'a gold neck-lace set with round, bright green stones. They think emeralds.'

'Right.' Toby rubbed his mouth with his hand. 'Soon as the tide goes down a bit we'll get the photographer in there. The stuff'll be safe enough till then. Look, take over here, will you, Milson? I'll be in the house. Let me know when the body's been recovered. I want to see it.' He turned his face away from the sea and climbed back up towards the house. Birdie picked her way after him in silence, her stomach churning, hands and knees trembling with fatigue.

And the sea pounded again and again at the body on the rocks, shattering the bones, smashing the flesh to pulp while seagulls wheeled, shrieking, above, sensing carrion.

ELEVEN

'He was here all along. I knew it!' exclaimed Isa. 'I told you. I told you. I could feel it. Oh, it's ghastly. He could have killed us all, one by one.' She rolled her eyes at the roomful of people and pressed her fingers against her mouth.

'I don't think he was in any condition for that.' Toby smiled at her benignly. With her softly-waving grey hair freshly brushed, and wearing a Liberty-print frock she'd unearthed from somewhere, Isa was looking very Auntie Dora today. From her garden she had brought Max roses, a glorious mixed bunch of gaudy, reds, yellows and pinks. They stood on the dressing-table in a white vase, a little battered from the rain the night before, but filling the room deliciously with their rich, glamorous scent.

'Lucky you thought of the cave,' Douglas said to Birdie. 'I'd forgotten all about it. Well, it was tucked into the back of my mind somewhere, I guess. But I don't think I'd have ever thought of it as a hiding place for an adult. It was a cramped little place for two kids, as I remember.'

'There wasn't much room, apparently,' nodded Toby. 'Still, all the signs are that Daley used it as a base from the time he killed his wife yesterday evening till we sprang him this morning.'

'But what was the point?' Berwyn leaned forward, her intense face curious. 'Why didn't he just get out while the getting was good? Why did he stay?'

'We can't be sure of that. He could have been waiting for his chance to attack Mr Tully. A chance he finally got this morning. Another theory is that he was disturbed after the murder, and made off towards the back of the house to hide. I gather there was a bit of coming and going. People coming home. Mr Tully calling out for his fiancée, and so on. Daley possibly didn't think it was safe to leave the front way. He could have hidden around the side of the house thinking he'd wait till dark, then fallen asleep. He'd been drinking at the pub all afternoon. And the bottle shop at the Paradise recalls selling a bottle of Black Label some time during yesterday afternoon, as well. The bottle in the cave was empty. He must have been pretty well tanked up.'

'And when he woke up, Mai's body had been found and the place was crawling with cops.' Max's eyes gleamed behind his glasses. 'I hope he sweated. I hope he felt like hell.'

'At that point we think he made for the back, to try to get out that way. But of course it was high tide at eleven last night. He could never have got around the headland. In fact, it's a wonder he wasn't killed getting as far as he did on that cliff in the dark. That's probably how he got that gash on his forehead, and the black eye. Certainly he wasn't a well man. He was violently sick, for one thing. Could have had concussion. The doctor'll have a look at that. And then there was the alcohol, no food in his stomach, according to the barmaid at the Paradise, and, presumably, the fear of discovery. Anyhow, he holed up, literally, under that

ledge and of course we could search around all we
liked, but all we could see were rocks and spray.

'By the time he woke up or regained conscious-
ness, or whatever, this morning, the tide was on the
rise again. He got himself up and crept up the side of
the house. That's probably when he looked in Birdie's
window. And, presumably, laid the trap for Mr Tully.'

'But the phone call!' exclaimed Wendy. 'Why
would Isa ring at just that time?'

'I didn't ring,' exploded Isa. 'How many times do
I have to say it, Wendy? I was still in bed asleep when
the cops—the police—called. I wasn't feeling the
best.'

'Another touch of the flu, probably,' said Toby,
without cracking a smile.

Douglas guffawed softly.

Isa lifted her chin. 'The fact remains—' she began.

'Dan thinks Warren Daley got through the fence
and into your house, Isa,' said Birdie. She watched the
woman's eyes widen with horror. 'Possibly he used
your kitchen phone. Put on a voice. It was only a four
word message. And Wendy said the voice sounded
odd.'

'But the door was locked. At least . . .' Isa put her
hand over her mouth. 'At least I think it was.'

'The back door was open when Constable Barassi
called.' Again Toby paused. 'You weren't answering
the front door, so he went round the back.'

'No. I didn't hear the bell. First thing I knew that
young man was calling me. I never thought to ask how
he'd got in.' Isa's lips trembled. 'My God, he could
have murdered me in my bed!'

'I'm sure Constable Barassi wouldn't hurt a fly,
Ma'am,' said Toby. But Isa made no response to this
mild attempt to lighten the atmosphere, and Toby
took another tack. 'Fortunately Daley was probably
concentrating on his campaign against Mr Tully at
that point, so you were safe. 'Course, if you'd disturbed him it might have been a different matter.'

'Yes.' Isa's eyes were still wide with fearful imaginings. 'One of the cats could easily have woken me to tell me there was a stranger in the house. In fact it's quite extraordinary that they didn't. Twinkle, particularly, is usually a marvellous watchdog. Very protective.'

Twinkle, Birdie seemed to recall, was the name of the fluffy white pyjama case on legs who'd persecuted her during her visit to Isa's house. It was hard to imagine that somnolent creature acting as a protector. It would be more likely to lie on you and smother you in the night.

'Anyhow, Daley made his call and then went back over the fence and around to the back of 'Third Wish' again. Maybe he waited in the side passage to see if his trap worked. He could've done. He certainly ratted the garbage bin at some point. These were in the cave.' Toby held up one of the plastic bags he had brought with him.

'Jesus Christ. Currant buns,' breathed Max. 'I made them—Thursday night, was it? Stale as old Harry now.'

'I gather they went out to the garbage this morning,' said Toby, nodding at Wendy.

'Why didn't he get some food at Isa's? If you're right, he would have been in the kitchen,' Birdie pondered.

Toby regarded her tolerantly.

'Your trouble is you expect everyone to think like you do, Birdie. The man was obviously half off his head. And not too bright to start with. He probably didn't think of it. Anyway, the fact remains he did take the buns, and seems to have eaten one or two. There were some odd bits left around the cave floor as well as these whole ones. And he took something else out of the garbage while he was at it.' He held out another three plastic bags. 'Recognise these?' he said to Berwyn.

Blushing deeply, she took the bags in her hands and held them by the edges, as though they were going to contaminate her. Birdie craned to look. Inside the bags were pieces of art paper covered with sketches of Mai. The crumpled, torn paper had been smoothed out, and reassembled. The charcoal was smeared, but the lines were decisive and firm, the touch sure. Mai looked out at them in profile and full face. In the corner of one page Berwyn had drawn Max, small and grinning, with a protective arm around her. Beautiful. Trusting. Naive. A natural victim, thought Birdie. And with hindsight, that's what she must have been. A sound between a groan and a sigh bubbled from Max's lips and Berwyn thrust the bags back at Toby. 'I threw those out this morning,' she said. 'Into the bin. With other stuff.'

He nodded with satisfaction. 'I thought so. He had them down in his hidey hole too. All set out in a gallery on the floor.'

'It's horrible,' she said, turning her head away. 'Brooding down there all alone with sketches out of a garbage bin. While the real woman—'

'Ah, pictures are one thing,' Max broke in. He was breathing heavily. 'You can get sentimental about pictures, can't you, and run no risks at all. But the real woman? The living, breathing thing with a mind of her own. That's too hard to cope with, isn't it?' There were tears on his cheeks. He struggled into a sitting position. 'So you just crush it, don't you? That's the only way to control it, isn't it? If you're a real man. A big, macho man. And if that doesn't work, you kill it. Why not? It was just an extension of your ego in the first place, wasn't it? It doesn't have a right to live independently of you!'

Douglas shifted uncomfortably in his chair. 'Maybe we should finish this off downstairs,' he offered. 'Max is supposed to be resting.'

'Embarrass you, did I?' Max chuckled humourlessly. 'Think I'm going off my rocker? Well you're not far wrong. But I'm not quite ready for the nuthouse yet.' He lay back on his pillows. 'Just get on with it. I'm all right.'

Toby cleared his throat. 'Well, as it happens we're almost through. Just wanted to bring you up to date. Now—ah—this would be the emerald necklace that your fiancée had with her, wouldn't it?' He held up another plastic bag. Inside, dulled gold winked and emeralds shone, clear and perfect.

Max nodded, and closed his eyes. 'That's right.'

'There were earrings, too.' Wendy spoke for only the second time since the conversation began. She was very pale. Her pleasant, motherly face was drawn and sober. She had stood with Birdie and seen the lumpy, covered stretcher carried from the clifftop to the waiting van. She had made the coffee and tea for the soaked police. She had answered the first questions about times and tides. She had heard the descriptions of the battered body, and the cache in the cave. She had done all this, while Berwyn and Douglas sat upstairs with Max, Marys to her Martha.

'There were no earrings in the cave, or on the body,' said Toby. 'He could have dropped them, I guess. Though I admit that seems unlikely. You'd think he'd have tucked them in a pocket for safekeeping. Anyhow, we'll have a look in the rocks at low tide. Quarter to six tonight that'll be, I think.'

'Yes. Something like that.' Wendy sighed.

Toby lumbered to his feet. 'He had the cash on him, sir,' he said to Max. 'All there but two hundred and ten dollars, from what we can see. I've given your daughter a receipt for everything. You'll get it back as soon as the experts have had a go at it.'

'Fine.' Max waved a negligent hand. 'It doesn't matter.' Then an odd expression crossed his face. 'That's the sort of thing that used to drive your mother out of her mind, Douglas,' he said. 'By God she hated it when I didn't watch the pennies.' He smiled, and rolled his head slowly on the pillow. 'She hated a lot of things about me. Clothes, friends, manners, house. Vulgar, no class, she said. Funny thing was, before we were married, she didn't seem to mind any of that. I s'pose she thought she could just change me to suit once we'd tied the knot. Like having a pair of strides altered. You can't do it before you've bought them can you? Then it's open slather. Doesn't work like that with people, though, does it? As she found.'

Douglas sat quite still, looking straight ahead, as if by doing so he could ignore what was being said, or avoid hearing it altogether.

'She was easy on the eyes.' Max closed his eyes. 'I'll give her that. When I met her I thought, this is what I need. This is what I want. Cool, lovely lady. Sophisticated.' He made a huffing sound that was probably a laugh. 'Got it wrong again, didn't I? God, she loathed me by the end. Lord preserve us. Took Douglas with her. Poor Wendy . . . lost her little mate . . . Couldn't understand . . .' His voice trailed off into indistinguishable mumbling.

Wendy stood up, pale as a ghost. 'I'll get you some coffee before you go,' she said to Toby. She went to the bedroom door and looked back at the others, frowning. 'We'll all have some coffee,' she added. 'Let Dad get some sleep.'

'I'll stay,' said Douglas. 'I don't want coffee. I'll stay and keep an eye on him.'

She hesitated, and then went out without another word. The others followed her. As she reached the door, Birdie looked back. Douglas was leaning against the bed, his chin on his clasped hands, watching Max. And Max, his eyes closed, was murmuring again. Words that only Douglas could hear.

Birdie saw Toby out. They stood together on the red-gravel terrace. The memory of that scrambling chase on the cliff-face, the shrieking, terrible fall of the man Daley, hung between them. Toby hunched his shoulders and turned away. Birdie put her hand on his arm. For some reason she didn't want him to go. Not yet. She had a sense of unfinished business.

'You haven't told me what was in Daley's bag,' she said. 'It *was* his, I suppose.'

'Oh, yes.' Toby shrugged. 'Nothing unexpected. Clothes. Pages about the engagement out of that women's magazine, *Hers*, or whatever it's called. Shaving gear, toothbrush, pen, writing pad and envelopes that matched the anonymous letters. That's about it.'

'Were any of the clothes new?'

'Oh, no. All pretty beat up.'

'Didn't you say about two hundred and ten dollars was missing from Max's cash?'

'Something like that.'

'What do you suppose he did with it?'

'Pissed it up against the pub wall. He didn't play the poker machines, apparently. Or eat anything. But there's the cab. And the whisky.'

'Even so, Dan. The barmaid said he was drinking beer. Two hundred and ten bucks is a lot to go through in a single afternoon.'

'Maybe he's a big tipper. You should see the barmaid. Bleached blonde, big tits. Eighteen going on thirty-five, if you know what I mean.'

Birdie said nothing.

'Your mates in there don't seem too thrilled the murderer's been dispatched,' growled Toby, after a moment. Birdie raised her eyebrows at him and he gestured impatiently. 'Well, we only got here last night and we've solved the case before lunchtime. And what do we get? Grim faces all round. If it'd taken us weeks to run Daley to ground, don't you think we'd've heard about it? You bet we would.' He threw down the plastic bags in his hand and pulled violently at his strangling tie.

'What's the matter, Dan?' asked Birdie quietly.

'What's the matter?' He almost smiled, staring down over the still, green garden. Then he turned round to face her. 'I get sick of it, that's all. Sometimes I just get sick of it, all right? Sick of—people. The violent, stupid louts like Daley. And the others. The ones I'm supposed to be protecting from people like him. The ones who snigger about me when they don't need me, and cling on to me when they do, and can't get me out of their houses fast enough when I've done the dirty work they can't do for themselves.'

'Dan—' Birdie began. But he held up his hand.

'I know what you're going to say,' he muttered. 'Don't say it. There's no way I could have known about the hole in the cliff-face. It's not my fault Daley smashed himself to a pulp. Those people in there don't blame me. They're just shocked. All right?'

Birdie nodded silently.

'All right.' Toby repeated. He stuck his hands in his pockets and looked away. Now, Birdie realised, he was going to feel embarrassed about letting his guard down in front of her. She began to talk, going back to his original complaint and ignoring everything he'd said since.

'Wendy and the others haven't quite realised what it all means, yet,' she said. 'It's all happened very fast. And Max isn't himself. It worries everyone. The house—sort of—revolves around him.'

Toby stirred, his hands still firmly hidden in his pockets. 'Pretty understandable if he's knocked around, isn't it? His girlfriend's dead. And an attempt was made on him too. Most people'd make heavy weather of that, wouldn't they?'

'But Max isn't most people,' said Birdie. 'That's the point. And the way it's got to him—all that talking about the past . . . it's so unlike him. He's usually so strong, Dan. Emotional on the surface, but tough as nails. A real survivor. I'd never have thought he'd re-act like this to someone dying. Even someone he loved, like Mai.'

Toby pulled his hands out of his pockets and slowly bent to pick up the plastic bags from the red gravel. As he straightened, he looked up at the lowering sky. 'Going to rain,' he commented. Then he rubbed his chin. 'Funny sort of business, isn't it? That little old man up there and that young girl. Doesn't seem—right, does it?'

'You were the one who said "half his luck".'

'Yeah. Well. Seeing them both . . . I dunno. The son, Douglas, would have been more her style, I would have thought. More of a manly sort of man. You know?'

Birdie thought about that. Thought of Max's brown wrinkled hand against Mai's soft cheek. And the infinite gentleness of its touch. 'Max is a manly sort of man,' she found herself saying. 'And he never makes you feel he's old. It's the last thing you think of.'

'It's the first thing I'd think of,' Toby said. 'Anyhow, I'll be off. I'll be in touch.'

He lifted his hand in farewell and strode off down the driveway, swinging his plastic bags with their strangely assorted contents.

He's right, thought Birdie. Seeing Max up there in that bed, it's the first thing you'd think of. He looks sick, and frail—and old. She shook her head, watching Toby's gradually receding back. Mai was dead. Murdered. Of course Max would be shocked. Of course he'd be sad and grieving. But he'd fight on. That had always been Max's great, abiding trait. The ability to fight on, whatever happened. In a way it was almost shocking, that hard resilience that had always left him basically intact whatever befell him. This—wandery, nervy stuff. It was so uncharacteristic. It was as if he'd changed overnight. What had happened to him? Did he love Mai so much then? So much that her loss was the only thing he had ever faced in his life that he couldn't bear?

Birdie didn't believe that. She turned away from the garden and faced 'Third Wish'. No. And yet—Max Tully had given up. She knew that as clearly as she knew something else. There were too many loose ends here. Little things. The missing earrings. The currant buns out of the garbage. The farewell note . . .

Birdie paced the red gravel, smelling the gardenias. She'd done this once already today, only a few hours ago. Had Warren Daley been peering at her from the side of the house, waiting for her to go inside so he could fix his primitive booby trap for Max? Or was the stick already in place by then? She wouldn't have noticed if it had been.

Warren Daley was dead. They would never know his side of the story now. Never know if Toby's reconstruction of his last day on earth was factual. And they would never know what had been going on in his mind. Mai, perhaps, could have told them. She knew him best. But Mai was dead, too. And there was no

one else. Isa had talked to him. But he'd been playing
a part when he'd been with Isa. The good-looking
young man down on his luck. The son she never had
doing her garden, helping her bury a murdered cat,
telling her his troubles over a glass of wine . . .

Birdie stopped. There was someone else. Someone she, at least, hadn't talked to. Julie Billings, the
barmaid at the Paradise Hotel.

'He's not!' Julie Billings's eyes were wide with excited
horror. She pushed the glass of beer towards Birdie
and automatically wiped the bar with a checkered
towel. 'Dead! My God!' She leaned forward. 'Did the
cops kill him?' she breathed. 'Did he get shot?'

'Oh, no.' Birdie took a sip from her glass. The
beer was icy cold. 'He fell over a cliff.' She casually
licked a line of froth from her top lip.

'*Really!*' Julie turned away to serve another customer, but dispatched the task in quick time and was
soon back, eager for more information.

'We're trying to reconstruct his last hours,' said
Birdie ponderously. 'And from what he said it was obviously important we talk to you.'

'From what . . .' Julie nibbled at her pink-painted
bottom lip and darted a glance over her shoulder.
'Oh. Well, I already talked to the police, yesterday, you
know.'

'Oh, yes,' Birdie flapped her hands dismissively.
'And that's fine for the record. You know. The official
story. You did awfully well there. But the people I'm
working for need more than that. Obviously.'

'Do they?' Julie thought about that. 'Who are you
working for?' she asked at last.

'Oh.' Birdie adjusted her glasses. 'It's safer you
don't know that, isn't it? Much safer. Now . . .' She
leaned forward conspiratorially. God, what am I going
to say next, she thought, keeping her gaze steady and,
she hoped, steely. Then she had an inspiration. 'Tell
me your side of the story while you can,' she hissed.
She watched the eyes widen again. 'And please! Be

quick! Time is very short.' She'd thrown that last one
in for good measure, but it worked. Like a charm.
Julie Billings talked her head off after that, well, whispered rather, hunched across the bar in her pink-
frilled blouse and gold chain, while other barmaids
looked daggers at her and the male drinkers on the
other side looked appreciatively at her round, denim-
clad behind.

Warren Daley drank in the bar all afternoon. He
seemed nice. He had lots of money. Hundred dollar
bills. Towards the end of the afternoon he'd given her
a hundred dollar note for a beer, and told her to
keep the change. Buy herself something nice. She'd
thought that was very sweet of him.

So when he said he'd meet her on the beach after
she got off at four-thirty, she thought, well, why not? It
wasn't as if she had a boyfriend at the moment. Well,
no one serious. He said he was going somewhere after.
But that was OK by her. And they talked a bit, and
played round a bit, and one thing led to another, as it
does . . . Here Julie passed and looked at Birdie rather
doubtfully, as if wondering whether for bespectacled
thirty-ish women who wore no make-up and talked
like librarians things actually did lead anywhere, ever.
But Birdie nodded sagely and Julie went rattling on.
They ended up having a cuddle in the bushes at the
end of the beach, she said, where it was nice and private.

'Thing was,' she whispered, leaning even further
across the bar so that the drinker directly behind her
became too involved with the view and tipped sauce
from his pie all down his chest, 'he'd had too much to
drink.' She giggled, pressing a small, dimpled hand
with sharply pointed pink nails against her mouth.

'He couldn't . . . you know? He just couldn't. Well,
then he got mad. Said it was my fault, would you believe it?' She bridled, and tossed her blonde head. 'I
said to him, "You're pissed. That's what's wrong with
you. Don't go blaming me." So then he started swearing at me and I said, "All right, well that's the finish.
You can't talk to me like that." And I got up and left.

Well, it was raining, anyway. And Mum has tea on the table at six.'

Birdie sat motionless on the bar stool. Warren Daley was on the beach with Julie Billings from four-thirty till at least five-thirty, when the rain started. He couldn't have got to 'Third Wish' in time to kill Mai. He couldn't ... She had had doubts. Of course she had, or she wouldn't have taken the trouble to seek Julie out. But even she hadn't expected to be confronted by such incontrovertible evidence that the man wasn't anywhere near 'Third Wish' when Mai Tran died. She pushed her bushy hair back behind her ears, thinking. There was no arguing with this. Even if the watch, stopped at 5.05, was some sort of trick, the evidence of the dry ground beneath the body was something that couldn't be faked. Warren Daley hadn't killed his wife. Then who had? She became aware that Julie was still talking, and forced herself to pay attention.

'... so he was dancing round and shouting after me and everything, with no pants on and his thing flopping up and down and everything. In the rain and all. God, he looked such a dork! And, this is the best bit. He got sprung. It was low tide, see, and someone came round the rocks right then, and caught him at it! Bet he felt small. He ducked down into the bushes and hid. God, I laughed!' Julie chuckled reminiscently. 'Don't think the other bloke saw him really, worse luck,' she added. 'He had his head down. Watching where he was going. Well, you have to. The rocks are slippery. 'Specially in the rain. Don't know what he'd've been doing round the point, anyway. There's nothing there. Only more rocks. He probably thought you could walk round to Long Beach that way. But you can't. Anyhow ...' she grinned. 'It was funny.'

'Julie!' shrilled one of the other barmaids. 'Get your arse into gear, will you?'

The man with sauce on his shirt grinned. He muttered behind his hand to his companion who roared with appreciative laughter.

Julie twisted around guiltily. 'Sorry, Carol. Be right with you.' She looked back to Birdie. 'Got to go. That's all there was to it, anyway. Really.'

'Julie! Did you see the other bloke?' called Birdie, as the girl turned away. 'The man who came round the headland. What did he look like?'

'Oh—' Julie shrugged, world weary at eighteen. 'Just a bloke. Big. Good tan. White t-shirt. Sunglasses. Just a big ocker. Like Warren. They're all the same.' She jiggled away to her work.

Birdie pushed herself away from the bar. *All the same.* She went to make a phone call.

TWELVE

—

Wendy finished packing the dishwasher, and began methodically wiping the kitchen benches. She noticed that the copper hood over the stove was dulled by a fine layer of dust, and wiped that too. Thank goodness the cleaners would be in tomorrow. The place was starting to look a bit grimy. Dad had said Angus Birdwood would be coming to see him at four o'clock. She must try to get the living room dusted off by then.

The house was very silent. Isa had gone back to her cats, Verity was out, Douglas was sitting with Dad, and Berwyn was in her studio doing heaven knows what. She wished Berwyn would go home. Verity, too, if she was honest. It would be so nice for Wendy and Dad and Douglas just to have the place to themselves for a while. Especially now, with Douglas and Dad finally seeming to have made things up. That terrible fight they'd had. Well, maybe it had been a good thing. Cleared the air. Dad had just been angry, of

course. There was no way he really thought Douglas
wasn't his. That was ridiculous. That would mean . . .
her thoughts propped and sheered off into safer territory. She gave the copper hood a final polish. That
was better. She peered at her distorted reflection in
the burnished metal. She looked middle-aged and
tired. Overweight, too. She should diet. Do some exer-
cises. People could take her for Douglas's mother,
though there was only eighteen years between them.

The thought displeased her, though she'd had it
before, many times, over the years and had always
quite enjoyed it. She had always looked mature for her
age, even as a teenager. It had been fun, at eighteen,
to walk Douglas in his stroller along the Paradise Parade and have people smile and say what a darling
baby she had, what a sweet young mother she was. It
had been pleasurable, at twenty-five, to have people
congratulate her on her lovely, strong little boy when
they went to the beach at holiday time. She had never
corrected them. Her heart had swelled at these moments exactly, she thought, as if he were her own. And
in a way he was, for Ingrid had never mothered him
at all, as far as Wendy could see.

When he was a baby it was Wendy who had carried
him round, played with him, sung him to sleep at
night. There had always been a nanny there, of
course. But the nannies had never really stayed long
enough for Douglas to get very attached to them.
None of them lasted more than a few months. Ingrid
would hire them, sing their praises for a day and a
half, then start complaining. In the end, she'd give
them the sack. She didn't seem to understand that no
matter how efficient they were they couldn't stop
Douglas crying sometimes. All babies got fretful. They
couldn't keep him squeaky clean every moment of the
day. He was into everything. They couldn't stop him
drooling or pooing on her when she made one of her
rare forays into motherhood—usually for the benefit
of some photographer. Babies did teethe, and plastic
pilchers weren't foolproof. So in a way Wendy was the

only continuing loving presence he had in his young life.

In the afternoons, when she got home from secretarial college, the first thing she'd do, after kissing her father, would be to go and see him in the nursery. Even as a tiny thing he'd look up and crow with pleasure when he saw her, opening up his little gummy mouth and grinning, clapping his hands. When he was older he'd sit in the garden, bouncing solemnly in a canvas swing that hung from a tree branch, his feet just touching the ground, for an hour at a time while she read on the grass beside him. At a year old he'd toddle along beside her almost all weekend, holding on to one of her fingers with a chubby hand. Even now she could feel that hand in hers. He called her 'Win' in those days.

It had nearly killed her, when Ingrid took him away. He was just two. She grieved for months. She hadn't thought her father had noticed. Not until he'd mentioned it today, murmuring as he tossed his head on the pale blue pillowslip. He hadn't given any sign of it at the time. Just joked and carried on exactly as before. In fact, he'd barely referred to Ingrid's abrupt departure at all. Just said to her, once, as they sat down on the terrace to eat a meal the housekeeper had cooked for them, that he was glad they were alone in the house again. Perhaps he assumed she knew as much as she wanted to about the matter. For after all she had heard all the arguments. For years.

She may have grieved for Douglas. But she was glad Ingrid had gone. Very glad. She'd disliked Ingrid intensely. Not just because her mother had said the things she had about her, though obviously they were true. But because it had been so obvious to her from the first that her father's wife didn't want her at 'Third Wish', despised her for her lumpy figure and homemade clothes, and felt she spoiled the elegant ambience Ingrid felt to be her rightful setting. Not that Ingrid ever said this in so many words. And not that Dad would have put up with it if she had. Wendy had never doubted Max's affection for her. It was something she had counted on since her earliest years. Being separated from him when he and her mother split up had been hard, very hard. She'd grieved then, too.

So much grieving. She regarded this idea almost with surprise. She'd never before thought of her life in these terms. But it was true, wasn't it? She'd lost her father, whose darling she was, who had carried her around on his shoulders and thrown her into the air, and laughed, as her mother never did. She'd got him back only at the cost of losing her mother. In terror she'd seen the bedrock of her life turn to sand as the sturdy woman she'd loved, fought with and taken for granted grew thin and weak and finally died in pain, weeping and bitter because Wendy would be alone, now, except for Max.

She'd lost her little brother, whipped away overnight without even a goodbye, his favourite stuffed dog left behind because Ingrid wouldn't have known what he played with anyway and the dog was old and tattered. She'd got Douglas back in the end, if only part-time, because Ingrid quickly twigged that the convenience of free babysitting at 'Third Wish' far outweighed the satisfactions of maintaining the rage and denying Max access to his son. But Douglas had grown up a bit, when he started to come to stay again. He no longer called her 'Win'. It wasn't the same. It was good, but not the same.

Wendy wandered around the kitchen, trailing her hand around the bench tops. She found the cinnamon pastries Max had made, and ate one, licking the sugar off her top lip, biting greedily into another without tasting it. Then, in a way, she thought, she'd lost her father again. To Berwyn Kyte.

She remembered how it had been when Berwyn first came. She'd been—shut out. That was the only way you could describe it. Not that either her father or Berwyn had been unkind. Berwyn, thin, quiet, intense and so highly strung that you always felt that you could see the nerves jumping under her fine, white skin, really hardly noticed her. Her whole attention, when she wasn't locked in her studio, painting, was focused on Max. While he was talking on the phone, or swimming, or talking to friends, she would stare at him from across the room under her heavy brows as though she wanted to absorb him utterly in that black gaze.

And Dad *was* absorbed. Berwyn's odd, sad paintings filled the house. She wore old shirts and jeans. She never did any housework. Never swept a floor or made a meal more complicated than tea and toast or maybe a plate with crackers, tomato and cheese on it. She lived in 'Third Wish' but never took charge of it. Left it to housekeepers—and Wendy. Just as Ingrid had left Douglas to nannies—and Wendy. Yet her presence was everywhere. It was as though she radiated a nervous energy that filled the house's every corner. She possessed it, as, at that time, she possessed Max.

Wendy had come to realise that her father and Berwyn were so wrapped up in each other that there was no room in the house for anyone else. She had felt—for the first time at 'Third Wish'—like a fifth wheel. She had suddenly discovered that she had no real place here. And that as a result she had—funny, Douglas had said this too—no life.

It was like waking up from a dream, almost. She was already seeing Roger Laidlaw then. Had met him at a tennis afternoon held by one of her old school friends. He was awkward, stodgy, predictable, older, kind, reassuring, lonely. They'd gone to a few films and dinners together. Her friend had fluttered with excitement. Matchmaking was her favourite sport. Roger had proposed. She'd married him, riding with pleasure the crest of the small wave of interest and glamour that arose with such affairs, and then settled, quickly, with gratitude, and with a sense of familiarity and rightness that she never analysed, into a life that was as different from her previous one as the tranquil, netted fish pond in Roger's garden was from Max's ever-changing open sea.

Then, after years of growing mutual dependence, the smooth surface of their daily lives only shallowly disturbed by occasional gnats of irritation, she lost him, too. She remembered the feelings she'd had, the night after his heart attack. She'd been angry. She considered this now, almost with surprise. She'd been angry because he'd left her. Left her to be alone, and gone back to his first wife, Lynette. Roger believed in life after death.

Perhaps now, wherever he was, with Lynette, Roger didn't even remember her. Wendy gazed straight ahead, thinking about him, and with a little shock suddenly realised that she was having difficulty recalling his face. All those years—and yet her memories of them now, as she stood here, were misty. It was as if their whole life together had receded into dimness. As if it had been an interlude, a small detour that had no relevance in the separate journeys of their lives, and so was easily forgotten.

She took another pastry, looked at it, and put it back, closing the tin and pushing it away from her. She gripped the edge of the bench, in a sort of panic. Where was her place, then? What was her life? She looked around the kitchen. The clear colours, the copper pans hanging above the island bench, the smell and taste of the air—these were real. What else was? She pulled her hands away from the bench and clasped them firmly. She pressed her lips together. She had to stop thinking like this. It was unlike her. It wasn't good for her. She'd always believed in looking on the bright side. For what was the point of looking too deeply into things, if what you found was unhappiness and confusion?

That was what was wrong with Berwyn's paintings, in Wendy's opinion. They were depressing. Like her picture of Dad. It was like him, of course. Berwyn was very clever at drawing, there was no doubt. She was enormously talented. But why make him look so thin, and odd, and—ugly? He was so attractive when he grinned, like in his publicity photographs. Why not paint him like that? And why paint him with his socks all falling down, for example? Berwyn could have asked him to pull them up, surely. And why put a look in his eyes that made you feel uncomfortable, even sad? Dad wasn't sad.

Wendy's mouth turned down at the corners. Ironically, the painting of Mai had looked as though it would have been quite nice. Maybe that was because Berwyn was doing it as a favour to Dad, not because she wanted to. It would be like her, to be only capable of producing a pretty picture when she didn't care. She wanted to paint Isa. If Wendy was Isa she wouldn't let Berwyn anywhere near her. She could just imagine what Berwyn would do with Isa's face.

'Wendy?'

She jumped. She hadn't heard anyone come down the stairs. But Douglas was standing there in front of her. 'You OK?' he said.

'Oh—yes. I was just thinking.' Wendy looked up at him and smiled. He smiled back, and instantly the clouds that had gathered around her lifted. Douglas's holiday was doing him good. He looked so much happier than he had when he'd arrived. She hoped his job hunting was going well. If he could find a way of settling in Sydney, now that he and Dad seemed to have come to some sort of understanding ... Hope fluttered timidly in her heart.

'Could I borrow your car again, sis? Sorry. It's a bugger, being without a car. I'll get one as soon as I can.'

'Oh, don't worry, Douglas. I'm not using it. You may as well have the benefit. The keys are on the table in ...'

He jingled his pocket. 'Got them already.'

Wendy walked with him to the front door. 'Is Dad all right?'

'Berwyn's sitting with him now. He might sleep. He's been—ah—talking quite a lot.' Douglas folded his arms uncomfortably across his chest. 'He's not making much sense. I hope that doctor knows what she's doing.'

'Oh, Heather's really marvellous, Douglas. She's been Dad's doctor for years. And he had all the tests and everything. She says he's just shocked. Shaken up,

she says. After all, he is seventy. He hasn't got the resilience. We've got to expect this sort of thing, at his
age.'

'I guess so.' Douglas fidgeted. He was impatient to
be gone, she realised. He'd done his bit at 'Third
Wish'. Now he had other things on his mind. She
wondered vaguely what they were. The job hunt, of
course. And a girlfriend, perhaps. A woman, Dad had
said. Could that be true? Of course, Douglas had always had lots of girlfriends. He was a very good-
looking man. But she wished he wasn't so secretive
about it. Wendy had never actually met any of them,
though he'd seemed quite serious about one or two
he'd mentioned. Still, that was in Perth, so it was understandable. Maybe she could suggest he bring this
one home for dinner.

As she opened her mouth to speak the doorbell
rang, startling them both. And when she opened the
door she was surprised to see Detective-Constable
Milson and the dark young uniformed policeman
called Barassi standing there. 'Oh!' she heard herself
say. 'Oh, can I help you?'

'Mrs Laidlaw.' Detective-Constable Milson ac-
knowledged her presence with a brief nod, and then
turned to Douglas. 'Detective-Sergeant Toby was wondering if you'd be so kind as to come down to the station at Paradise for a chat, sir,' he said. His voice was
quite courteous, but his eyes were cold. 'Just a few
things that need clearing up.'

Douglas flushed slightly and flashed a broad
smile. 'No problem,' he said heartily. 'As a matter of
fact I was just going down to Paradise anyway.' He
showed them the car keys. 'Bit of business to do down
there. But it can wait a while.'

'We'll follow you, then, sir,' said Milson. He stood
aside to let Douglas pass.

'How long do you think you'll need me?' asked
Douglas casually. He threw the keys in the air and
caught them again.

'Hard to say, sir,' Milson replied.

Douglas raised his eyebrows and made a face of

comical dismay at Wendy. 'Sounds bad,' he chuckled. 'Better not expect me for dinner, Win.' Still chuckling, he walked off down the drive, with the two police following him closely.

Wendy shut the door behind them and went into the silent living room. She sat down in one of the big leather chairs. She felt breathless. There was something wrong. She'd seen the baffled fear and guilt in Douglas's eyes as he left. It was exactly the look he used to get as a child when he'd done something wrong and came to her for help. But Douglas had done nothing wrong now. Then why was that look in his eyes? And why, for the first time in twenty-five years, had he called her 'Win'?

In the bedroom upstairs Max stirred. 'The door,' he mumbled. 'Who is it?'

'Wendy'll fix up whatever it is, Max,' said Berwyn. She ran a nervous hand through her cropped hair. He looked so pale and helpless, lying there. 'Please try and rest. Try to sleep.'

'Can't sleep,' he groaned.

'Does your hand hurt?' she asked awkwardly. She wasn't good at this. She never had been good at looking after other people. She wasn't even particularly good at looking after herself. Why was that? she wondered. She could feel, all right. Max's pain and despair hurt her physically, almost. But the feeling translated into action only with rusty difficulty. The little attentions that seemed to come so naturally to someone like Wendy were foreign to her. Perhaps it came from being too much alone. And yet she'd always been the same, even as a child, in the silent shadowy house of her parents. Maybe she just didn't like people enough. She'd had no real friends at school. Or art school, later, really. There'd been one lover before Max. But he'd never been a friend. In fact, now that she came to think about it she hadn't even really liked him, let alone loved him. Just kept company with him, for a while, till he got bored and drifted off. Max

had been different. Like a lightning bolt out of a clear
sky. As unexpected, and thrilling, and dangerous.

The man in the bed had closed his eyes again. It
seemed to bring him comfort, anyway, that she was
there. She wondered why he'd been so insistent she
stay in the house. She wished she hadn't. Max . . . She
sighed, looking down at him breathing shallowly beside her, a deep line of strain between his eyebrows.
His unbandaged hand twitched on the sheets. What's
going on in your head, Max? For once, she didn't
know. She sat on, listening to the sea. There was no
movement in the house at all now. It was absolutely silent. She wondered who had been at the door.

The Paradise police station, set on a small, bald block
of land adjacent to the parking area that ran behind
Paradise Parade, was a new red brick building that
bore a strong resemblance to a well-kept lavatory
block. Douglas had thought this every time he passed
it over the last week, and now he found that the mim-
icry did not stop at the front door. Inside, the place
even smelled like an institutional convenience, being
redolent of disinfectant of the more basic sort. From
the hard sheen of the ultra-serviceable pale green
paint on its walls to its harsh white lighting and the
brutal practicality of its heavy-duty grey vinyl floor covering, the Paradise police station assaulted the eyes
and dulled the senses, a fact that the one small, sad
palm in a white plastic pot by the front desk did nothing to mitigate. It reminded Douglas unpleasantly of
the boarding school where he had spent ten years of
his life. Not the front rooms or the headmaster's study
where parents were received, of course. These were all
fine old rugs, portraits and oiled cedar. But the back
parts, where the boarders lived their Spartan and reg-
imented existences, endured major and minor tor-
ments in the same peer-pressured silence and thus
learned, it was said, to be men.

The cop at the desk, busy on the phone, barely
raised his eyes as Milson marched past him, with

Barassi and Douglas trailing along behind. Douglas slipped a sweaty hand into his pocket and attempted a saunter. His mind was all whirling confusion. There's nothing wrong, he told himself. Don't act as though there is. This is just routine. I'm Max's son. It's natural they'd call on me if they needed to clear anything up. It's all quite natural.

Milson led the way around a corner into a small maze of offices. In a glass-fronted cubicle to his right Douglas saw Dan Toby in conversation with a solid-looking individual in a checked shirt who looked faintly familiar. They looked up as Douglas passed, and he grinned and raised his free hand to Toby in casual greeting.

'In here, sir,' said Milson, pushing open a door and holding out an arm to guide Douglas through to the tiny interview room beyond.

Douglas went inside and immediately felt claustrophobic. He sank into the chair Milson indicated, facing a pint-sized desk, and waited for further developments. They arrived in the person of Toby himself. He was carrying a manila folder. He nodded to Douglas, squeezed past Milson to get behind the desk, and sat down. He wriggled his shoulders as if his suit coat was too tight, pushed his chair back as far as it would go and looked around. 'Snug in here, isn't it?' he commented.

Douglas said nothing. He wondered what was in the folder. He had a strong urge to get up, push past Milson, who had now closed the door and was standing against it, and get the hell out. But he knew that was foolish.

'Now.' Toby leaned across the desk with his hands clasped and regarded Douglas with a slight smile. 'Thank you for coming in to see us, Mr Tully. We'll get through with this as quickly as we can. There are just a few discrepancies in our records we thought you could clear up for us.'

'Oh, sure.' Douglas could feel that his smile was stretching too widely, and hear that his voice was pitched a little too high. Toby's own smile broadened.

'We appreciate your cooperation,' he said. 'You'd be surprised how reluctant some people are to assist the police. But as I always say, the innocent have nothing to fear.'

A few people'd argue with you on that one, thought Douglas, but of course nodded responsibly, trying to keep his eyes sincere.

Toby unclasped his hands and opened the folder. He held it up and squinted at it, effectively preventing Douglas from seeing what was inside.

'Yesterday, Friday, you borrowed Mrs Laidlaw's car and went out at about one-thirty. And you returned, as you said you would, around six. That's right, is it?'

'Yes.'

'Could you go through your movements during that afternoon again, please Mr Tully?'

'Why?' The question burst out more aggressively than Douglas had intended. He watched Toby's face assume a rather injured expression.

'We have to complete our records, Mr Tully,' he murmured.

'It's just that I've told you everything once already,' said Douglas. He tried to prevent himself from squirming. That's what this big bugger was waiting for. 'I went to the beach to meet a girl . . . who didn't turn up.'

'The girl called Karen whose last name you don't know?' Toby enquired.

'That's right.'

'And whose address you don't know and who you haven't seen since?'

'That's right!' Douglas felt his face flushing.

'Quite the mystery woman,' Toby commented easily. He consulted the contents of his folder again. 'You waited about forty-five minutes and then left the beach and proceeded to the Paradise Hotel. There, on your way to the beer garden where you prefer to take your ease, you saw Warren Daley?'

'Yes. He was in the public bar. I saw him through the door. I didn't talk to him. In fact, I'm sure he didn't notice me. He was too busy trying to impress the barmaid.' Careful! Don't lose your head. Don't volunteer too much, the dim voice of experience whispered. Remember all those lessons. All those catastrophes. School. Max. Bosses. Say enough, but not too much. He'll think there's something funny going on if you're too eager.

Toby was nodding understandingly. 'So you state that you stayed in the hotel from two-thirty till just before six, when you drove home.'

'Guess I must've.' Douglas essayed a sheepish grin. 'I'm the family wastrel, you know. And here's the proof.'

'Aha ...' Toby looked at the folder again.

Douglas sat back in his chair. He hadn't even realised he'd been sitting forward. Bad move, that. He felt that his shirt was soaked with sweat. He wondered whether that sour-looking detective Milson behind him had noticed.

'Now ...' Toby's forehead wrinkled in apparent puzzlement. 'The thing is, Mr Tully, that just this afternoon I heard something that confused me a bit. The girls serving in the beer garden remember you quite well. Your first name and all. You've been there a few times in the last week, I gather. Sometimes with a friend, sometimes alone, they said.'

Douglas nodded, his stomach churning. 'So?'

'Well, sir,' drawled Toby, 'the shifts at the Paradise change at four-thirty. And the new lot of girls who came on ... sorry ...' he consulted his notes again while Douglas waited, and sweated, 'the one bloke and two girls who came on, say you didn't stay long into their shift at all. Finished the drink you were on, they said, and left.' He smiled comfortably at Douglas. 'They notice these things, you see,' he remarked, 'because of the tips.'

Douglas said nothing.

'That means you probably left at quarter to five, rather than quarter to six.' Toby paused. 'What do you make of that?'

'I don't bloody make anything of that!' Douglas burst out. Don't lose your temper, his inner voice warned. But the walls of the tiny room were closing in on him, and he had had enough. He raged on. 'What does it matter, all this, anyway? You're just wasting my time. So I fucked around for a while before I went home. So what? You've been investigating a murder, as far as I know. Not perfectly innocent people's private doings. And you've got your man. Scared him over a bloody cliff so he smashed his brains out, didn't you? What does it matter, how I was spending my time? It doesn't bloody matter a pinch of shit!'

'Oh, it matters, Mr Tully.' Toby's voice was very cold, now, and the eyes were hard. 'It matters a lot. Because it turns out Warren Daley had more luck with the ladies than you. He was with a woman friend at the time of Mai Tran's murder. He didn't touch a hair on his wife's head. But you were taken by taxi to 'Third Wish' at quarter to five on Friday night. The taxi driver'll swear to that. He got a good look at you. He originally responded to our description of Warren Daley. Big, brown hair, good-looking, the worse for drink . . . After all, as someone else said today, all you blokes look alike. But you can't mistake a face you've sat next to for ten minutes, can you?'

Douglas sat staring at him, gripping the seat of his hard chair. Now he remembered where he'd seen the big man in the checked shirt before. He'd seen him in a cab. While they were driving. On Friday. At four forty-five. To 'Third Wish'.

THIRTEEN

—

'The bloody idiots! What do they think they're playing at?' growled Max. He'd insisted on coming down and sitting in the living room, but hunched in the big leather chair in navy silk robe and pale blue pyjamas he looked, if possible, even frailer than he had lying in bed upstairs. He glanced irritably around the assembly and focused on his daughter. 'Wendy, stop crying, sweetheart,' he said through clenched teeth. 'Go and ring Travers again.'

Wendy continued to sob and wring her hands. 'It's Saturday. He's playing golf, Dad. I told you that.'

'Well, get him at the course, then!' stormed Max, losing his temper. 'What's the point of having a lawyer if you can't get him when you need him?'

'I can't understand it,' Wendy wept. 'It's—crazy. Why do they keep saying Mai's husband didn't do it? Of *course* he did it. He's the only one who *could* have done it.'

'On the contrary, Wendy,' said Berwyn dryly. 'It now appears he's the only one who *couldn't* have done it. He was somewhere else at the time.'

'He had the emeralds,' Isa pointed out. 'You can't get away from that.'

'Look,' spluttered Max. 'Forget all this and keep to the point, for God's sake. The point, you silly women, is they think Douglas—Douglas, of all people, killed poor little Mai. Good God, the boy's a fool, and I'd be the first one to say it. But he wouldn't kill anyone. And he had no reason to kill Mai. The whole idea's ridiculous.' He glared at Birdie as though she was arguing with him. 'That so-called friend of yours, Toby, had it in for this family all along, you know. Remember him asking about everyone when he first got here? I wondered what he was up to at the time. He's one of those pinko coppers who love to see someone with a bit of dough come undone. I can smell it.'

'Max, that's ridiculous,' Birdie exclaimed. 'Dan's not like that. Of course he had to cover what all of us were doing when Mai died. It was likely Warren Daley had killed Mai. But it wasn't a certainty. And now it turns out it was a complete furphy.' She hesitated. 'And actually, Max, I know you won't like it, but you'll have to face something else. We all will.' She looked around at their faces. Max's twisted in a grimace of irritation; Berwyn's, frowning and intense; Isa's, avid; Wendy's, red and puffy with tears.

'Douglas lied about when he came home,' she said slowly and carefully. 'He lied to us, and he lied to the police. He said he drove home at six. So he did. But he'd already been home an hour before. He first came back to "Third Wish" by cab at a quarter to five. The cab driver recognises him. And anyway, Douglas now admits it.'

'But he's explained!' cried Wendy, in an agony of fear. 'He's explained how it happened. It could have happened to anyone, Verity.'

'No it couldn't,' snapped Max. 'Only a wrong-drummer like Douglas'd booze himself into such a state he had to get a cab home, then think better of

it and go back for the car. Around the bloody headland! Pissed! Of all the boof-headed, bone-
brained . . .' He subsided into sulky silence.

'He was embarrassed because it was my car he'd
left, Dad,' pleaded Wendy. 'He was thinking of me.
And it was low tide. Or lowish. He got here, felt bad
about coming in and telling us what he'd done, and
decided to go back. That's not so silly, really.'

'But if that's really what happened it was pretty
silly not to come clean about it in the first place,
Wendy,' Birdie pointed out. 'Unfortunately Douglas
only told the truth when he was forced to. Now it
looks as though he has something to hide. Mai died,
they're certain of it now, at five minutes past five. That
means she was still alive, and probably in the garden,
when Douglas arrived. He could have seen her. He
could have gone to talk to her, maybe to try to get her
to leave, maybe to try again to inveigle her into some
sort of indiscretion with him. They could have argued.
And he could have killed her.' She ignored a stifled
cry from Wendy and went on: 'Then he could have
panicked, realised no one knew he was home, nicked
round the side of the house, climbed down the cliff
and gone back to Paradise round the rocks. Like we
used to do as kids. Then all he had to do was pick up
the car, kill a little bit of time, and get home at six,
when he was expected, acting innocent. That's the
cops' scenario, I'll bet, and it fits the known facts just
as well, you see, as Douglas's version.'

'Balls!' cried Isa with spirit. 'If ever I've heard a
story with the ring of hideous, embarrassing truth to
it, that story of Douglas's is one. I've known that boy
all his life. I love him dearly, but he's as stubborn as a
mule and as silly as a wheel and as cunning as a barn
rat. Since he was two years old he's been getting himself into messes and then trying to cover them up so
Wendy and Max wouldn't find out. And just about always he got himself into even worse messes for his
trouble.' She sighed, and thoughtfully examined her
chipped pink nail polish. 'This time, mind you, he's
excelled himself. But still . . .'

'There's something else.' Birdie saw them all turn back to look at her. Resentful, scared, irritated. She pushed on regardless. They had to come to terms with this. Max, particularly. 'If Warren Daley didn't kill Mai, then someone else did. And as far as the police are concerned that someone is almost certainly Douglas, or if not him, one of us.'

They stared at her, apparently shocked into silence.

'Their best bet is Douglas at the moment, because Douglas, the one person who claimed not even to be near the house at the time Mai died, has been found to have lied. But if he convinces them he's innocent, they'll come back here looking for the answer elsewhere.'

'Now look,' Max began menacingly. 'I don't want to fall out with you, Birdie, but—'

'Don't shoot the messenger, Max,' interrupted Isa. 'What d'you want? You want her to lie to us to make us feel good? Christ almighty you're irrational sometimes. She's perfectly right.'

'Claptrap!' mumbled Max. 'Anyone could have come in off the street and done it. You probably left your bloody security door open, or that bastard Daley did, and they came through your place into mine. I told you we should've got that side fence fixed up. Replaced with something no bugger could get past. I was a fool to let myself be talked into leaving it alone. For the sake of a few bloody trees . . . and now look what's happened.'

'Why would anyone do that, Max?' said Berwyn in a low voice. Her cheekbones were so white they looked bleached. 'Why would anyone just come in off the street and kill Mai?'

He made an impatient gesture. 'Well, they obviously did, didn't they? We won't know why till we catch them. And the cops are fiddling around wasting time with Douglas. Wendy! Ring Travers again!'

The security door buzzer sounded, shockingly loud. Everyone jumped as though it was a pistol shot.

'That'll be Angus,' growled Max. He glanced at his watch. 'He's early. Said he'd be here at four.'

Wendy stood up stiffly and went to the blinking red light by the front door. 'Yes?' they heard her say. 'Who is it, please?' There was a short burst of static and a distorted female voice. 'It's—I'm a friend of Douglas's. I need to talk to Max Tully.'

Wendy turned around to Max, her eyes wide. 'She says—'

'I heard, I heard.' Max looked exhausted and confused. He struggled to regain his equilibrium. 'Let her in.'

Wendy hesitated. 'It could be a journalist.'

'If it is she'll wish she'd never been born,' growled Max. 'Let her in.'

Wendy pushed the button and stood with her hand on the doorknob. They waited in thick silence for the bell to ring, and when it did, a minute or two later, Wendy opened the door as reluctantly as though outside waited a ravening beast.

The gasp she gave, the little stagger back from the doorway, gave the same impression. Strange, then, that it was only a slight, blonde young woman in jeans standing there.

'Who's this, on earth?' said Isa loudly.

It was the girl Birdie had seen walking up Paradise Parade with Douglas. And she was angry. Her fair brows were knitted, her chin was stuck out, and her small hands were clenched. She strode, ponytail swinging, towards the group by the windows and focused belligerently on Max. He blinked at her, his expression an almost comical mixture of shock, anger, interest and dismay.

'Remember me, Mr Tully?' she demanded. Her voice was high and almost shrill, with a nasal undertone.

He nodded. 'Trish,' he said after a moment. 'You haven't changed.'

'Oh, yes I have,' she spat. 'I'm a different person now to what I was when you broke Douglas and me up. Eight years as a single mum's seen to that.' She

put her hands on her hips and scowled down at him.
'But you're not different, are you? You're exactly the
same. Someone's a thorn in your side, you just get rid
of them, right? Except now you're throwing your own
son to the wolves. Well, I gather you're claiming he's
not your son at all. now, so I suppose you think that's
OK. Well, it's not. You'll never get away with it. Whoever you're shielding better watch out. Because there's
no way you're going to get away with what you're
doing to Douglas. No way in the world!'

Max stared at her in silence. Then his brow wrinkled and he lifted his hand to it. A hand that trembled
slightly.

The girl nibbled at her bottom lip. Her eyes
darted around the room. Perhaps she had expected
anger, Birdie thought. Perhaps she had expected a
fight from the foe she remembered in his arrogant
prime. If so, she had been disappointed.

'Well, that's all I came to say,' she said. She turned
on her heel.

'Wait!' Max roused himself to speak at last. 'Look,
I don't understand what's happening here. Where did
you spring from?'

The girl swung around to face him. Her hazel eyes
seemed to shoot sparks. 'I didn't "spring", as you put
it, from anywhere. I've been alive and kicking all
along, you know. For all these years. Much as you
might have wished I'd drop dead as soon as I went out
of your sight eight years ago.'

Max's mouth twitched. 'I knew you were alive and
kicking, my dear,' he said grimly. 'I should. My bloody
cheque's been going into your bank account every
month of those eight years, if you'll recall. And it's
never been sent back marked return to sender, as far
as I know.' He paused and narrowed his eyes. 'You
might also recall that there was a condition attached
to those payments.'

She laughed, showing small, even white teeth.
'Oh, yes. Keep away from Douglas. Why do you think
I refused to see him for years? Told my folks to send
his letters back? I wasn't going to risk my son's security

for a man who'd let himself be talked out of sticking by me when I needed him most. For all I knew he'd just dump me again if you kicked up rough. Then I wouldn't have the man or the money, would I?'

'Tough little cookie these days, aren't you?' A glimmer of what could have been grudging respect lightened Max's drawn face. 'You have changed.'

'Too right I have.' The girl's fair brows drew together again. 'But like I said, you haven't. And neither has Douglas. Except for one thing. He's finally decided what matters to him. Finally. And he's gone for it. He tracked me down last year, and he started writing me letters from Perth every day. Wanted me to go over there and marry him. As if I'd give up everything I've worked for here to do that. Not that I wasn't tempted.' She tossed her ponytail and for a moment her face softened. 'I'd thought about him a lot. Maybe almost as much as he thought about me. But I wasn't going to take any risks. So he just threw in his job and came here. Well, I had to see him then, didn't I? I couldn't turn him down.'

Wendy made a small sound and Trish glanced at her, turning away immediately with a curl of her lip. 'I know he told you he was retrenched. Well, he wasn't. He just didn't want you nagging and rousing on him like you always do. He resigned, and came here and for three weeks he's been trying to talk me round. Wanting to get back together. Wanting to see Jamie.'

Birdie remembered Douglas's afternoon absences, his eager, placatory expression on Paradise Parade, his frequent abstraction and depression, his tirade against Max the night before. 'I gather you weren't keen on that idea,' she remarked.

Trish raised her eyebrows. 'You're Birdie,' she said frostily. 'The detective. Douglas told me about you. Is this an example of your detecting?'

Birdie said nothing.

Max stirred restlessly in his chair. 'Listen, let's cut the crap,' he barked. 'You've been seeing Douglas on the quiet. Fact. He's been trying to talk you into getting involved with him again. Fact. Presumably you

wouldn't let him tell me about it till you'd made up
your mind, because of the money. Fact?'

She nodded, her mouth pursed into a tight rosebud.

'But now he's got himself into another bloody silly
mess and for some reason you've got it into your head
that it's my fault. Like every other bloody thing that's
ever happened to Douglas. Is that right?'

'Yes.' The rosebud opened just enough to let out
the word, and snapped shut again.

Max pushed himself forward in his chair. 'Well,
it's not my fault. Get that into your head. It's got nothing to do with me. The whole thing's ludicrous.'

She stared at him, and then slowly looked around
at all the other people in the room. Isa was nodding
vigorously. 'He's been saying that for an hour,' she
shrilled. 'Earbashing us all till we're sick of it. Ring
Travers, get Travers . . .'

'Who's Travers?' asked the girl.

'My solicitor,' said Max briefly. 'We've got to get
him in with Douglas as soon as we can.'

She smiled slightly. 'It's all right. My solicitor's
with him now.'

'Your . . .' Max almost goggled at her. Then he
made an obvious effort to pull himself together.
'Look, sweetheart, that's all very nice, but we can't use
some little local bloke on a thing like this. We've got
to—'

'My name's Trish,' the girl snapped. 'And my solicitor's perfectly capable of looking after Douglas.
Andrea Moore of King, Marley and Moore. You've
probably heard of them.'

Birdie had, at least. There was nothing wrong with
King, Marley and Moore. In fact, there was everything
right with them.

Max felt the same, apparently. 'What's someone
like you doing dealing with King, Marley and Moore?'
he burst out. Then he recollected himself, and cleared
his throat. 'Look—ah—sorry. I didn't mean to
imply—ah.'

'Of course you did,' retorted Trish crisply. 'But

you've forgotten. Eight years is a long time. I've changed. Other things have changed too. Anyway, we won't go into that. We'll concentrate on Douglas. If you haven't set him up, and I still don't know whether to believe you on that or not, then you'll help me get him out of this.'

Max pounded his fists on the arms of his chair. 'Good God, girl, what do you think—?'

'My name's Trish,' she cut in.

They glared at one another. Birdie decided it was time to intervene. 'It was you who Douglas went to see after lunch, on the day Mai died, wasn't it?' she asked.

'Yes. He told me he'd spun some tale about a girl he had a date with on the beach. Keeping his promise to me, see.' The tight mouth relaxed in a half-smile. 'But it was me he was with, and of course we've told the police that now. I'm only sorry he didn't stay longer.'

'Why didn't he?' Birdie asked. 'He'd obviously expected to. He told us he'd be home at six.'

Trish tossed her ponytail back. Her eyes were defiant, daring them to criticise. 'We didn't have an arrangement,' she said. 'He just rolled up. I was angry with him for just turning up like that. He was pushing me too fast. He asked again if he could see Jamie. I said no. I'm not having my son upset and confused by some strange man coming into his life, taking him up like some new toy and then maybe pissing off again. I want to be sure.'

The security door buzzer sounded again. Trish jumped violently, betraying the rigid tension that her anger had so far disguised.

This time Berwyn quietly rose and went to the control panel. She listened to the voice, then pushed the button without comment, opened the front door, and stood beside it, waiting. 'It's the police again,' she called to Max. 'Do you want to speak to them?'

'Only if they want to speak to me.' Max's brow was deeply furrowed. Birdie saw Wendy glance at him in concern. She twisted around in her chair to watch the official visitors arrive. It seemed a long wait, but finally two figures appeared in the doorway. One bulky, in plain clothes. Dan Toby. It was important, then. The other, hovering behind him, in uniform. Barassi, perhaps. They murmured, and Berwyn nodded. Then she closed the door and came back to the gathering by the windows.

'They want to check the garbage,' she said flatly. 'I said they could.'

'Good God!' groaned Max.

Birdie itched to go and see what was happening. The garbage? Why would they be checking the garbage again? They'd already been through it once, last night, after the discovery of Mai's body, in case the handbag had been disposed of there. Her thoughts raced. Was this to do with Douglas, presumably left to Milson at the Paradise cop shop while Toby supervised the combing of the rubbish bin? Or something else?

She forced herself to sit quietly. She'd find out soon enough. She pushed back her glasses and concentrated on the girl called Trish. 'So you wouldn't talk to Douglas yesterday, or let him see your son, and he stormed off to the pub?'

'That's right. And drank too much. Like a fool. And you know the rest. But then later that night he rang me, from the motel. He told me everything. Told me about the girl dying, and what his charming father had said about him. Said he'd left the house. Didn't ask to see me. He was, just, so . . . defeated and lonely. He'd always been so lonely. God!' She looked at Max almost with contempt. 'He always knew you didn't like him, you know. But this . . .' She shook her head again, so that her ponytail swung, and lifted her pointed chin. 'Anyway, I told him to just come. And he did. Jamie was asleep, but he saw him. And the next day he met him.' She smiled. A curious, sleepy smile.

'We didn't tell Jamie who he was, of course. They just talked. Watched cartoons together.' The smile broadened. 'Douglas was blasted out of the sky by him. Overwhelmed. Amazed. It was great. I told him it was great. I told him it was going to be OK.' There was a short silence, then her smile disappeared abruptly. 'So he comes back here happy as Larry to get some clothes. At peace with the world. Ready to hold out the olive branch to you and tell you everything. He finds you laid up, and decides to hold off on the revelations till you're better. Next thing I know, he's in the bloody Paradise police station. Helping the police with their enquiries, as they put it. Seems a bit sus to me. Seems to me he's being made the bunny. And I told Andrea so.'

There was a knock on the door. Max swore under his breath as Berwyn again rose to answer it. This time Toby followed her into the room. His grey suit was crumpled as usual, but unmarked. It had not been he who had fossicked through the Tully garbage, anyway, Birdie thought. Poor Barassi, who lingered outside, had probably borne the brunt of that. Toby's small grey eyes took in the assembled group with interest. 'Sorry to trouble you again, sir,' he said to Max, sounding as though he wasn't sorry at all. 'But could I ask you to identify these?' He held out a small plastic bag. Inside, covered with some whitish substance, were two exquisite gold and green objects.

'Mai's earrings,' hissed Max. 'D'you mean to tell me they were in the garbage?'

Toby nodded. 'Stuffed into the base of a currant bun, would you believe. As was the necklace originally, apparently. Tests showed that today. Seems that's how Warren Daley found it. Bit of a shock for him, eh? Could've broken a tooth.' He stuffed the bag into his pocket, and held out a piece of paper. 'A receipt for these, sir,' he said formally. 'They'll be given back in due course.'

'Wonderful,' grunted Max. He watched with hooded eyes as Toby smiled pleasantly and departed.

'They'll try to say Douglas did that,' said Trish, through clenched teeth. 'They'll say he could easily have got to the garbage bin. They'll say he stole the emeralds and then got scared after you had your fall and the police came back. I told you. He's being made the bunny.'

'If he's being made the bunny he's done it himself,' muttered Max. 'I played no part in it.'

Her eyes narrowed. 'Well, the fact is, someone put those emeralds in that bin. Or into the buns before they went out to the bin, I suppose. Whichever, someone here knows a lot more than they're saying,' she said. 'And you'd better think about that, Mr Tully. It's your girlfriend who got killed. And it's your family that's in the gun. Forget about Douglas if you want to. I'll look after him. He's my family now. But you'd better look to your own.' She swung around and made for the front door. As she swung it open she looked back over her shoulder. 'The cops certainly will be, anyway, after we're through with them,' she called. 'So you'd better get your stories straight.'

The door banged shut after her. The people in the room sat motionless. It was as if a whirlwind had passed through the room, leaving in its wake exhaustion, shock and slowly settling dust.

It was Wendy who finally broke the paralysed silence. 'Was she threatening us?' she whispered. 'How dare she?'

'She was only saying what Birdie said before,' murmured Isa. She had lost a lot of her bounce since the police visit, thought Birdie. She looked, in fact, rather ruffled.

'I'll make some tea,' Wendy said, 'I think we could all do with a cup.'

Isa stood up, pulling nervously at her skirt to smooth the creases. 'Not for me, thanks. I must get on home,' she babbled. 'I'm no use here. And it's nearly time to think about feeding the cats.' She moved forward quickly and kissed Max on the top of his head. 'God bless, my dear,' she breathed in his ear. 'I'll call later.' She swept the rest of the party with a rather confused, Auntie Dora smile. 'I'll let myself out,' she trilled, and whisked herself off with fairly obvious dispatch.

'How odd,' murmured Wendy, looking after her. Then adding, with uncharacteristic asperity, 'Not that she isn't always odd.'

'Not odd, on this occasion, I'd say,' Berwyn put in steadily. 'Disturbed. Worried. Scared. Not odd.'

'Now why would you say that?' cried Wendy in exasperation. 'Why does everyone keep talking in riddles? I don't understand!'

'That's because you won't try to understand, Wendy.' Berwyn stood up in her turn, and stretched. 'Think about it.'

Wendy flushed with anger. 'What—?'

'Berwyn means that we can't go on thinking about a stranger off the street any more, Wendy,' Birdie broke in. She glanced at Max. His ashen face showed only too clearly that he at least had taken the point. 'The buns only went out into the garbage bin this morning. Someone belonging to this house must have put the emeralds inside them either in the kitchen, or once they were thrown out.'

'So Isa's getting out while she can,' droned Max. 'She knows when a place isn't healthy. And she's got a great instinct for survival, has Isa.' He turned vacant eyes towards the sea.

FOURTEEN

—

Angus arrived punctually at four, parking his immaculate car behind his daughter's battered affair on the roadway and toiling up the stone steps. He was plainly shocked to find Max looking so frail, but made no reference to his old friend's state. Just shook his hand, murmured conventional words of condolence, accepted Wendy's offer of tea and sank down into a chair, making no waves in the room. His calm, familiar presence, his talk of things outside 'Third Wish', slowly began to diffuse the tension that had gripped them all since the police visit, and little by little the dark matters with which they'd all been grappling for nearly twenty-four hours began to receded into the background.

After a few minutes Birdie slipped away, and wandered out into the garden. She felt it would be good for Max to have some time alone with Angus. But Berwyn and Wendy seemed to be firmly fixed in their seats, and she doubted very much that either one would choose to be the first to move. Perhaps they were watching each other. Perhaps they were both concerned for Max. But anyway, she could certainly use this opportunity to get away and think. For thinking was what was required, now. Of that she was certain.

She paced down the stone steps. They were clear now of booby trap, police, pink tape and other obstacles to progress. The garden was absolutely still. No cats were to be seen. Probably they were all at home for a change. Four o'clock, as she remembered, was dinnertime. A flash of colour caught her eye. Isa was out and about next door, under the giant magnolia tree. She was bending down. She had something in her hands. Birdie craned her neck to see. Then she realised what was happening. Isa was tending the cats' graveyard. She was digging with a little trowel, and planting seedlings. Perhaps for Othello, dead in his prime. Rosemary, for remembrance? Not in that shade. Violets, probably. Isa's garden was full of violets.

Birdie had a sudden sensation of deja vu. She had walked down these steps on Thursday afternoon, the day she first arrived. It was hot, and quiet, like this. Max was locked in his study. Berwyn was sketching Mai. Douglas was out. Wendy was sewing her doll's dress. So she had walked down the stone steps and seen Isa, and Warren Daley, in the cats' graveyard. It all seemed a very long time ago. Yet it had been only two days. And now Mai was dead. Warren Daley was dead. And Max could so easily have been dead also, had the turn in the steps not broken his downward plunge.

They knew now that Warren Daley had not killed his wife. And it seemed to Birdie most unlikely that he had set the trap for Max either. She had seen the glazed look in the eyes of the man as he turned and ran, the terrible gash that disfigured the battered, ravaged face. It was the face of a hunted man, not a hunter. No one in that condition would have come out of hiding to set a trap. And what was more important, no one in that condition could have crept to Isa's house, made a bogus phone call and departed without trace. Or stood, starving, in a kitchen without taking food, thinking it more prudent to rummage in a garbage bin.

No. And Daley wasn't a planner. He was impetuous, full of shifting, grandiose ideas that masqueraded as plans. His every action showed that. Maybe in that long day of drinking at the Paradise Hotel his simmering resentment, fueled by alcohol, had culminated in some vague idea of storming back to 'Third Wish' and having it out with the rich man who thought he'd bought him off so easily. Then Julie Billings caught his eye. The idea changed and developed. First he would have this pretty girl, then he would have his revenge. He was a real man, a big man, and just for once the world was going to recognise it.

Then later, on the beach, humiliated and angry in the rain, he had seen Douglas coming around the headland. Another idea. An even better one. Creep around the rocks and storm the mansion from the sea. Take the rich man by surprise. But in the rain, Warren's staggering feet had failed him, and he'd slipped, and gashed his head on the jagged rocks Birdie remembered so well. So his glorious project came undone. A smelly garbage bin was the limit of the territory he conquered. Dazed, sick and confused, he skulked between the house and the sea, until he was finally flushed out of his hiding place to run and die.

Someone else had laid the trap for Max. Someone else had made the call that lured him down the steps at a run. Birdie thought of Max now, sitting weak, small and somehow crushed, in his big chair. Had he worked this out for himself? And if so, was this why he was afraid to go to sleep? Why he couldn't rest? Why now he was sitting in the living room surrounded by people when surely, with aching head and throbbing wrist, he would be more comfortable upstairs in bed? Was this why, with Angus Birdwood's arrival, the tension in the room had subsided? For nothing could happen to Max while Angus was by.

'Is your father here?' Isa's voice broke into Birdie's thoughts, weirdly echoing them. The Auntie Dora face gleamed through the dark shrubbery, as Isa bent and twisted to get a clear view of the woman on the stairs.

'Yes,' called Birdie.

Isa exclaimed. 'They never told me Angus was coming. I'm so glad. So good for Max. I'll be right in.' The face abruptly disappeared, and shortly afterwards Birdie saw a flutter of Liberty lawn on Isa's front path. She opened the security door and waited.

'Thank you, darling,' cooed Isa. She patted at her grey hair and dusted her hands off on her skirt. 'In and out, in and out, as the actress said to the bishop.' She began to toil up the steps towards the house.

Birdie watched her go, and wondered. The woman's moods changed like the wind. She was mad, Max said, at the party. Mad like a fox, Angus had responded. Perhaps both things were true. That was the trouble here. There were too many truths. Too many different ways of looking at things.

She sat down on a step and thought. Go back to basics. Accept that Mai wasn't running away. But the note was on the dressing-table, and the emeralds were gone, when Max went to look for her in the bedroom just after six. The note had been planted, then. By the same person, presumably, who had taken the emeralds. To give the impression that Mai had run. But the note was genuine. Birdie struggled to recall it. She closed her eyes and visualised the careful, rounded hand:

I have been trouble to you. Now I have brought more trouble to your house. My husband is a bad man. I see now that I must go. I am sorry. Mai.

The note wasn't dated, or addressed to anyone in particular. Of course the assumption had always been that it had been written on Friday and was intended for Max. But it could easily have been written to someone else on Thursday night, after Warren Daley had declared himself. Receiving it, that someone would have believed Mai would soon be troubling them no longer, only to find the next day that Max had 'fixed' things, and the marriage would go on after all. That someone had seen Mai in the garden, joined her there, and killed her. And put the note in place and taken the emeralds, to make everyone believe the girl had run. In the hope, no doubt, that her body would not be found.

It had all the earmarks of an impulsive crime. A matter of moments, perhaps since bitterly regretted. Birdie could imagine how it would have been. A wave of anger and bitter frustration. The garden thick, still and silent. The back of the girl's white neck, encircled by its leather thong, exposed. A quick dart of the hand. Fingers slipped under the plaited band, to twist and pull it tight. The briefest of struggles. Black hair tumbling down as the jewelled comb fell away. The thudding of a small body on the leaves, half under the tangling jasmine vine. Then the panicking rush away. The frenzied planning. The note recalled. The way found to get into the bedroom and plant it. The emeralds taken. Mai has gone. Mai had fled her husband, and her own shame. The eyes of all are directed away from the house, away from the garden, into the streets leading down to Paradise.

But then Birdie found the body. And the note became an embarrassing irrelevance, the emeralds a white-hot burden. The police have already searched the garbage bin. So into the garbage the emeralds go. Tomorrow night the bin will be wheeled down to the street. Sunday night is garbage night at 'Third Wish'. The collection truck will come roaring and grinding up the hill at first light Monday morning and the bin will be emptied, its contents crushed and carried away. The emeralds will never be seen again.

How ironic that it was Warren Daley who upset that plan, unearthing the emerald necklace, covered in dough crumbs, in his search for food, and leaving it for the police to find.

Birdie ran her fingers through her heavy mop of hair. It was wet around the nape of her neck. Even in the shade the air was hard to breathe. Soon she would go inside. But first she knew that she'd have to do what she'd been avoiding all this time. She had to actually focus her mind, instead of skirting round the issue. Who had killed Mai Tran?

Douglas? He was Toby's pick. And on the face of it, he seemed most likely. He had lied about his movements on Friday evening. What's more, Trish's spirited defence of him had only gone to show that he came back to 'Third Wish' that night in a state of desperate frustration and anger. Mai, serenely in possession of the garden, his father's bride, the proposed mother of his father's children, the future controller of his father's vast wealth, could have symbolised for him everything that had gone wrong in his life. He was a big, powerful man. If she had taunted him, in her quiet way, as they stood under the trees together, he could have seen red and killed her with two fingers of one hand.

It could have been Douglas to whom Mai wrote on Thursday night. He was Max's son. Mai could have been traditional enough to feel he was the one to whom such a note should be addressed. He, moreover, had approached her in intimate terms earlier that day. They hadn't heard his side of this story yet. More may have gone on than Mai reported to Max.

And Douglas could have planted the note and taken the emeralds. He had gone up to change on arriving home, because he was wet. It would have been a simple matter for him to slip into the master bedroom at the head of the stairs on his way to his own room down the corridor.

Yet Douglas had come back to the house this morning in a soft, gentle mood, brimming over with pleasure because he'd been reunited with his lost son, roughly loving to the father who had repudiated him only the night before. The father for whom, in this scenario, he had set a death trap that same day? Was he such a good actor, then? Douglas?

Maybe. All salesmen were actors, in a way. And Douglas's ability to deceive was well established. But it was upon the trap for Max that the case against Douglas fell down. Douglas could have made the bogus phone call. But Douglas wasn't home, at least to all appearances, when the trap was set.

Berwyn was another matter. She was home when the trap for Max was set. What's more, she had been outside to the garbage bin that morning. She could have hidden the emeralds then, as well as placing the stick in place on the stone steps. There were extensions to both Max's private line and the house phone in the studio. Berwyn could have rung Wendy from the private line extension and mimicked Isa's voice, knowing that Wendy would go rushing down to tell Max about the call, whatever anyone said.

Berwyn had been painting Mai. And she was a famous person in her own right, and Max's wife. Mai could then, easily, have felt that it was Berwyn to whom she must apologise, and explain her decision to leave the house. Berwyn had been painting Mai that afternoon. Instead of brooding over the portrait she could have gone out to the garden after the sitting, and seen Mai there. She could have joined her, and killed her. She could have placed the note and taken the emeralds as easily as Douglas could have done.

Berwyn said little, but her feelings were intense. She had obviously found Max's relationship with Mai distasteful. And she was Max's wife, being ousted by a girl half her age and losing the money she would inherit if he died intestate. But Berwyn had plenty of money of her own, and anyway money didn't matter to her. Besides, unless she was a truly great actress she'd been quite sincere when she echoed Isa's prediction at the party: Max would tire of Mai in six months. He'd feel regretful, pay her off, and go back to his old way of life. It was one of the things about the match she found offensive.

If she believed that, why kill the girl? Why not just bide her time? Because of the planned babies? Birdie thought about that. No. Max had cast babies aside before, when he tired of their mothers. There was no reason to think he wouldn't do it again. Then, as predicted, all would be as it had been.

And again, the trap for Max was a stumbling block. Birdie couldn't believe Berwyn would hurt Max. You could see by her portrait of him that she loved Max cocky, confident and strong, weaknesses and fears hidden where only an intimate could reach. That was what she respected in him. That was what fascinated her. She'd have no wish to see him crippled. There would be nothing she could gain by it, and if he was killed, everything to lose. Berwyn knew Max very well. She would have seen that his regard for her had continued as strongly as ever throughout this affair, despite his infatuation with Mai. If anything, it had strengthened during her stay at 'Third Wish'. At the end of Mai's predicted wife-span, Berwyn would still be there.

As would Wendy, Max's familiar before Berwyn, and appalled by the thought of the approaching marriage. Wendy, who had had such plans of moving back to 'Third Wish' and housekeeping for her father in his retirement. Moving her doll-making projects, perhaps, into Berwyn's light and lovely studio facing the sea. Wendy was sorting papers on her bed while Mai died. But she could have gone to the window. She could have seen Mai going into the garden. She could have gone out to speak to her, as she had wanted Douglas to do. She could have suddenly seen her chance to rid her family of a menace. And who more likely than Wendy to have received the note from Mai? It was she who had hired the girl. It was she who had wailed about the scandal, the newspapers, the disgrace, after Warren Daley dropped his bombshell.

Wendy could have gone to the master bedroom to plant the note and take the emeralds as easily as Berwyn or Douglas could have done. And she, like Berwyn, went out to the bin this morning. She could have set the trap for her father.

But would she? She wouldn't want to kill her father. She adored him. It would, in fact, be true to say that he was central to her life. And how could she organise the phone call? For the house phone had definitely rung, and Wendy had no extension of the other line in her room, as Berwyn did.

And Isa? Always Isa. She too would remain with Max when Mai's allure grew stale. She seemed per-

fectly confident of that. Would Isa have killed Mai over
Max? In a way, her personality was the most likely one.
Isa was quite capable of white-hot rage. She was impetuous and in her own way, absolutely callous. But she'd
been superbly cynical over Max's latest folly, and, chatting with Birdie in her pretty living room, with Max's
delphiniums and lilies scenting the warm air, she had
been obviously secure in his affection, however com-
promised. It was hard to imagine her killing out of
jealousy. And anyway, of course, she'd been with
Birdie while the murder was committed. Unless the
police were wrong about the time of death, which
seemed extremely unlikely, Isa was out of the running.

Birdie plodded on, however. Alibis were always
suspect. You had to go over all the other points, just in
case. Could Mai's note conceivably have been written
to Isa? Yes, it could. It was Isa, after all, who had Mai's
husband on her premises. It was Isa who had had a
bitter fight with Max, shouting on the phone that he
was selling out his friends and family for Mai. She had
been the only one to speak out frankly at the earliest
stage, and say what others were certainly thinking.

But Isa couldn't have planted the note or taken
the emeralds, could she? Shifting uncomfortably on
her hard stone seat, Birdie thought back. And realised
with surprise that yes, Isa could. Isa had run upstairs
on arrival at 'Third Wish' on Friday evening, to call
Wendy and Berwyn down to drinks. She in fact was
the one who had alerted Max to the fact that Mai
wasn't in her room. It would have been a matter of
seconds to plant the note. The emeralds, lying there
on the dressing-table, could have been taken on impulse, to gild the lily.

Isa had easy access to 'Third Wish' over the fence.
She could have put the emeralds in the bin. She
wouldn't have used her own, just in case they were
found. She could have set the trap for Max. And rung
up to call for help. She claimed she hadn't made the
call, but that didn't mean she hadn't.

And if Berwyn wasn't an actress, Birdie reminded

herself, Isa was. But the motive was weak. And she herself was Isa's alibi.

She slapped idly at a mosquito. There were thousands of them down here. Breeding away in the dimness and the warm damp. Every female with a hundred and forty eggs pumping through her body. Every water-filled cranny filled with wrigglers. The spiders didn't breed so quickly. So much for the balance of nature. She should go inside. She was hot, wet and being eaten alive. But there was one more person to think about.

Max himself. The person, next to Warren Daley, most emotionally involved with Mai and therefore, statistically, the most likely person, next to Warren, to have killed her. Max was impulsive, passionate, quick-thinking and clever. Theoretically he could have done all that was necessary as easily as anyone else. There were two small problems, of course. One, Max would hardly have set a trap for himself. And two, he was in no position to commit the murder. For at the time he was locked in his study, reading his copy to technicians at the other end of the cable. From five o'clock to ten past five, every weekday, without fail, no exceptions. They rang him. He didn't ring them. He had no way of juggling the time. If he had adjusted it—arranging for the taping to be done earlier or later, giving some excuse, it would be on record and could easily be checked. And Birdie was positive that Toby would already have done so. It would be a matter of routine for him. He was well aware of the statistics too.

There was a small sound from the other side of the garden. Birdie stood on her toes and twisted her neck to see what it was. The driveway doors were opening. With a slight crunch and skid of gravel Wendy's neat car began to climb up to the house. The doors swung shut behind it. Douglas was back. Toby had let him go, at least for now.

Birdie stood up and paced restlessly back down the steps to the security door. There might be some way, though, that Max could deceive the system. She couldn't see it at the moment, but that didn't mean it didn't exist. As with Isa, she should ignore the alibi. All right, then. Max could have been floored, as Berwyn said he would be, by the revelation of Mai's dishonesty. He could have been driven to violence. It was possible. He could have waited till Friday to kill her, pretending all was well, to draw suspicion away from himself and re- inforce the idea that Mai had run away. But that would mean killing in cold, cold blood. Holding the thought for nearly twenty-four hours, and then carrying it out. Birdie shook her head. No. That wouldn't work. Max was the sort of person who could plan infinitely to get something he wanted, or catch an enemy out, or take a subtle and complex revenge. But it was impossible to imagine him planning in that way to take a young girl by the throat and kill her. That wasn't Max. And that wasn't the crime. None of it fitted.

Nor did Max's present state. As she'd told her fa- ther, he was shattered. He wasn't acting. Could he be so shattered, if he had coldly planned such a crime? Lady Macbeth was. Yes. But Max was no Lady Mac- beth, biting off more than he could emotionally chew.

Parrots began to chatter in the trees above Bird- ie's head. She squinted up into the leaves, but in the glare still cast by the white sky she could see nothing. If Max belonged in Shakespeare at all it wasn't in a tragedy, she thought. Something like 'The Tempest', maybe. With Max as Prospero, Ariel and Caliban all rolled into one. Did that make Wendy Miranda? God, no. But Mai could be. If Mai . . .

She shook her head impatiently. She was wander- ing. And again, she was wondering about Mai. The girl's face floated in her mind. Innocent victim, or subtle schemer? Why did it matter? How many times had she asked that question? She knew why. It was the central piece in a jigsaw. And around it floated other pieces. The note, the emeralds, the trap for Max. The emeralds. The trap for Max . . . Birdie rubbed her forehead. She couldn't get her thoughts in order.

She got up and began walking rapidly up towards the house. She'd been down here long enough. Her head was spinning. Names and faces loomed out of the chaos and receded. Max, Isa, Wendy, Berwyn, Douglas ... all possible, all impossible ... Douglas, Berwyn, Wendy, Isa, Max ... not strangers, pieces on a chess board to be moved around at will. Real people, familiars of her childhood, small parts of herself, all of them, and for that very reason her mind failed to sense in any one of them the element of danger a stranger could rouse.

Yet one of them *was* dangerous. One of them had killed. One of them could kill again. Which one? Which one? Pictures, faces, facts, scenes from the last two days, the last three weeks ... the ringing of the phone, the sound of a voice. Berwyn standing in front of a painting: *The spaces are just as important as the lines.* What we don't know is just as important as what we do. Pictures, facts, forming patterns, changing, re-forming ... Mai's face ... the emeralds ... the trap for Max ... Suddenly they clicked, and formed a whole. A whole that took her breath away. That solved all the problems. Turned the chaos into some sort of grim, dark order. Could it be? Her mind started away from the thought. The pictures spun again. And again, stopped, fitting and arranging themselves into the same murky pattern. Was this, then, the way it was? This? It could be. It must be. And yet there was something ... something ... nagging at her. *Look at it another way ...*

As Birdie climbed higher the sound of the sea grew louder, and the air grew tangier and fresher. She turned and looked back at the garden closing in lush and green behind her. It was oppressive down there. It was as though a miasma clung around you, filling your nose and mouth, blearing your eyes, clouding your mind. She reached the red-gravel terrace and, deliberately clearing her mind as, with relief, she drew the fresher air into her lungs, walked towards the house.

And then, without warning, as she put her foot on the bottom stair, everything just turned itself over, shifted, slipped into place and stayed there, clear, simple, undeniable, self-evident. She blinked at the familiar front door, unbelieving. She knew.

FIFTEEN

—

Birdie stood motionless, amid the scent of gardenias. She knew. She knew who had killed Mai Tran. She knew who had set the trap on the garden steps. The facts were there. Take away the confusions, the conjectures, the unknowns, and the facts remained like firm, black lines on a blank sheet of paper, etching out a portrait of a murderer. But, like Berwyn's portrait of Mai, it was unfinished. Birdie contemplated it in her mind. It was very clear. But there were still vital pieces missing. Even now, there were things she didn't understand. Perhaps later she would. The really disturbing thing was that she might see the answer, but there was no way she could prove it. And—she faced the fact full on—for the first time in her whole career she didn't know that she wanted to.

She climbed to the front door and lifted her hand to ring the bell. She could forget about all this. It wasn't her responsibility. Trish's lawyer would get

Douglas off—if the matter even reached the courts, which she doubted. The evidence was far too weak to hold without a confession. Toby would know that. The matter would quietly drop, unsolved. Birdie could take herself off, today, if she wanted to, and leave 'Third Wish' and its people to go on as before.

But even as the temptation crossed her mind, she rejected it. The people wouldn't go on as before. The shadow of the past days would hang over them forever. And forever they would know that one of them, one of them, was not what they seemed. One of them had crossed the boundary between anger and destruction. One of them was dangerous. One of them, having killed, could kill again. And she would know. She, too, would have to keep a dark secret forever. Living with it. Smothering it. Never betraying a flicker of suspicion. To the family. To Toby. To her father.

She rang the bell. Wendy opened the door to her and she went in, scratching absent-mindedly at her forearms.

'The mozzies have been eating you, Verity Jane,' scolded Wendy. 'Dear, oh, dear, look at you! I'll get the calomine.'

'No, no, don't worry. I'm OK,' said Birdie. But Wendy had already gone off on her mission of mercy.

'Come and have a drink, darling,' called Isa.

Birdie waited for Wendy, took the calomine lotion and cotton wool from her with a nod of thanks, followed her over to where Angus was sitting by the windows with Max, Isa, and Berwyn. Douglas was nowhere to be seen. Presumably he was upstairs, or in the kitchen.

Strange. Now she knew, she saw them all with different eyes. Yet they didn't know she knew. To them, she still looked the same. She perched on the edge of a couch, next to her father. He patted her knee.

'She's very like you, your girl,' Max said. He was lying back in his chair, his face sagging and old. 'In more ways than one, Angus.'

'Is that so?' Angus regarded him mildly. Only the

slightest crease between his eyebrows betrayed, to Birdie at least, his apprehension.

Max smiled. 'Cold as ice and tough as nails,' he murmured. 'Mind like a computer.' He sighed. 'I always thought she and Douglas might get together, you know. Remember how we used to talk about it, in the old days?'

Angus said nothing. Birdie squirmed slightly and began dabbing the bites on her arms with thick pink calomine lotion. A smell that reminded her irresistibly of beach holidays filled her nose.

'Mosquitos love Birdie. Always did,' said Max. 'Remember, Angus? Remember the time we lost Douglas because of it?'

'How could I forget?' smiled Angus.

'Do you remember, lovey?' Max was addressing Birdie now. She shook her head. She didn't remember and she didn't care. Nor did anyone else in the room, she was sure of that. But Max was persistent. He was going to tell his nostalgic story come hell or high water. To take his mind off his present troubles? To make a point? Or just to indulge himself? Who knew, but Max.

'Douglas was about eighteen months old,' he began, 'and Birdie was—oh, I don't know, about eight. And Angus and Jane got this party going at Palm Beach, in a house they were renting there for the summer. Anyhow, Ingrid and I got there and for some reason we'd taken Douglas. Between nannies as usual I suppose. And Wendy . . .'

'I was in camp,' Wendy put in rather sulkily. 'Tennis camp. Ingrid made me go. I hated it.'

'Ah, yes.' Max's eyes glazed over. He didn't want to think about Wendy's troubles at this moment. 'Well, Birdie had this big double bed, and we put Douglas down with her in that. There were mozzies everywhere, and we tucked the mosquito net in all round them—remember Angus?—and just went off and forgot all about them. They were safe enough. Or so we thought.'

'What happened?' asked Birdie, interested in spite

of herself. She wondered why she'd never heard this story before.

'Ingrid went in to check on Douglas, see, oh, hours later, and blow me down, he's gone! There you are, peacefully asleep, and there he is, not there! So of course she throws ten fits and starts rushing around screaming blue murder. She can't find me, see, because Jane and I are on the beach. Having a talk, you know, and just wandering around getting cool . . .'

Birdie saw her father's eyes flicker. She felt a tightness in her chest. No wonder she'd never heard this story before. Max and her mother. Of course. It would have been inevitable, really. It probably never came to anything. Just a flirtation. But it still made her feel sick. She concentrated on not letting her father see she'd registered anything amiss, and smiled at Max encouragingly. I'm letting the old man have his therapy, her smile said, to anyone who might be watching. Letting him reminisce. She listened absently as Max's story drew to its climax.

'So Ingrid is yelling for me and carrying on, and I come rushing in and everyone else starts looking in the garden and on the beach and talking about ringing the cops. And you know what Angus does?' Max looked around the room, his eyebrows raised.

'Cool as a cucumber he goes into the bedroom, and he looks at the bed, and he thinks for ten seconds and then he goes around to the far side, where Douglas is supposed to be, but isn't. And then he calls me. And when I come in he just points. And there Douglas is! The little bugger has turned over in his sleep and slipped right down between the side of the bed and the tucked-in mosquito net. There he's been all the time, fast asleep, while we've been all over the place like a madwoman's breakfast. And only Angus thought to look.' He leaned back and closed his eyes. 'Calm, logical old Angus,' he said. 'Angus worked it out and Angus found Douglas for me. And his daughter found Mai, in just the same way.'

There was a heavy silence in the room. Max's eyelids fluttered. His eyes opened. 'A bit of logic,' he said.

'Logic and sense. Runs in the Birdwood family. Not in ours.' He looked steadily at Birdie. 'Shame you had too much sense to get involved with Douglas, lovey,' he went on. 'Douglas could have done with a clear head on his side. By God he could.'

'Trish seems to have a clear enough head,' said Berwyn, curled up at the end of the couch beside him. 'And she's certainly on his side.'

'Oh, well.' Max shrugged. He moved restlessly and looked at Birdie narrowly. 'What do you think about all this?' he asked abruptly.

She stared at him, not quite knowing what to say. She felt her father tense beside her. 'I—don't think the cops have got enough on Douglas to charge him,' she said at last.

'Of course they haven't,' sneered Max. 'They're fools. We were just saying the same thing before you came in. Did you see him come home? He's making himself a sandwich in the kitchen. Cops didn't feed him. Bastards.' His eyes wandered out to the sea. 'Getting late,' he said. Then he looked back at her, and he frowned. 'But what do you think? You must have an opinion. You've been here all through this. You've seen us all going through our paces. You've said the cops think someone here killed Mai. Berwyn and Isa agree with you. So who is it?'

'Come off it, Max,' Angus Birdwood muttered. But Max was intransigent. His tired eyes gleamed behind his glasses.

'No. I really want to know. She's the private detective, Angus. And it'd be obvious to a drover's dog that she could run rings around that aggro stirrer Toby. If she can't help us, who can?' He struggled upright and leaned forward, half-grinning at Birdie. 'Come on, girl. Give!' he ordered. 'What does the computer say? The data's been going in for days. And you've been doing more than donating blood, out there in the garden. You've been computing. I know that. So give me the print out. What're you waiting for?' The tone was jocular, but the knuckles on the arms of the chair were white.

Birdie made her decision. She looked him straight in the eye. 'It's a bit like your mosquito net story,' she said. 'It's been a matter of looking at things as they really are, not as they appear to be. You see an empty bed, so you think no one's in it. But someone is. They're just not where you're looking. You hear the phone, and you assume someone's calling you. But it could be a wrong number, or someone might have arranged a Telecom call-back, to trick you. A wake-up call, maybe, or that service where you simply ring a number and a minute or two later they call you back. People use that service all the time to check their phone, or to play practical jokes on one another. You take what you see and hear for gospel, but what you don't see and don't hear can be just as important to the truth.' She screwed up her nose. 'Oh, look, I really can't say anything else, Max. Not till I've talked to Dan Toby. And I can't do that till tonight, apparently.'

Wendy made a small sound of protest, immediately stifled as Max glared at her. Douglas came in from the kitchen, swallowing the last of his sandwich. 'What's going on?' he asked. He looked haggard.

'Oh, nothing much,' shrilled Isa. 'Birdie's just telling us she knows who killed Mai but can't let on.'

Angus Birdwood stood up. His face was grim. 'Isa, behave yourself! Max, this isn't fair,' he said. He turned to Birdie. 'Why don't you come home with me for dinner? I could do with some company.'

Birdie looked at him steadily. She quite realised that this was as far as he would permit himself to go in asking her to leave. This was, in effect, her last chance. She dropped her eyes. 'Oh, look Dad, I can't. I'm sorry. I'm seeing Dan in Paradise at nine,' she said carelessly. 'How about tomorrow night?'

He nodded, rigidly controlled. 'OK. Fine. Well, look Max, I'll be off,' he said shortly. He held out his hand and Max took it. Their eyes locked for a moment. 'Take it easy,' murmured Angus. He turned away. 'Bye, all.'

'Bye, darling,' quavered Isa. 'I'll be going too, soon. God bless.'

'I'll come down with you, Dad,' said Birdie brightly. 'Heat myself up again. Then I'll have a swim.' She followed him to the door and stepped into the humid air outside with relief. She had deliberately chosen the path she was going to take, but her stomach fluttered and her head felt as if it was full of bees.

'What are you playing at?' asked Angus abruptly, as they walked down the steps. 'This isn't like you.'

She said nothing.

They reached the door in the wall and let themselves out. Birdie propped the door open with the half-brick the police had thoughtfully left behind. At the car Angus turned to her again, but she held up her hand. 'Don't ask me, Dad. Please don't,' she said.

He shook his head. 'You're crazy,' he said. 'Look, Birdie, I know you don't want me to ask anything, and I won't. I won't ask a bloody thing. But I'm going to tell you something, no charge. Max didn't hire you to find Mai's killer. You were hired to find out about some poison-pen letters. You owe Max nothing. He can't make you take responsibility like he's doing. He's not thinking straight. He's whacked out. He barely knows what he's saying. You can see that, can't you?'

Birdie nodded.

'If only I could've got a word with him alone! But those damned women were hanging round all the time, and of course he wouldn't talk in front of them.' Angus frowned. 'This morning I only got a few words out of him. I thought I'd do better face to face. But not with a crowd I won't. Shit, he's in a bad way. I've seen him down before, but never like this. Never like this.' He tightened his lips.

Then he looked up at her. 'I don't like it. He can be a bastard. God, I know that. A selfish, egocentric bastard. He's been a bad father to his kids, in the ways most people would think count, anyhow. And probably a bad husband to his wives. There'd be plenty of people who say he deserves everything he gets. But I'm not one of them. He doesn't deserve this. What he's done with his life—' He paused. 'While you've been doing this book business, has he said anything to you about himself as a kid?'

'Not much. Just what I knew already. There's no need, really. It's pretty well documented. Everyone knows about Max's childhood.'

'Everyone knows what he tells them about his childhood. It's one of his ploys, to talk about it. Everyone knows he was poor, that his mother struggled to keep him. All that. But have you ever heard him talk about his father?'

'I assumed he didn't have one.'

'Oh yes. Until he was twelve or so he did. A violent drunk. Max hated him. Hated him like the devil. He never talks about him. He told me about him the night after your mother died. He'd come to see me. We both got very drunk. I don't know why he told me then. He said he'd never told anyone else. I guess he was—sharing grief, if you know what I mean. Or maybe it was a way of—apologising for what he was. He and Jane were—well, the relationship was always complicated.' Angus looked down at this small, plump hands resting on the car bonnet. 'I understood. I always understood. People are what they are. You take them whole, or you keep away. To me, Max was Max. And Jane was Jane. I knew her and loved her for exactly what she was. Beautiful, funny, full of life, greedy for it, loving it. She made me very happy, and part of me died when she did. That's it. Max didn't need to tell me anything.'

Birdie drew breath. Her eyes were prickling behind her shielding glasses. She dug her nails into her palms. She never cried. Never. Her chest ached. She felt as though a door to a dark little room in her heart was being prised open. She fought the feeling. Her father's face was calm. She realised that he didn't know the effect his words were having on her. He thought she was like him. He thought she'd come to terms with all this long ago. But she was still a child when Jane Birdwood died. She thought like a child. She had a child's strange logic. She dealt in images and imaginings. And she'd never gone beyond that, where her

mother was concerned. She blinked, swallowed, and
frowned, putting the unwelcome feelings aside, turning ruthlessly away from them. Angus was still talking,
in his soft, unhurried voice.

'Max's mother was a little, dark, harried woman.
You'd pass her in the street and never look at her
twice. He showed me a picture of her. As far as I know
he'd never shown that to anyone else either. She'd
been pretty once, probably, but she was quite worn
out by the time this picture was taken—with Max at
about ten or eleven, by some street photographer. He
made her have it taken, he said. He paid for it, with
money from his paper round. It's a touching little picture. This scrawny little kid grinning at the camera,
and he's got his arm round his mum sort of bracing
her up. You can practically hear him. "Smile, Mum!"
But she isn't smiling.

'The dad lived with them when he felt like it,
drinking his way through what little money they had
in the house—her cleaning money, Max's paper-round
money—' Angus half smiled, 'till Max cut out a floor-
board in his room and made a cache there. He'd lie
around drinking, beat and terrorise them both, then
leave for months at a time.

'Max said what he hated, hated worse than being
beaten up, worse than being poor, was that he felt so
powerless against this bastard. Not being able to stop
him hurting his mother, or taking their money. He
wanted his mum to get away. He thought the two of
them could set up somewhere else and start again. He
asked her over and over. He saved up his money
under the floorboards as a fund for them. Poor kid.'
Angus looked back at the high stone wall. Above and
beyond it Max's palace rose above the trees.

'But she was too scared, Max said. She just
wouldn't do anything. She didn't have the strength to
fight for herself, or for him. He tried to give it to her,
but no matter how hard he tried, he couldn't rouse
her.

'When the cops came to tell them his father had
been killed in some pub brawl, Max said it was the

happiest day of his life. The tragedy was, his mother died too, only a year later. Some smallish thing—pneumonia or something. She didn't have the will to keep herself alive, Max said. She just couldn't try. Or wouldn't. And so she died. And he was alone. He said he realised that he always had been, really.'

Birdie thought of the portrait on the wall in the living room. Max. Alone. The man who still carried inside him the child he had once been. As we all do, she thought. Of course. But it hadn't struck her quite as forcibly before.

'What did Max say to you, this morning?' she asked. 'Why did you come?'

'He said he was going crazy,' her father answered bluntly. 'That's about all he said. Except come and see me. So I came. A lot of good it did, except to worry me sick about you as well as him.' He thumped the heel of his hand against the shining metal of the car. 'What am I going to do with you?'

'There's one thing you can do for me,' said Birdie, pushing gently past him. 'And then stop worrying. I know what I'm doing.'

Did she? Thirty minutes later, alone in the sitting room of 'Third Wish', she wondered. But there was no point in thinking like that now. She'd decided what to do. The wheels had been set in motion. All she could do was play her part, and hope. She looked out at the lowering sky. It was nearly six. Drinks time, usually, at 'Third Wish'. But tonight was different. Max had gone back to bed. Douglas had gone, finally, to pack his things. He'd spend tonight in his motel. Wendy was in her room. Berwyn was upstairs in the studio. Isa had left, slipping, presumably, over the fence, for she was gone when Birdie arrived back at the house and she hadn't come out through the security door. No wonder, after what had been said. No wonder the family had dispersed so rapidly when Birdie came back into the house. She had risen to Max's bait, and in doing so had fixed a gulf between herself and them that wouldn't be breached until the murderer was un-masked.

Upstairs floorboards creaked as people moved around their rooms. Downstairs the house was abso-lutely silent. Birdie tiptoed to the phone and lifted the receiver. As she had expected, there was no dial tone. Someone had one of the extensions off the hook. She couldn't ring out from here now, even if she wanted to.

She went into the housekeeper's apartment and changed into her swimsuit. It was still hot outside. The water in the swimming pool would be refreshing. But as she looked out into the garden for the last time she found that she was shivering. She wrapped her towel around her shoulders and let herself back into the kitchen. She walked through the lobby towards the sit-ting room. The front door was slightly ajar. She turned her back on it and moved towards the pool doors.

Outside there was barely a breath of wind. The ocean was humping and oily-looking. The sky was low-ering, with a suggestion of thunder. And the humidity was stifling after the dryness of the air-conditioned house. Birdie put down her towel and took off her glasses. Immediately the world became a mysterious and dangerous place. She had always known that this was the real reason she disliked the water. She was half-blind, swimming. Out of her element, and handi-capped as well.

She let herself down into the tepid water and began to swim. One lap. Two. Her heart was beating violently. Her ears strained. There was water in her eyes. She couldn't see. She finished the second lap and held on to the ladder, wiping the water from her face. She could hear nothing but the waves and the seagulls. She turned and swam to the other end of the pool. And just as she was turning again, she thought she heard it. The gliding of the pool door opening, just far enough to let some-one out.

It could have been her imagination. It could. She forced herself to keep her head down, though with all her being she wanted to look, to strain her useless eyes and see.

She concentrated on listening, but now there was no sound. No sound at all, except the rushing of water in her ears. She abandoned the idea of another lap and swam to the side, reaching for the edge and clinging to it, panting. She shouldn't have swum those laps so fast. She hadn't swum for years. She'd been nervous. She'd have to rest. She opened her water-filled eyes. And a figure, looming above her, bent down.

'Who is it?' panted Birdie. But she knew. Knew even before the hand came down, tangling in her hair, banging her head against the tiles, pushing her down. Knew even as the water rose over her nose and eyes, filling her mouth so her screams were gurgles and bubbles and her feet kicked uselessly in deep, pale blue water.

And the hard hand held her down, while her straining, clutching fingers slipped from the edge. *This is really happening to me. This can't be happening. Not to me. I'm not ready* ... The thought came to her, almost with surprise, as the roaring in her ears became a crescendo and her lungs ached for air. She felt her wriggling struggles, so small, barely rippling the water probably. She knew that soon she would have to breathe. Breathe the water. *I'm not finished yet. This wasn't supposed to happen* ... And then everything was red. She could see red, everywhere. And the ache in her lungs had gone. She wasn't frightened any more. Or surprised. Or anything. She was asleep, dreaming, floating ...

Then rudely, roughly she was torn awake. She was choking, and blind, and the pain in her chest was like knives as she heaved and gasped for air. What was happening? Someone was shouting at her. Shouting her name. Shouting at her.

'Breathe! Breathe! Yes! Birdie! You bloody fool! Didn't I tell you? Didn't I warn you ... ? Oh, thank God!' It was Dan Toby's voice, cracked and shaking. He was panting, and calling her name. Then he was shouting something else as he rolled her onto her side

on the hard paving while she coughed and vomited
water, groaning and pulling her knees up in agony.
But breathing. Someone was covering her with a
warm, rough towel. Someone was wiping her face and
putting on her glasses. And she could see now. Her
eyes were stinging and watering, but she could see.
She could see Toby's face, wet and anxious, close to
hers. And behind him were the people who had come
running when the shouting started, so nearly too late.

They were clustered together, pale and aghast,
clutching one another. They were shocked, so
shocked. Birdie was sorry. She wanted to explain, but
she couldn't speak. It had been the only way, she
would have said to them, if she could. I had to do it.
I wish you hadn't had to see. But there was no choice.

Milson and Barassi were both gone. Both. Birdie
didn't find that surprising. She had felt that hand
twisted in her hair, pushing her down. She shuddered.
Berwyn Kyte was a small woman. But her strength was
the strength of desperation, and her hand had been
hard as iron.

SIXTEEN

—

'You knew, didn't you?' Birdie's voice was a husky croak. She swallowed, and sipped at the tea Wendy had put into her hands after tucking her firmly into her armchair with a mohair rug. Her head was still spinning slightly, and her chest and throat ached. She was weak, and shocked. But at its deepest level her whole body was infused with a warm feeling of well-being and gratitude. The tea was hot, the rug was warm, she was alive. She glanced at her father, summoned back to 'Third Wind' before his car engine had had time to cool. He smiled at her. She looked again at Max. 'You knew,' she accused.

He nodded, his face sober. His eyes were dull behind the glasses. 'I think maybe I would have from the start,' he said, 'if it hadn't been for Warren Daley. She—Berwyn—was always very—well, she was intense about everything. But I always knew she was particularly intense about me.' He dropped his eyes. 'We were so close,' he went on, shifting in his chair. Almost squirming, Birdie thought. He didn't like to think about this. But he was forcing himself to go on. He knew he needed to say it. 'It didn't suit either of us,' he said finally. 'She always said she wasn't cut out for marriage. She wasn't. And neither was I. Neither of us, really, should get too close to anyone. It's not our way. We're scared of it. It's—' he forced a grin—'not good for our mental health.'

'Don't say that, Dad,' protested Wendy, beside him. He patted her arm absently.

'I tried to have my cake and eat it,' he said. 'I tried to have her, and hold back. I went out. I worked. I put everything I had into looking after her—getting my control back. Holding her off. That's what a shrink'd say, I guess. It nearly drove her crazy. It stopped her working. But she was braver than me. She just broke it off, clean. Left, and stayed away. After a while I realised it was for the best. We saw each other, but not too much. I had girlfriends—it didn't worry her. She knew how much they meant to me. A bit of fun. Nothing at all.'

'Old lech,' said Isa comfortably. She bent her head and delicately sipped tea from a china cup. Toby regarded her appreciatively. Auntie Dora to the life.

'Then Mai came along,' croaked Birdie.

Max nodded. 'I told Berwyn, at this dinner we had the week before the party. She took it well. She thought I was being stupid, I could see that. But it didn't worry her. I could see that too. Mai—well, see, Berwyn wouldn't think there was anything to Mai. I don't suppose any of you did.' He smiled again, sadly. 'Poor little Mai,' he murmured.

Birdie saw Wendy and Douglas exchange furtive glances.

'So I got cocky,' growled Max. 'I—well, I tried to have my cake and eat it too again, I guess. I got Berwyn here, to paint Mai's picture. Then I had them both, didn't I? In a way. Then I had everyone here, with me, under my eye. Berwyn. Mai. Isa.'

Isa. As always. Birdie smiled.

'I knew it was a mistake,' Max went on. 'After the first few days. Berwyn sees too much. She realised Mai was—different. And she was painting her. All those sketches Berwyn does before she starts a portrait. She did it with me, too. I remember it so well. She talks. You talk. You say things to her. And she drinks them in, and they flow out through her hand and turn into . . .' His face contorted. 'Oh, God. If she goes to gaol . . . they'll let her paint, won't they?'

There was a heavy silence in the room.

Angus Birdwood spoke for the first time. 'Berwyn knew about your father.' It was a statement, not a question.

Wendy, Douglas and Isa looked at him in surprise. But Max nodded, his head in his hands. 'I told her the day we—the day I saw my portrait finished.'

Berwyn said she and Mai didn't talk, thought Birdie. But of course they did, as Mai had said. Mai wrote Berwyn a note, the night Warren Daley came to the door. A note saying she was sorry, and would go. But the day after, relieved and happy, Mai told Berwyn that Max had intervened, and saved her. And she told the woman she had grown to trust about her marriage. Just as she had told Max. And so Berwyn found out about the beatings, and the years of terror, and the escape. Then she knew. She knew that now Max would never abandon Mai Tran. Never. In Mai, Max had found someone he could love and protect unconditionally. With her, thanks to Warren Daley, he could satisfy his most primitive, irrational need. With her he could succeed, where with his mother he had failed. Mai would depend upon him utterly, unthreatened and grateful. She would allow herself to be saved, swallowed, absorbed. She was his chance finally to heal the pain he'd carried around all his life.

And in the late afternoon, Berwyn had gone with the girl into the garden. The portrait had no background. What better setting, for Mai, than the wild place she loved to go? Berwyn wanted to see her there. It must have happened that way. For why else would Mai have worn the clothes she was being painted in to walk in the garden? And left her hair up, when for preference she wore it loose?

So Berwyn and Mai had walked in the garden, and Berwyn had felt the heat, and the isolation, and a desperate rage and jealousy she finally couldn't control. And so Mai had died, and fallen abandoned among the smothering vine. And Berwyn had run back to the house, and placed the note, and taken the emeralds, and tried to forget. Mai Tran had disappeared. She was gone.

But then Birdie found the body. And Mai came back. The real Mai. Not smug, hypocritical, dishonest, vacuous, manipulative, as in those first sketches stuck around the studio walls—the first impressions Berwyn wanted to remember. But Mai shatteringly naive, innocent, trusting, betrayed. As she was in the sketches torn and crumpled and stuffed in the garbage bin.

Max was speaking again. 'After we found out it wasn't Daley, I—I thought of Berwyn straight away. I couldn't help it. But there was that stick over the path. I didn't believe Berwyn would hurt me. Not in cold blood. I can still hardly believe it.' His shoulders sagged.

'That was my stumbling block with Berwyn too,' rasped Birdie. 'But then once I thought about what actually happened that afternoon, I realised. She didn't set the trap for you.' She coughed, clearing her aching throat. 'She set it for me, Max. Maybe not to kill me. The stick was halfway down a flight. Just to hurt me and get me off the scene, I'd say.'

'Why would she do that?' queried Douglas, almost idly. He was sitting on the edge of his chair, with his bag beside him, as though he was waiting for a bus. Trish was coming to pick him up, Birdie guessed.

'I think she probably thought I was getting too close to working out what really happened. She didn't know where Daley was, then. Any minute he could have turned up and been proved not to have been anywhere near "Third Wish" when the murder was done. As, in fact, later happened. Then the spotlight would have been back on the family. She didn't have

much faith in police . . .' Birdie pushed up her glasses
and met Toby's amused eyes. 'But I'd already been a
thorn in her side. I'd found Mai, and blown the runaway idea. I was still on the spot. And I was starting to
wonder about things that frightened her. Why Mai
had gone to the garden dressed like that, for example.
And that stiff, vacant portrait. It was so uncharacteristic of Berwyn. She told me it was because she couldn't
get to know Mai. But she knew I knew she was lying.
She'd painted enigmas before. Brilliantly. She won her
second Archibald with Harriet Deal.

'She couldn't paint Mai properly because she *did*
get to know her. She couldn't bring herself to tell the
truth on canvas. But she couldn't successfully paint a
lie, either.

'She decided to try and get rid of me. This morning she knew you were on the private line, Max. There
are extensions of both phones in the studio. She
thought you were safely out of commission for a while.
So she arranged for a dummy call to come in on the
other line. When Wendy answered the dummy call
Berwyn picked up her receiver too, and gave the message. She offered to go to Isa's herself, but she knew
I'd want to do it. She knows people, by God she does.
It makes her dangerous.'

'You're pretty dangerous yourself,' said Max
slowly. 'You talked about call-back numbers. You said
you knew who'd killed Mai. You said you hadn't talked
to the cops yet. Then you rang them from Angus's car
phone. You went out to the pool, on your own. You
knew she'd see you from her window. You let her try
and kill you. You trapped her.'

'She had a choice,' Birdie answered. Again the
memory of that hand in her hair flooded through her.
Pushing down, down, remorseless. She shivered.

'I thought you were talking about me, with that
call-back crack,' shrilled Isa. 'I thought you thought
I'd rung myself while we were having drinks on Friday,
and snuck outside and seen the girl and killed her,
while I was supposed to be on the phone. And the
woman I was talking to didn't leave her number. I

couldn't even remember her name! God, I thought, I'm for it! I'll be up in front of the beak fighting a murder charge, next. Revenge killing for Othello, I suppose. How will the Springdale ads go then, I thought. "Springdale, the margarine for murderers! Trust Auntie Dora!" '

'I thought you meant it for me,' whispered Wendy. Her eyes filled with tears. 'I really did. I thought you'd decided I killed Mai because I wanted—you know—Dad for myself. And tripped him up so he'd be crippled, and need me and everything. I saw a film once, where . . .' Her lips trembled.

'Well, I didn't think so,' said Birdie firmly. 'And I didn't think it was Isa, either. Or Douglas. Because of the emeralds.'

They stared at her. Max's sad face relaxed into a half-smile. 'She didn't reckon any of you blokes could have faced throwing them away. All that lovely moolah, in the tip? You'd have died first. That's it, isn't it, Birdie?'

She shrugged. She wished this hadn't come up. She should have known better. Wendy would be insulted now.

'So that left Berwyn.' Max looked out at the darkening sky.

Berwyn, and you, Max. Birdie met her father's eyes. They both glanced at Dan Toby. Max would never think of it. And they would never tell him. But there was another way it could have been. A way that had come over Birdie like a dark wave, in the garden this afternoon, as she climbed up towards the air. Long ago, it seemed now, at the very beginning of all this, before the body was found to dismiss the thought from his and Birdie's minds, Toby had had another scenario for Mai's abrupt departure, another face for Mai. Mai the conwoman. Warren Daley her accomplice. Max their dupe.

What if this had been true? What if Max had suspected? What if he had laid a trap, slipping out of the study to hide in the garden and watch, leaving the answering machine to spout forth his message to the country when the radio station rang at five? What if he saw Mai come slipping like a shadow down the steps, and begin to wait, with the emeralds, for her accomplice? He would be able to see she was waiting. Waiting in the garden for the signal that would lead her to open the security door and creep away. What if Max had watched her waiting, looking at her watch, pacing impatiently, hidden in the trees, because Warren Daley was late, because Warren Daley was drunk and playing around with Julie Billings on the beach when he should have been coming to fetch the woman who'd played her part so well, but was now impatient to be gone.

Max wouldn't have planned to hurt her. Only to trap her. But if he'd confronted her ... If she'd laughed at him ... If he'd seen himself betrayed by the woman he'd thought was his salvation, he could have caught that leather band. He could have twisted it. He could have killed her. And then later, nearly mad with fear and guilt, staged the booby-trap incident, to divert suspicion from himself once and for all.

Birdie would never have to face that nightmare now. It was a phantasm that had melted away as soon as she realised that there was another answer to the mystery of the trap no one would set.

'I never liked Berwyn,' Wendy whispered. She shook her head, watching Max as he lay back in his chair, his eyes closed. 'I never liked her. But I never thought ...' Her voice trailed off.

'She would have been all right,' murmured Max, without opening his eyes. 'If she hadn't come here. And Mai would have been all right, too. Mai died because she trusted me. You nearly died because I couldn't face the truth, Birdie. Because I wanted you to face it for me. This is—all of it—my fault.'

'It's not your fault, Max,' said Birdie steadily. That's what Berwyn said, she thought with surprise. She swallowed. 'Mai's death wasn't your fault. And I knew what I was doing. I was doing it for myself, not just for you. I just wasn't careful enough. I rang Toby

on Dad's car phone, but I didn't give him enough
time to get here. I rushed things. I swam too fast and
got tired. If I hadn't, things would never have gone so
far.'

Max was hardly listening. 'I knew Berwyn had
done it,' he muttered. His lips were hardly moving. 'I
knew for sure when I saw those pictures Toby found in
Warren Daley's cave. The ones she'd thrown away. Mai
like she really was—and—' He fumbled in the pocket
of his dressing gown and pulled out the battered cigarette tin Birdie had seen before. He opened it, with
fingers that fumbled and shook. Inside was a picture.
Small, rectangular, faded black and white. Birdie took
it from him. Young Max stared out at her, skinny, grinning, full of life. His arm was protectively hugging a
small, dark woman. We're happy, his grin insisted. We
love each other, and we're a family. Just like other
people. Aren't we, Mum? We'll be fine. Won't we?
Won't we? But the woman's dull eyes were hopeless
and her mouth barely curved.

Birdie looked up. At Max and her father. She'd
seen this picture before, or something very like it. A
little corner drawing, a scribble, on one of Berwyn's
discarded sheets of sketches. But there, Max, small
and smiling, had had his arm around Mai.

Max gave a sigh that was almost a groan. 'She was
too close to me. Knew too much. Much too much. She
killed Mai because of it. Christ,' he whispered. His lips
were stretched and pale.

'Max,' began Isa, half-rising from her chair. But
he held up his hand.

'It's all right,' he said. He clenched his fists and
looked down at the little tin on his lap. 'When my
mother was—dying, she just lay in bed. She wouldn't
let me get the doctor. She wouldn't let me do anything. She just lay there. She was coughing. She could
hardly breathe. And she was burning up. I took my
money—I used to keep it in this tin.' He touched the
tin with a shaking finger. 'I went to the chemist and
got some stuff. It took almost everything I had. The
chemist said it'd help, but it didn't. I stayed away from

school and got her food, and gave her the medicine
every four hours like it said. No matter what I did she
got worse. She wouldn't eat, hardly drank. Finally I
couldn't even get her to take the medicine. Then
some people came. Social welfare, I suppose, because
of school. They took her away. And me. I never went
back. I never saw her again. She died in hospital, they
said. She didn't ask for me. She didn't remember me.
She didn't know where she was.'

Tears were rolling down his cheeks. 'I couldn't
help her. I tried so hard. But I couldn't make her want
to live.'

'Max.' Angus's voice was steady. 'She had a
choice. And so did Berwyn. Like Birdie said, she had
a choice too. We all choose, in the end. And no one
else can make us choose one way or the other. We
choose to be weak. We choose to be strong. Sometimes we choose to live. Or to die. That's the way it is.
You can't run people's lives. Not even you.'

Max, huddled in his chair, went very still.

There was a knock at the door. Trish's head appeared around the jamb. 'Hi,' she said, rather tenta-
tively. 'The door in the wall was open and we just
came on up. Hope that's OK.'

Douglas leapt to his feet. 'Of course it's all right.
Come in. Both of you.' He was rigid with tension,
Birdie saw. His hands clutched each other behind his
back, the strong fingers twisted into a knot.

The door opened more widely. Trish came in,
chin up, eyes gentle as they rested on Douglas. And
behind her walked a boy.

'This is Jamie,' she said to Wendy, to Isa, to Max,
whose head was still bowed.

The boy shuffled awkwardly, and looked up at
them with dark, suspicious eyes.

'Hello, Jamie,' faltered Wendy. She glanced at
Douglas, pale-faced behind her.

'Hi,' said the boy gruffly. He stuck his hands in his
pockets.

At the sound of his voice, Max looked up. And
saw. Saw a thin, dark, eager face, a wiry little body,

clever black eyes. He sat forward. He stared. His mouth opened. *Three wishes . . .*

'You were at the beach this morning,' said the boy, almost accusingly.

'Yes,' said Max.

'No one goes that early.'

'I do,' said Max. 'And so do you, I guess.'

'Yes. I like it. Our house is just there. I'm allowed.' The boy's eyes swivelled to his mother. 'As long as I don't go too near the water or talk to strangers,' he added.

Max nodded. He met Douglas's eyes. They looked at one another for a long time.

'On the beach you looked really weird, then you ran away,' said the boy conversationally. 'I thought you were nuts!'

'Jamie,' warned his mother.

'I thought I was nuts, too,' said Max. 'I thought I was seeing things. You—I thought you were someone else.'

'Who?'

'Someone I remembered from a long time ago.'

The boy's eyes brightened. 'A ghost?' he breathed.

'Something like that.' Max stared at him, fascinated.

'He's the image of you, Max,' breathed Isa. 'The image.'

The boy glanced at her darkly, then his face changed. 'I've seen you on TV,' he said with interest. He turned to his mother, his eyes alight. 'It's Auntie Dora!' he whispered out of the side of his mouth. 'See, Mum? It's her. Does Douglas know Auntie Dora?'

She nodded, smiling, but her hand on his shoulder tightened. She doesn't want him to get sucked in, thought Birdie. She's had him to herself so long. This must be hard for her.

Douglas must have had the same idea. 'We'd better be off,' he said, standing up and moving close to them.

But the boy was whispering again, in a lower voice this time. Trish put her hand on Douglas's sleeve. I'm a big girl, her smile said. I can cope. 'Jamie was wondering if he could have your autograph,' she said to Isa.

'Aw, Mum,' growled the boy, as if embarrassing him was all her idea. But he took the pen and notebook Douglas passed him and sidled over to Isa's chair. Embarrassment wasn't going to stop him obtaining his prize, anyway. Isa beamed. They began murmuring together.

Angus pushed gently at Max's arm. 'Isa's overshadowing you,' he said slyly. 'She'll get above herself. You'd better look to your laurels.'

'What do you suggest?' Max's eyes were still startled as they flicked from Douglas to the boy and back.

Angus felt in his jacket pocket. 'Want to see a dirty picture?' he hissed. He pulled out a Polaroid photograph. Max looked at it, with his eyebrows raised. 'I've been carrying it round for a week. It's worse now, Max. Over twice as bad. And the switch is still jamming,' said Angus. 'Ferdie French is dying in the bum. They hate him. They want you.'

'Sorry to hear that,' Max's mouth twisted at the corners as he passed the picture over to Birdie. It showed an office packed almost to the ceiling with bags of mail. A woman sat wedged behind a desk heaped with letters. She had her hands up in the air, in a gesture of mock despair. In felt-tip pen someone had drawn a bubble coming from her mouth. 'Max, He-elp!' said the words in the bubble.

'We're taking more shots this week. We could release them. Great publicity.' Angus paused. 'For when you come back.' He waited for Max's snort and pressed on. 'The place is a morgue, Max. And, come on, you hate retirement. Admit it. Give us five more years. Three. One, even. You can keep the ten-to-six spot on too, if you like.'

'Angus, I'm seventy years old,' Max said. 'I can't keep going forever. God, I could croak at any tick of the clock.' But in his eyes a spark began to glow.

'So die in harness,' smirked Angus. He knew he'd won.

Douglas put a self-conscious arm round Trish. 'We'll have to go in a sec,' he said. 'But we'll be around for a while. Trish is working in Paradise, and she's got the beach house for the school holidays. We'll be in touch.'

'What're you doing in Paradise?' Max asked Trish. It was the first time he'd spoken to her directly, and even now his eyes had drifted to the boy at her side.

'Have you heard of Milly's Bakehouse?' she said.

Max looked puzzled. 'Yes. Of course I have. The hot bread chain. New one just opened on Paradise Parade.'

She spread out her hands. 'Well, that's me.'

'You mean you have the franchise for that shop? You personally?' He was obviously surprised and impressed.

She smiled. 'Oh no,' she said. 'I own the whole chain. But with new branches I always—'

'What!'

'I own the chain,' she repeated impatiently, but with a gleam of triumph in her hazel eyes. 'Your money didn't go to waste. I did a business course. I had the idea. Bread and buns and just a few extras. I started with one shop, and it took off. So I got another one. Now there are thirteen. Paradise made the baker's dozen.' She grinned more widely, enjoying his reaction. 'They're branches, not franchises, by the way. I don't like franchises. You don't have enough control. Anyway—well, there you are.'

'There you are.' Max regarded her in some confusion. 'A chain of bloody cake shops. That's what I was always going to do. Before I got into radio.' He looked at Douglas. 'You fell on your feet,' he said dryly.

'I fell on *my* feet,' snapped Trish. 'I need a good salesman. Doug's already set up a nice little New Zealand deal for me. Gingerbread men.'

'Gingerbread men,' murmured Max. 'My God.'

'The doughnuts are better,' Jamie volunteered. 'The ones with jam in. You know?'

Max nodded.

'Will you be at the beach tomorrow?' asked the

boy. He stuck his hands in his pockets and planted his feet firmly apart. 'Now you're not a stranger, and I know you're not nuts, I can talk to you.'

Isa screeched with laughter. 'It's incredible,' she cackled. 'Blood will tell.'

'I'll probably be there,' said Max slowly. 'And maybe you—and your mum—could come back to "Third Wish" sometime.'

'What's "Third Wish"?'

'This place.' Max waved his arm around the big room. 'This house.'

'Why did you call it that? Did you make three wishes?' The thin, eager face tilted towards him.

'Oh, yes. Once upon a time. I wished I had a house by the sea, like this. That was the third wish.'

'Jamie, we'd better think about going, I think.' Douglas was restless, but the boy was insistent.

'What were the others?'

Max sighed. 'The second wish was to be rich and famous.'

'Is he?' the boy asked his mother. She nodded, with a wry smile. She's lived with this, thought Birdie. Lived with a mini-Max all these years, and loved him. Thinking all the time, I suppose, what an irony.

'So what was the first one?' Jamie demanded. 'To be ruler of the universe?'

There was a short silence.

'No,' said Max finally. 'I didn't think of that.'

'What, then?' Jamie waited, listening intently. As indeed, did they all.

Max looked around. 'I was just a kid, see,' he hedged. 'Just a kid.' Then he saw there was no help for it, and gave in. 'My first wish was to be six-feet tall,' he said. 'One point eight metres to you. Silly, huh?'

Jamie looked him up and down. 'That one didn't come true,' he noted.

'No.' Max lifted his arms, and stretched. His eyes were still sombre, but on his face a slow smile began, and broadened to a grin, with a glint of gold. 'Still,' he said. 'Like I always say, two out of three's not bad. Is it?'

ABOUT THE AUTHOR

Jennifer Rowe is an award-winning Australian writer whose first murder mystery, *Grim Pickings*, established her as a mystery writer of the first order. Editor of *The Australian Women's Weekly*, she has also written *Murder by the Book* and the forthcoming *The Makeover Murders*.